DEAD INNOCENT

STEVE DAVISON

Alice&Fred Books

Alice&Fred Books

First published in Great Britain in 2011
Revised and republished in 2020

A & F Books
Sydney House
34 Station Road
Tiptree
Essex
CO5 0AZ

ISBN: 978-1-8380691-2-4

Design and typesetting by Ashdown Creative
www.ashdowncreative.co.uk

Cover photographs © Adrian Assalve/iStockphoto.com
© Johanna Goodyear/Dreamstime.com
© Ali Rıza Yıldız/Dreamstime.com

DEAD
INNOCENT

'While we are free to choose our actions,
we are not free to choose the consequences
of our actions.'

Stephen R Covey

For Harry and Louis

'Tell the repo man and the stars above that you're the one I love, you're the one I love.'

David Gray

Acknowledgements

There are so many. I'll try to be brief:

JD, thank you for everything – oh and 143 xx
M, M & J, much love (as always)
PB & DS, oldest and most beloved friends
The SHC crew – inspiring, energetic and cuddly

Thank you to:
The A&F project
J, M, A & A for reading the manuscript
and giving great feedback
Dan N and Steve K for your wonderful names!
AA for giving the series a cool, gritty look
DI AW for an 'insider's view'
on all things Met Police

Thank you also to:
DB for inspiring me to start writing again
LC for inspiring me to continue

————

AUTHOR'S NOTE

This is a work of fiction.
The characters and events are fictitious.
The scientific principles, however, are not.
It's the details I've had fun with. Enjoy.

Prologue

The car was a Bentley. A Mulsanne. Metallic blue with white leather upholstery, thick carpet and a wooden veneer drinks cabinet in the back. It had two passengers – the driver, Frank Davies and his boss James Pine. James Pine was the twenty-eight year old son of the industrialist, Charles Pine. Pine was sitting in the rear, deep in conversation on his mobile phone. Light coloured hair, just the blond side of sandy, a face tanned from a bout of skiing in Verbier. His suit was Armani – dark grey and fitted – with a starch white shirt. His tie was blue and folded neatly at the neck.

He pulled the phone from his ear for a moment and said: 'How much longer?'

He never used the driver's name because – as the driver knew well – he didn't know or care what it was.

The driver said: 'About twenty minutes, Sir.'

'Twenty? Put your foot down. I'm running late.'

Frank watched Pine in the rear-view mirror as he spoke into the phone once more: 'Twenty minutes. Tell them to wait.'

Then he rang off.

Frank Davies negotiated Milk Street and turned east onto Cheapside. The phone burst into life again and Pine snatched it up. 'Yes? I know. I arranged it. Of course it matters. About twenty minutes if this prick puts his foot down. Deal with it until I get there.'

Frank Davies flicked his eyes back to the road. He would have liked to smack James Pine in the mouth. He might just do it one day too. But not right now. That would be very dumb indeed. He had a wife and two young kiddies at home and this was probably the best paid chauffeur's job in London.

They reached a stretch of open road near Bank and Frank hit the accelerator. At last they might make some progress.

That's when the child suddenly appeared in the road. A blurred shape from Frank's left. Running from nowhere – running fast. Frank had no place to go. He hit the brakes hard. The child hit the Bentley's fender harder.

Then Frank's world went dark.

He stumbled from the car. The child was down on his left side and bleeding from the ears. His eyes were fluttering like moth's wings. Frank reached out and touched the child's hair. Then a small crowd gathered. There was screaming from a woman. Frank saw Pine get out of the car. He had his phone stuck to his ear. Frank was sure he was calling the hospital but Pine shouted into the mouthpiece: 'He's knocked down a fucking kid. Can you believe it? The meeting's off. We'll rearrange.'

'Someone get an ambulance. Please!' screamed Frank.

The crowd pushed forwards. Frank was on his

knees near the child's head.

'Be brave,' he whispered to him. 'Help is coming. I promise.'

The child's blood soaked into Frank's trousers. Frank stroked the boy's skin very gently. On the edge of the crowd, Pine had opened a packet of cigarettes. He lit one up and took a deep drag. Frank glanced upwards and Pine shook his head like he was disgusted. He blew a narrow plume of smoke skyward, then he turned and walked away.

Two Years Later

The house is a small one. A terraced dwelling in a road full of them. Low-end cars are parked in the curb-ways and on small blacktop driveways. A few kids gather on a brick wall at the end of the street. They smoke cigarettes and waste time. Beyond them, in the middle distance, an endless stream of cars and buses crosses the Canning Town Flyover towards Canary Wharf.

I am in the man's front room. I sit on an upright chair in a space that is oblong in shape, maybe twelve feet by eight. It is decorated with light blue paint and prints from Ikea. The carpet is also blue but darker than the walls and thready in places.

It is two o'clock in the afternoon yet the man wears a white, coffee-stained, towelling robe and a pair of cheap, foam slippers. His name is Frank Davies. He sits in a fat armchair and stares past me to a space on the wall beyond. I have asked him lots of questions and I watch him struggle with each one. He appears drugged. Sedated probably, yet he is desperate to give me the information I seek. Some of the questions I prepared in advance. Others arise because of information he provides. His answers are often laboured and jumbled, yet he responds honestly.

I appreciate that.

In fact it has just saved his life.

1

Rita Sidhu sat high up on a lab stool and grabbed a handful of her long, dark hair. She bunched it up and tied a red ponytail-band around it. She undid a couple of buttons on her white lab coat, adjusted her Calvin Klein spectacles and smoothed her grey skirt over the top of her long, slender legs. 'Go ahead,' she said at last.

Opposite her was a thin young man in tight, black jeans clutching a camera. An expensive, chunky kind with a fat, extendable lens. He held a light meter in his hand and fiddled with the flash mechanism. Finally satisfied, he pulled the camera to his face and fired off a flurry of shots. He stopped, flipped the camera around and inspected his work in the digital display. 'Couple of good ones,' he said to an older man who waited out of shot clutching a laptop computer to his chest.

'Are they usable?' he asked.

'Think so,' nodded the cameraman. 'I'll shoot a few more just in case.'

Every now and then he gave Rita some direction. *'Lift your chin … Lean forward slightly … Smile! …'*

Finally he declared himself satisfied and the other man moved forward to take his place. He pulled up a stool opposite Rita's, flipped open his laptop and began to hit the keys. After a few moments he stopped, smiled awkwardly and finger combed his bright red hair over to one side. 'Okay, Rita,' he said. 'I've prepared a list of questions I think will appeal to our readers. I'll call them out and you answer them in any way you want. Don't worry about going too fast,' he added, wiggling his fingers, 'I can touch type at one-twenty words a minute.'

Rita nodded. 'No worries,' she said, 'ask away.'

'Alright-ee,' he said, squinting at the screen. 'Let's see. Here we go. There are gifted scientists who will work all their lives and never have the success you've enjoyed in your three years as a PhD student. How do you feel about that?'

Rita cupped her chin and thought for a moment. 'Bad, if I'm honest,' she said. 'I feel like an interloper. Many of my colleagues have better brains than I will ever have so I'm not claiming any intellectual credit for it. I've worked hard of course, but my success owes as much to luck as anything else.'

The spurt of staccato at the keyboard paused for a moment. 'Why do you say you were lucky?'

'Because I happened to find a lab that was on the brink of something special. I didn't know that at the time. There was no clever design to it, or some insight on my part that led me to come here.'

'Ah, yes,' he said. 'Tell me about the path you took to arrive at Retnel.'

Rita pushed her glasses up onto the bridge of her nose. 'I applied to various labs in my field and finally found one that I liked and that liked me. I can't even claim to have Googled Robert Fleet. It would – '

'Dr Fleet is head of the molecular genetic laboratories here, am I right?'

'Yes, he is. I didn't assess him for the work he had produced. It would have been usual for me to do that. In fact it's in my character to do that. Yet in this case I didn't. It just felt right, I guess. I left uni, packed my stuff and headed for London.'

'Can you tell us a bit about the infra-1 gene and how you managed to isolate it?'

Rita puffed out her cheeks. 'It was two years ago. I can't remember the exact date, but I do remember the excitement when I first saw the thin black band on the electrophoreses gel. I immediately called Robert who came bounding over as if he knew something special was about to happen.'

'A light bulb moment?'

'Very much so,' said Rita, thinking back to that fateful day. The day that started all of this.

She had called him over and he'd held the culture plate up to the light and begun playing with his goatee beard. 'You cloned it?'

There were a half dozen Polaroids spread over her desk. 'Take a look.'

He had quickly pulled out a pair of half moons and peered at the evidence.

'See the high molecular weight band?' she asked. 'I doubled the EDTA concentrations.'

'That's all?'

'That's all.'

He traced the ladder with his finger, counting each band in turn.

'Convinced?'

'I can hardly believe it,' he said, kissing the Polaroid. He grabbed Rita's shoulders and gave her the biggest hug. The significance of this moment wasn't lost on her. Robert Fleet had been her mentor and friend these past few years. He saw something in her when she arrived fresh faced from Durham. Now it was time to pay him back. Cloning the infra-1 gene was a perfect way to begin. All the dreams they had for this project were now suddenly possible.

'Reet,' he said, 'we've got to celebrate this.' He bounded towards his office and emerged a few moments later with a champagne bottle.

'Where did *that* come from?' Rita asked.

'I bought it a few months ago,' he laughed. 'I was beginning to wonder if we'd ever drink it.'

The cork popped and the froth drizzled over the white floor tiles. He grabbed two lab mugs and poured. 'It's the first step, I know,' he said, 'but what a way to start! Well done, Rita, I really mean that.'

She savoured the compliment. For the first time she felt she deserved to be there. This eminent man, this awesome lab. She could hold her head up with everyone else now and it felt great. They clinked the mugs together and she took a swig, savouring the bubbles and their sweet flavours.

'You know,' she said, after a few minutes of silence, 'I think this is the proudest day of my life.'

Robert smiled and topped up her mug. 'I'm glad. After today there'll be no stopping you!'

'You think?'

'I know,' he said. 'I always have.'

2

Friday

A studio flat, especially one in Bloomsbury, owes much to the art of squeezing a lot into very little space. The architect that designed Rita's made sure it was everything a first-timer looks for in an apartment: minimal and uncluttered with more branded appliances than an electrical superstore. The flap table was different though. It was just a piece of pine cut into a long rectangle. Mark made it for her when she first moved in and she probably spent more time in front of it than anywhere else.

Meg drained her coffee and got up from the stool. 'I'm done,' she said. 'You ready?'

'As I'll ever be.'

'Let's go then.'

Rita pulled on a jumper and threaded her arms through a beaten-up rucksack.

'What about Barry?' Meg asked.

'Asleep,' Rita replied.

'No change there then,' said Meg, rolling her eyes.

'I'm not biting,' said Rita, ignoring the sarcastic remark.

They descended the two floors of Lancaster

House and came out onto Southampton Row. Even though it was early – 5.53am according to Rita's watch – the crowd was starting to build as they headed for the tube. The early May sun cut through a light morning mist. They ducked into Holborn and rode the escalator down to the eastbound platform.

'How *is* Barry?' Meg asked as they jostled for position with dozens of other commuters.

Rita had worked with Meg for just over two years. She knew that once she focused in on a topic she pursued it ruthlessly.

'Fine,' Rita replied.

Meg didn't answer.

The tube pulled in and they bundled into the carriage. The morning rush had started to bubble.

'But you're not fine, are you?' said Meg as the doors bounced shut.

'Yes, I am.'

She shook her head. 'No, you're not.'

Rita opened her mouth to reply, but Meg got there before her. 'It's not working, is it?'

They shuddered into St Paul's and were bumped and pushed as people got on and off. 'It's just gone a bit stale, that's all,' Rita said, trying to make light of it. 'That's what happens when people get past the first six months. It'll turn around.'

Meg clutched the grab bar above her head and said, 'Do you love him?'

The question was like a slap.

'The answer is either yes or no,' said Meg.

Rita noticed a man glancing at her over his paper

at her. He looked away when she glared at him. 'Why does everything have to be black or white with you?' she whispered.

'It's a simple question,' Meg said.

'I don't know.'

'Then the answer is no.'

The train screeched loudly as they thundered into Liverpool Street. The doors opened and they joined the swell of commuters shuffling towards the up escalator and Broadgate. Meg fell in behind.

'I'm in a funny place, that's all,' Rita said over her shoulder. 'It felt exciting in the beginning. He was in finance, which impressed me, he was funny. Good-looking.'

'Yeah, I get the picture,' said Meg.

Rita pulled an oyster card from her back pocket. 'You've never liked him,' she said.

'He hasn't had a job for six months,' Meg replied.

'That's because he's trying to find the right one.'

'Oh, come on, Reet. Barry's as wet as a flannel. You need someone dynamic.'

'He's a nice guy, Meg,' said Rita.

Meg shook her head. 'Rita, he screwed that Polish girl while you were working your arse off at Retnel.'

Rita waved the oyster card over the reader and the barrier flipped inwards. 'We've been over all that,' she said over her shoulder as Meg also negotiated the barrier, 'it was a one off. I was doing too many hours; we weren't seeing a whole lot of each other. Relationships are delicate, Meg.'

'Oh, please.'

About six months ago, Barry was spending his days surfing the internet at The Coffee Bean on Kemble Street. He was looking for what he called 'five star' job opportunities. Rita was happy he was leaving the flat every day and doing something positive. Turns out, so was Marcianna. She was a barista there and the two of them would spend lunchtime at Marcianna's place. Rita found out after coming back from Retnel one particular lunchtime and seeing them holding hands outside All Bar One on Drury Lane. They had a big fight about it, he admitted what had happened and why. Truth was they were hardly seeing each other. Rita was working flat out and he felt neglected. She understood that on one level. Thing is, it didn't hurt her like she thought it should do. She didn't feel emotional; gut wrenched or anything like it. She didn't analyse it either. She just got on with life. He promised it wouldn't happen again and as far as Rita knew it hadn't.

'You're so clinical. You know that?' Rita said.

'I'm realistic. He screws someone else and you view it as a minor detail. Like he's just said your bum looks big in tight jeans.'

'Oh, come on.'

'I'm serious. You don't care, Rita. That's what I'm trying to say. If you did you'd be hurting and you're not.'

'Yes, I am.'

'Then you're a great actor and I know that's not true. I watched you in last year's Christmas panto. You were terrible.'

'Thanks,' said Rita shoving the oyster card back

into her pocket.

'Why don't you admit what the problem is?' said Meg.

'Why don't you tell me?' said Rita.

'He's not Mark.'

Rita's breath caught in her throat. An image filled her brain. The one that returned again and again. Him lying there. On their bed. The woman sitting up on top. Naked flesh. Pale. Lean and sinewy.

She opened her mouth to reply. She wanted to say something smart and cutting. Something that would counter everything Meg had said. But she couldn't. Meg was right. 'No,' she said softly. 'He's not Mark.'

* * *

Barry Townsend woke suddenly. A noise had brought him around. Something light and tinny like keys jangling on a ring. His eyes probed the semi-darkness. They flicked left towards the curtains that were drawn against the window. He could see brightness behind them. That meant it was morning. But it was early morning. Too early for Barry to get up. He glanced at the space next to him; to where Rita slept. It was empty. Barry was confused for a brief moment before he remembered where she was. At the lab giving a demo. She had been talking about it last night. Had to be up at the crack of dawn to get there on time. *Better her than me*, he thought. He listened briefly to the silence. Then he turned over and prepared to go back to sleep. He settled and adjusted his position on the bed. Closed his eyes once more. Then the sound came again. This time close to his ears. He sat up. An intruder stood by the window watching him. Dressed in a black sweater. Black trousers. Wearing gloves.

Barry pulled the covers to his chest. 'What do you want?' he heard himself say.

'Where is Rita?' the intruder asked casually.

'Rita?' Barry tried to clear the fog from his brain. 'Gone,' he said.

'Why?' the intruder asked.

'Sorry?'

'*Why?*' came the reply.

Barry stuttered. His body felt stuck to the bed. The shock of another person in his bedroom held him still.

'When was it arranged?' the intruder went on.

'What?'

The intruder stood for a moment as if lost in thought. As if trying to work something out.

Barry pushed the covers back. Forced himself out of the bed. Tried to assert some authority. 'Who are you?' he said. 'Get out of my flat!'

'It's not yours. It belongs to Rita.'

'How the hell do you know that?' asked Barry.

The intruder pushed Barry back down on the bed. A casual shove. No big deal. The way it was done frightened Barry more than the act itself. It was polished and sure.

Barry struggled to get his breath. Tried to control his panic. Tried to make sense of what was happening.

The intruder sat down on the bed. Smiled. Spoke

softly. 'Rita never leaves this early.'

Barry stared back. 'She has a demo to perform,' he said.

'A demo?' said the intruder.

Barry nodded.

'What does that mean?'

Barry tried to think. He didn't know what it meant. They never talked about what she did. They mostly talked about him. 'I'm not sure,' he said.

'Was it hastily arranged?' asked the intruder.

Barry had no idea if it was hastily arranged or not so he said the first thing that came into his brain. 'Probably.'

The intruder smiled once again and produced a small red tube from an inside pocket. It looked like a cigarette lighter. A fancy one with chrome edging and metallic paint. The intruder flicked it as if igniting the flame. But a flame did not appear. Instead a four-inch blade exploded from the shaft. The intruder turned it quickly and drove it downwards and at an angle into Barry's leg.

Barry's breath caught in his throat. The shock of the sudden violence stopped the air. It was as if his throat had closed. He struggled to breathe. Then he felt the pain. A roasting, charring burn. Like a poker – white from the fire – penetrating his flesh. The intruder was up. Moving around the bed. Pushing him down. Grasping his arm.

It was a nightmare. One that was about to get worse.

3

Retnel Biotechnology was a beautiful glass-fronted edifice located in the round at Broadgate. Its design was typical of the sleek, glazed skin structures that now dominated and overpowered the less garish stone buildings of the old city. With Liverpool Street station just below it, the Retnel building was in the centre of the financial district. Very useful when touting for funding from private equity or VCs. Like many commercial enterprises in bioscience, Retnel had partnered with an organisation that shared the same philosophy as their own. It made commercial sense to pool resources and share technology. Both would then work under the same umbrella name. Usually the name of the more powerful partner. Hence, the third floor of Retnel was dedicated to The Institute for Molecular and Developmental Biology, or IMDB for short, that Meg, Robert and Rita worked for. Any progress made in terms of commercial application of IMDB's work would go down as a Retnel success. IMDB was happy with that as long as profits were shared.

The two women shouldered through the revolving door at Retnel's entrance and groped for their passes. The interior was cool and empty.

Empty except for the security guard, a tall and thin man with a peaked cap and a stay-pressed shirt. He smiled and said, 'Early today?'

'Got a presentation to prepare for,' answered Meg, flashing her pass.

'Good luck with that,' he said.

'Thanks.'

Rita hit the call button on the elevator and they rode it to the third floor. The corridor on three was narrow, but it was bright and familiar. The labs were all to the left. One after another. Lab number 3467 was three doors down. It was open already. Robert Fleet was inside, pinning a rota to a notice board.

'Ladies!' he said as they stepped through. He often referred to Rita and Meg in the plural. They had spent so much time together over the last couple of years it was as if they came as a package. Robert had introduced them soon after Rita cloned the infra-1 gene. They were well matched. Meg's work ethic was easily as torrid as Rita's. After the initial success, they had spent thousands of lab hours characterising infra-1, studying its structure, its interaction with other genes, always trying to understand how it worked, what it did and why it did it. Often working far into the night before catching a few precious hours' sleep at their pods, then going straight back to work early the next morning. The experience had been exhilarating for both of them. In Meg, Rita had found someone who seemed to be in tune with her way of thinking. She liked her from the very start. It was a typically brilliant bit of social engineering by Robert Fleet. The work they had produced together, especially in the last six months or so, had been so original; so far reaching that neither of them could believe what they had begun to uncover.

'Morning, Robert,' they chanted together.

'You prepared for today?' he asked.

Rita heaved off her rucksack. 'As I'll ever be.'

'And you, Meg?'

She was already unpacking. 'You kidding? I've been up most of the night with this stuff.'

'Good,' said Robert. 'They've set it all up in the conference suite upstairs.' He checked his watch. 'We need to be up there in an hour.'

'I want at least one run through before we go on,' Rita said.

Robert smiled. 'I knew you'd want to check.'

Rita flopped into her chair. She unlocked her desk drawers and said, 'I'm a control freak.'

'I know that too,' replied Robert, tossing over a set of keys. 'That'll open the conference room. They'll be arriving at eight.'

Rita caught the keys and stashed them into her pocket. She surveyed her pod. It was littered with diagrams, half written notes, torn-off sheets of lined notepaper. She and Meg had been here late last night preparing for the presentation. They had stopped all lab work to concentrate on it. Rita tidied the notes and got them into a numbered order. 'You finalised the slides, Meg?' she called as she stapled the lot together.

Meg leaned against a cleared lab bench and peered into a white MacBook. 'Yeah, it looks nice and pretty,' she said tapping the space bar. 'Doesn't mean it'll fly but it's very pretty.'

Rita got up from her pod and leaned over Meg's shoulder. 'Ooh, very slick. The graphics will win them over even if I don't.'

'Umm,' said Meg, checking the final slide. 'What you planning on wearing?'

'My dark power suit, of course,' said Rita. 'What do I always wear for formal?'

'Where is it?' asked Meg.

'In the rucksack.'

'So what about creases?'

'They'll fall out,' said Rita, fishing the crumpled material out of the rucksack.

'Show me,' said Meg, holding it up to the light. She shook her head. 'I'll take it to James.'

'Who's James?'

'He owns the dry cleaners in the station mall. He'll be open by now. I'll get him to put an iron over it.'

'Aw, thanks, Meg,' said Rita.

'Don't thank me,' she replied. 'Just go and learn your lines.'

* * *

I've made a mistake. An error of judgement. One that I usually do not make. The preparation in my work is everything. I stand or I fall by it. It gets me the reward I deserve or it throws something up that could harm and damage me forever. The stakes are high. They always are.

But I *have* made a mistake and I need to reason through my next move.

Rita was out. That should not have happened. She leaves at 7.15. Always. You can set your watch by it. Day after day. I've staked her out. Followed her movements. I *know* when she comes in and when she goes. I have to know. I'm not playing a game here. *Not* knowing means the end for me. So I am patient and careful and thorough.

But she was out. On *this* particular morning. The morning I chose to make the hit. Is it a coincidence? Are there other factors at play here? Factors I know nothing about? The boyfriend was there in her place. That never happens either. But today he was there.

Today, today …

I wanted to know if the boyfriend was part of the conspiracy. So I killed him. Bled him out. It's an old trick. He had the time it took to bleed to death – about twenty minutes if it's done right – to tell me what he knew.

He knew nothing.

I assumed that would be the case, but I wasn't taking any chances.

So what to do?

I'll not rush to make amends. To kill her in an unfamiliar place for example, or in a scenario that has not been rehearsed over and over again. In other words: to make a rash decision. An inexperienced gambler who loses a stack on a bad bet will hurry to double up on the next. I'll not make that mistake.

No, I need time out. Space to think through what comes next.

It means Rita will have another day or two to live. That's okay, I can cope with that.

4

The polished mahogany table that usually dominated the centre of the boardroom had been removed. Instead the space was filled by four rows of five leather office chairs. At the front of the room was a flip chart, a white screen, a projector that drove a power-point presentation and, moving nervously between all these, Rita herself. The presentation had lasted twenty minutes. She scoured the room. Twenty odd faces stared back. Most were male, although there were two women at the back; all of them – including the women – were wearing corporate suits. Most had notebooks and leather document cases. A few had i-Pads. With the exception of Rita, Robert and Meg, none of these people were scientists. They were from the City and represented private equity, loan investors and other bioscience outfits. All looking for the next big drug in which to invest. If what Rita had just said pleased them then maybe some of it would come the way of IMDB. There was a lot riding on this.

Rita glanced at Robert and Meg and they each nodded back their approval. Meg gave her the thumbs up. Rita quickly stole a look at IMDB's president, Ronald Bell, now well into his seventies, who was sitting against the back wall resting his head against the panelling. His large, banana-like fingers, so often wrung together in excitement when they made progress, were now laced over the top of his crossed knees. He gazed benignly in Rita's direction. Everyone loved him. He treated all of them – from research scientists to canteen staff – as if they were part of his own family. Without him IMDB would have perished years ago and everyone knew that. This was for him as much as anything else.

Rita's mouth felt dry.

A hand went up from the back and the questions began. They wanted to know more about Interleukin 50 and what it did, its effects on macrophages, how IMDB could make it so specific, and turn it on and off at will; how IMDB could incorporate a gene which coded for it in the way Rita had proposed, and above all else – step by step in layman's language – how the macrophages could eat through arterial plaque. All of this Rita had covered already, but she was happy to repeat it. They would never understand the technology fully, but that was okay. They didn't need to.

A man in the front row raised his hand. He was suntanned, wore a dark blue pinstripe suit and sat side-on in his chair with one arm slung over the back of it. 'The experiments you've completed in mice look impressive,' he said, glancing down at a note pad balancing on his lap. 'Any similar data using human subjects?'

'Human?' she asked. 'No, not yet, it's too early.'

'How much funding do you require to get that data?' someone else asked.

Rita was waiting for a question like that. The Retnel accountants had been working on this for weeks. She flicked the power point and showed the slide that gave the breakdown including manpower, equipment, fees, raw materials, overheads. Everything.

'We calculate an investment of ten million sterling will be required to bring this technology to the stage where it will be licensed for human trial. Assuming success at that stage, the rewards, both in terms of amelioration of human suffering and financial profitability, are off the scale.'

There was no denying that. Most of the heads in the audience nodded as she said it. Even if they didn't understand the mechanism in the same way a molecular immunologist did, they knew the ramifications of its success. These people studied the numbers and the numbers told them that heart disease accounted for 38% of deaths in the UK alone. Of those, most were suffering from arterial plaque build-up. It was directly or indirectly responsible for 233,000 deaths per year in the UK and 600,000 in the US.

A sobering statistic.

An awful lot of heart disease sufferers stood to benefit from this technology should it fly.

That was Rita's cue to get off and let the Retnel business development team take over. They loved numbers as much as this audience did and were just aching to talk about projections, business planning, cash flow, and size-of-prize forecasts. Rita received polite applause and made her exit.

Robert and Meg had moved to the far door and were making frantic hand signals for her to follow. She got to them and was bundled through in a flurry of backslapping and frantic giggling from the pair of them.

'Well done, Rita,' said Robert, almost jigging as he spoke.

'You nailed it, kiddo,' said Meg, linking her arm through Rita's.

'You think?'

'Yep. It was impressive.'

'Nothing's been signed yet,' Rita said as they led her through the corridor towards Robert's office.

'Of course not,' said Robert, 'but seeing it brought together in a presentation like that. Well, I reckon we should celebrate. Come on!'

They ran to his office like giggling school kids. There were papers all over his desk; books and files piled on an office chair. A bundle of *Immunology Today* journals balanced on top of his clunky PC. Robert busied himself moving the piles to the edge of the room so they could all sit down.

'Give him a hand, please, Rita, ' said Meg, 'while I work on something much nobler.'

Meg rummaged by Robert's desk and pulled a bottle out of a carrier bag. She busied herself with the cork.

'Where did you get that? ' Rita asked.

'Ah, that would be telling,' she said, fiddling with the twine.

'I thought we'd have a small celebration,'

said Robert, flopping into the chair behind his desk. 'We all deserve it.'

'Couldn't agree more,' added Meg, easing the cork forwards. 'And even though this office is a complete mess and I've no idea how you work this way, I couldn't think of a better place to have it.'

'I'll take that as a compliment,' Robert replied, giving Rita a wink, 'and don't let appearances fool you. The disorganised professor routine is just to impress visitors!'

You're not joking, thought Rita. Robert was one of the brightest people she knew. The disorganisation did not translate to his work. He was as sharp as a tack. He knew it and so did they.

Meg popped the cork and poured three slugs into white IMDB coffee mugs. 'Remember the last time we did this?' asked Robert.

'After we spotted the infra-1 band on the gel,' Rita said. 'How long ago was that?'

'Long enough to turn this field on its head.'

'I'll drink to that,' said Meg.

They each took a good slurp and Robert reached for the bottle and began to re-pour.

'Hey!' Rita said, covering her mug. 'I've got an assay to set up this afternoon. It won't happen if I get trollied.'

'Relax,' said Robert. 'I'm giving you the day off. You too, Meg. This is a time for reflection not for work. Make a long weekend of it. There's a whole mountain of exciting work ahead of us but it can wait till Monday.'

Meg downed her champagne in one and held

her mug out for a refill. 'You are without a doubt the best boss in the whole wide world. Have I ever told you that?'

'Never,' said Robert, filling the mug.

'Well, that's very remiss of me.'

'I'll remember that the next time you complain about being here half the night working on something that can't wait.'

'Complain? Me? You must be mistaking me for someone else.'

Rita plonked her mug down on Robert's desk. 'If we've got the weekend off, I know what I'm going to do with it and, with the greatest respect to the two most amazing colleagues anyone could ever work with, it's not here.'

'Where you going?' asked Meg.

'Can't say,' she said, hitching on her rucksack.

'Why?'

'Because I'm a secretive soul.'

'Yes, you are,' said Meg. 'I hate it.'

Robert smiled at the banter.

'I'm off to get *your* kids, you idiot!' Rita grinned. 'Jungle Café! You up for it?'

'Of course,' laughed Meg. 'Wait for me!'

5

Detective Chief Inspector Terry Varcy's office was a small room at the far end of a large open space. The space housed tidy rows of workstations. They were part screened, had a desk, a monitor with keyboard and a small area to handle paperwork. The sort of place that might have belonged to an insurance firm or a team of accountants.

Varcy's office had been refurbished during the late winter. He'd spent most of March and April squashed in a corridor with his desk against the wall and piles of files spilling onto the floor. Not that he was complaining. His office badly needed something doing. It had been years since it had been touched. He didn't mind the choice of colour either. Magnolia was inoffensive enough. It was the lighting that was annoying him. He preferred fluorescent strips or even naked bulbs. Instead they had fitted half a dozen modern spotlights in four rows of two. It made the task he was currently trying to complete particularly awkward. A few moments earlier he had positioned a chair under one of the spotlights to see if that would help but it was useless. Now he was standing on his desk on tippy-toes so that his left eye was as close to the spotlight as possible. In one hand he held a circular shaving mirror and in the other a dropper from a bottle of Optrex. He had positioned the dropper just a couple of centimetres above the lower lid of his left eye and was just about to release the rubber bung when the door opened. It was Kendrick.

'What you doing up there?'

The droplet of Optrex missed Varcy's eye and plopped onto his shoe. 'Damn,' he said, shaking his leg. 'Don't you ever knock?'

Kendrick shrugged. 'I didn't realise you were doing your make-up.'

Varcy blinked his eyes a few times and repositioned himself for another attempt.

'Seriously, what are you doing, Gov'nor?'

'I've got an ulcer on my eyelid.'

Kendrick screwed up his nose. 'Never heard of that before.'

Varcy released the bung once again and this time a satisfying whoosh of cold liquid filled his eye. He blinked hard to ensure an even distribution of the mixture. 'Better,' he said, peering in the mirror. 'Here, help me down.'

Kendrick took his weight and Varcy eased himself towards the floor. He boxed up the Optrex, and went around his desk to replace the mirror in the top drawer.

'Can I have a look?' asked Kendrick.

'At what?'

'Your ulcer – I've never seen one.'

'No, you can't,' said Varcy, swivelling his eyeballs left and right to check for any further discomfort. He pulled a linen handkerchief from his top pocket and carefully dabbed his face.

'Are you sufficiently sighted to have a look at this?' Kendrick said, waving a frayed sheet of A4 in the air.

'What is it?'

'Just came in,' said Kendrick, handing it over and moving around the desk. 'Holborn. Southampton Row. 7.45am. Dave Edmond was in the HAT car.'

Varcy nodded. 'Yes, Ray Johnson came and spoke to me about this.'

'A neighbour noticed the apartment door gaping open,' said Kendrick.

On the sheet were a couple of photographs. Both were of the same young man; dark hair, mid-twenties perhaps, lying face up on a bed, his eyes open, mouth sagging, what looked like blood splatter both on his chest and on the light coloured sheets that surrounded him. The second photograph showed the source of the splatter. His right arm was turned over and a deep gash had been cut from his mid forearm through to his wrist and into his palm.

'This all we have?' asked Varcy.

'For the moment.'

Varcy glanced back at the sheet. Back at the photos. Back at the dead young man. Then his office phone rang. He picked up.

'You get to see the photos?' asked Ray Johnson.

'Just seen them,' said Varcy.

'Gruesome, huh?'

'I've seen worse.'

'So have I,' said Johnson. 'I want you to handle this one. You okay with that?'

Varcy nodded. 'I'm okay with it.'

'Who do you need?'

'The usual suspects,' said Varcy.

'No problem. Let me know if you want anything else.'

Varcy replaced the handset.

'*His eminence?*' asked Kendrick.

Varcy nodded.

6

Bloomsbury was a mixture of residential and business buildings, the latter resulting from an overspill from the successful square mile. The classical residential buildings intended for the rich Georgian folk had survived and were laid out in neat squares and even their mews , once the stables, were worth a fortune. Boltholes for celebrities and media people, business tycoons and rich Arabs.

Lancaster House was on Southampton Row, near the Theobalds Road end. It was a tall, grey building sandwiched between a tinted glass office front that had 'Macadam Associates' across the entrance, and a large retail unit selling hand-made furniture. Once a downmarket office building, it had been gutted during the property boom and turned into two dozen one-bedroom apartments.

Varcy stood outside the entrance and scanned the apartment windows that overlooked the road. Not a bad view. The traffic moving down Southampton Row was heavy and slow. Varcy checked his watch. It was barely ten o'clock. The weekend exodus had already begun. He had planned to go away himself, that wouldn't happen now.

'What floor?' asked Varcy, moving towards the

entrance and nodding at the constable who guarded it.

'Second,' said Kendrick, following him inside. 'Flat 24. We can take the stairs.'

They arrived at the landing of three apartments which were arranged in a triangle. Number 24 was screened off with tape. The door was open and a plastic sheet covered the entrance. There were a couple of partially gowned SOCOs in front studying a set of photographs, and a pale and sweating Katz, who came to meet them.

'You all right?' asked Varcy.

Katz had a narrow face and thinning, blond hair which he now pushed back off his face. He wiped his brow with his sleeve. 'Yeah, just been a bit of a rush that's all.'

'You look ill,' said Varcy.

Katz nodded and looked down at his shoes. 'It was my birthday yesterday, Gov'nor. Some of the lads took me out last night and I had a few too many.'

'Ah.'

'Lightweight,' said Kendrick.

'You well enough to fill me in on what happened here?' asked Varcy, moving to a couple of cardboard boxes that were stashed against a wall adjacent to the crime tape.

'Yes, Gov'nor. The neighbour from number 22,' Katz gestured to the flat directly behind them, 'came out this morning around 6.15 and saw the apartment door was open. He went in and found the body.'

'Where is this man?'

'He's gone off to work, Gov'nor. He's given a statement and knows we'll need to talk to him later.'

'How was the neighbour when you saw him?' asked Varcy.

'Bit shaken but okay.'

Varcy peered into one of the cardboard boxes and fished out a clear plastic bag. 'The photos I've seen are quite gruesome. Not pleasant for a professional let alone a civilian.'

'No indeed, Gov'nor,' said Katz.

'Have we identified the body?' asked Varcy.

'Yes, Gov'nor. One of the SOCO boys found the victim's wallet. His name is – *was* – Barry Townsend. Twenty-six years old.'

'Anything else?'

'The medic has just left. He thinks the corpse is around four hours old.' Katz checked his watch. 'That would put the murder at around 6.00am.'

'That it?'

'For the moment, Sir.'

'And what about this flat? Is it his?' asked Varcy.

'Ah, no, Gov'nor. That much I do know.' Katz checked his notebook. 'It's registered to a female called Rita Sidhu.'

Varcy tossed the name about in his mind. 'Do we know anything about Ms Sidhu?'

'Not yet, Gov'nor.'

'Okay, keep me updated.'

Katz nodded.

The plastic bag contained a scene-of-crime gown, overshoes, gloves and a paper cap. Varcy tossed one over to Kendrick then turned to Katz. 'I don't suppose you want to go back in there given your delicate state.'

'Not if I can help it, Gov'nor.'

'What's the smell like?' asked Varcy, knowing that this was the thing liable to make him feel sick.

'He's recent so I've smelt a lot worse but he's shat himself, Gov'nor.'

Varcy winced and pulled a small tub of Vick from his coat pocket. He dabbed a smear of the mentholated grease under each nostril before handing the tub to Kendrick. 'Okay, log us in.'

Varcy ripped open the bag and hurriedly got into the garb. When he was done he caught sight of himself in a wide window set in a recess by the stairwell. Behind the thin, white fabric his stomach bulged and the hat squashed his face.

'You look like Susan Boyle,' said Kendrick, pulling on his overshoes.

'Who?' asked Varcy.

They moved towards the plastic sheet that covered the door.

'You don't know who SuBo is?'

'Should I?'

'She's the greatest singer ever to emerge from Scotland,' said Kendrick, shaking his head.

'Tell me you're joking,' said Katz, filling in the details in the log book.

'Yeah, I am,' said Kendrick after a few moments. 'She's third greatest. I forgot about *The Proclaimers*.'

Varcy and Kendrick ducked under the plastic and emerged into a small lobby. Ahead of them was a living room. Varcy could see a light brown, leather couch and the edge of a flat screen TV through the doorway. To their right was a small galley kitchen. He peered in and noted the generic white units, chrome knobs and the fake marble worktop. It was tidy – there were no abandoned dishes from the night before – and the surfaces were clean and clutter-free. Near the entrance to the kitchen was a high wooden table with two stools stashed neatly underneath. Behind them, next to the front door, was a small, red-tiled bathroom not much bigger than a closet. To their left, the bedroom. Varcy moved slowly and braced himself for the horror that awaited him. It had been twenty-five years since he'd signed up and fifteen since he'd joined CID. In that time he had seen all manner of dead people in a hundred different ways. It made no difference. He never got used to the shock of it. Nor the smell of them either. The putrid odour that made him want to vomit his guts up.

Two SOCOs were collecting either side of the bed. One was crouched by a small table to the victim's left while the other, a set of tweezers in hand, was picking at an area of pillow above the dead man's head.

'Gentlemen,' said Varcy as he came in.

They nodded a solemn greeting.

'Christ,' uttered Kendrick as the full horror emerged.

'Indeed,' said Varcy, surveying the body on the bed. It was naked except for a pair of yellow boxers. The legs were splayed slightly with the left foot externally rotated. The insides of the upper thighs were stained with a caramel-coloured faeces and the skin was pale and mottled. At the lower part of the left thigh – near the knee – was a coin-slot wound about half an inch long. Blood trails from this puncture had run over the lower part of the leg and onto the foot. His arms were resting at his sides, the left hand clenched into a loose fist and the right open with the palm upwards. Varcy moved to the side of the bed and examined the wound in the victim's right forearm. This was the injury the photograph had depicted so clearly back in his office. The flesh was raised and pulled back where the cutting tool had snagged. The burgundy valley it revealed was deep enough to expose what looked like bone. The blood beneath the arm had pooled on the sheets and the splatter had hit the carpet, the wall to Varcy's left and the ceiling above his head. There were two yellow markers on the wall where the bulk of it had hit, one on the ceiling and one on the floor next to a green, plastic bucket. Varcy was surprised by the bucket and bent forwards to peer inside. A dark, reflective liquid covered the bottom.

'Is this blood?' he asked the SOCO with the tweezers.

'Yep,' he replied. 'About three pints of it.'

Varcy tried to imagine a scenario in which this young man's blood ended up in a bucket.

'You seen this?' asked Kendrick, hunching over by a wardrobe near the foot of the bed. On the floor was what looked like a Swiss Army knife. The blade was free from the shank and a thin, ochre-coloured stain stippled the steel. It too was tagged.

'I can't believe this blade caused all that,' said Kendrick nodding towards the victim.

Varcy shook his head. 'It may have caused the wound above the knee, though. Remind me of this young man's name.'

'Townsend,' said Kendrick. 'Barry Townsend.'

'*Barry Townsend, Barry Townsend.*' Varcy repeated the name slowly over and over. Trying to connect with it. Trying to connect with the young man who lay dead in a flat which was not his own, in a pool of blood and excrement that most surely was. He closed his eyes and stood motionless. He was aware of the gentle sounds of the SOCO boys working the scene. He pushed those away and focused. He felt the air against his skin. He tried to envision its particles drifting and floating past him. Trillions of vibrating molecules that formed the space in which this murder was committed. He considered how they might have been shaped during the act. The way in which they were moulded by the presence of the aggressor and his quarry. Like a pin-art face print, they formed the negative of this gruesome scene even if for a brief moment. He tried to picture what that might have looked like. The elements that were in play. The prevailing emotion that was felt.

Reconstruction was always his first step and that is what he would do now. He opened his eyes and traced his steps back from the bedroom out into the hallway. He checked the doorway, the frame and architrave for evidence of forced entry. He found none.

The kitchen was often the heart of a home. This seemed too small to be much more than a functional space. He moved slowly to the living room. It was compact and minimal with an oatmeal-coloured carpet. Again he noted the cream sofa. The walls were cream too, but relieved somewhat by a print of a red rose above the fake fireplace. The generic kind found in department stores. Dominating the wall next to it was a casement window framed with fawn, tab top curtains. Varcy pulled them aside and peered down at the traffic below on Southampton Row. The May sun glinted off the car roofs and the windows of the office buildings opposite. He turned away and focused back on the room. In front of the couch was a glass coffee table. Its surface was clear but on a plastic shelf below it were a few journals. Varcy got on his knees and peered at the small pile. The top one was a computer magazine called *MaximumPC*, underneath this an issue of *Country Home*, and on the bottom a copy of *Scientific American*. He stood up again and saw Kendrick at the door.

'You okay?' Varcy asked.

'The smell's getting to me a bit.'

'You need some air?'

Kendrick shook his head. 'Nah, I'll be okay. How's it going with you?'

Varcy blew out his cheeks. 'I'm trying to make sense of it.'

'And?'

'The sex of the killer worries me. This Rita Sidhu

owns the flat and, judging by the décor, she lives here too. So she has to be in the frame.'

Kendrick nodded.

'The dead man is her boyfriend no doubt. It's possible she murdered him for some reason. It would take a lot of strength and force of will. But it's possible.'

'That fits a non-forced entry,' said Kendrick. 'Other than the front door there are two points of entry to this flat. The window in here and the one in the bedroom. Neither has a balcony and both are about sixty feet above the street.'

'Agreed,' said Varcy. 'So she used her key to get in and came into the bedroom unexpectedly while Barry was sleeping.'

'Then a dazed Barry wakes and she starts cutting him?'

Varcy shrugged. 'The trouble with it is I don't believe the average woman would have the strength to do a job like this. And there's something else about young Barry that disturbs me,' said Varcy. 'Something I can't get past.'

'What?'

Varcy moved out of the living room back into the hall. 'I'll show you what I mean.'

They entered the bedroom again and Varcy pointed to Barry's leg. 'See the wound above the knee?'

'Of course,' nodded Kendrick.

'It's familiar.'

'How?'

Varcy thrust his hands behind his back. 'I don't

know. I'm trying to figure that out. But it's like a déjà vu. You know?'

'I suppose,' said Kendrick.

Varcy was silent for a moment. 'I'm interested in what Barry was feeling in the moments leading to his death,' he said.

'Terror I should imagine,' said Kendrick.

Varcy nodded. 'Yes, but there's something else.'

'Something like what?'

'I think Barry was passive and compliant.'

'Passive?' said Kendrick.

'I think so.'

'I would have screamed the fricking place down if I'd been lying there,' said Kendrick.

'Maybe you would,' said Varcy. 'But maybe you wouldn't given certain circumstances.'

Varcy moved to the right side of the bed and bent forwards to study Barry's knee wound. 'Let's assume that Barry here was sleeping. That seems reasonable since the murder was committed some time around 6.00am. Something brings him to his senses. He wakes up and before him is a stranger.'

'Not his girlfriend?'

'Not in this scenario.'

'Okay,' said Kendrick.

'What would you do if you woke up to find an intruder at the foot of your bed?' asked Varcy.

'I'd attack him.'

Varcy nodded. 'Maybe. But suppose the intruder acted as if his being in your bedroom was the most natural thing in the world? Maybe he sits next to you or gets out a mobile phone to make a call. What then?'

'God knows,' said Kendrick.

'Well, first up he's mad, isn't he? Not operating with a full deck. He might be harmless, but to act as if nothing is wrong is weird and scary to the bravest among us. You feel violated, confused, but you try to cajole him.'

Varcy tried to picture young Barry attempting to fathom out what was going on. Talking softly, talking loud. Shouting, going silent. Perhaps trying to gain common ground. Subjugating himself. 'You'd talk him round,' Varcy went on, 'or soothe him while you desperately tried to think of ways of alerting someone. You'd certainly not want to get him excited.'

'You might just punch him in the head and be done with it,' said Kendrick.

'You might,' said Varcy. 'But Barry didn't because he was terrified. And he was terrified because the intruder did something so unexpected, so violent, that all his calculations about him were shot. The killer drove a Swiss Army knife deep into Barry's leg. Think of the pain. Think about the shock of that. It gives the intruder enough time to do what he came to do.' Varcy moved around the bed and pointed to Barry's arm. 'That.'

'So why?' asked Kendrick. 'For fun? Because he's sick?'

'I don't think so,' said Varcy, 'and that's what's disturbing me. That cut on the knee leaves Barry docile long enough for the intruder to assert his authority. The lethal cut of the arm here gives Barry the time it takes to bleed to death to tell the intruder something he badly wanted to know.'

'So what does Barry know that's worth all this?'

Varcy stared at Barry's lifeless body for a long moment. 'I don't know,' he said at last. 'But I'm going to find out.'

7

Reet-Reet was godmother to Charlie and Max. Charlie was six years old and Max was three. The best kids anyone could wish for. Both of them cute and edible. They were as excited to see Rita as she was to see them when she and Meg picked them up from nursery.

Meg leaned against the bonnet of her beaten up Toyota, smiling as the kids charged Rita. Both of them enveloped a thigh each and wouldn't let go. They were great huggers and kissers. Rita loved them for that. They didn't judge or probe, they just cuddled and Rita adored it. She picked each of them up in turn and looked into their eyes. All kids have something about their eyes, but these two boys melted her away. They were her special babies.

'What about me?' Meg said from the car. 'I'm the taxi service *and* Mummy!'

Rita staggered towards her with two koala kids clinging to her legs.

The kids' seats were in the back. High and proud with soft head huggers. Rita strapped in Max while Meg took Charlie. Max had a stash of plastic *Transformer* toys kept in a pouch in the seat in front.

'That's his show-and-tell stash,' said Meg as Max dived in and scooped out a handful.

'What's show-and-tell?'

'Max takes a special toy to nursery once a week, then stands up in front of the class and tells everyone about it.'

'Aw, that's so sweet.'

Max leaned forwards and whispered in Rita's ear. 'I'd like Optimus Prime more than anything else.'

'Max, stop being so devious!' said Meg as she checked Charlie's seatbelt.

He was old enough to know that *Reet-Reet* would buy him pretty much whatever he wanted this weekend.

Rita gave Max a wink.

'What's devious mean?' asked Charlie.

'Never mind. You all set?'

Rita strapped in next to Meg who hit the accelerator.

* * *

Jungle Café was buzzing. Formerly a warehouse on the edge of Camden, it had been converted into a tangle of gaudy colours, cartoon walls and soft-play areas. A super magnet for stressed out parents – and godmothers – of kids with too much energy to burn and nowhere to burn it. As the name implied it had other advantages for adults too. Specifically, a never-ending supply of caffeine.

They got a table by the entrance. Meg piled the boys' gear onto a plastic chair while Rita removed their shoes.

'Watch the kids while I get the coffee,' said Meg as the boys charged towards the play area.

8

Charlie's face was about six inches from Rita's and he was staring intently into her eyes. 'Will you come into the ball pool with us, Reet-Reet?'

The ball pool was not exactly what she had in mind at that moment but what was she going to say? How could she resist him? She leaned forward and kissed the end of his nose. 'Come on then, mister.'

'Yay!' shouted Charlie and Max together before charging towards the caged area.

Rita started after them. Then her phone rang in her pocket. She picked it up, held it to her ear and began to chase after the boys. 'Rita speaking,' she said without looking at the ID.

'Rita Sidhu?' said a male voice.

'Yes, can I help you?'

'Ah, yes, I hope so. I'm Detective Chief Inspector Terry Varcy from the City Police in London. Is this a good time to speak?'

'Police?' said Rita.

'Yes, CID.'

Max and Charlie were now at the entrance to the cage. 'Come on, Reet-Reet!' they shouted.

She put her finger to her lips. 'Is everything okay?' she said into the phone.

'You are the owner of flat 24, Lancaster House, in Bloomsbury?'

'Yes, I am,' she said. 'Is something wrong?'

'I'm afraid so,' said Varcy. 'I must speak to you right away.'

9

Robert Fleet reviewed the last few hours with as much concentration as he could muster. He remembered having the type of feeling that he had rarely experienced before. He had been satisfied. Satisfied with his lot, satisfied with his life, satisfied with the enormous progress the infra-1 gene project had garnered. He had often thought about what it might feel like to discover something profound; something that would make a difference. Names like Flemming, Watson and Crick, and Jenner were legendary. The people he'd read about even as a small boy. In that sense he had always known what he wanted to do with his life. To be on the cutting edge of science, to be like them. It had been a long, hard road, but he wouldn't have changed any of it for a second. Nothing was certain. He knew that and he accepted it. He took nothing for granted, but now the project was on the brink – on the brink of something great.

He had been slumped comfortably in his office chair with his feet up on his desk. He remembered that very well. In his hand was the last of the champagne. After Rita and Meg left he had enjoyed another glass. This was a time for celebration after all. He had felt happier than he could remember feeling.

It was after the telephone call that it all went bad. The guard from the lobby called and told him his car window had been smashed. Robert parked his car in the Retnel underground lot. He went down to assess the damage. It had indeed shattered. He yanked the door open and began to clear the shards of glass. Then he felt a sudden sensation behind his shoulder. Sharp at first. Burning a moment later. Then a flame searing at his flesh. Boring a hole. He reached backwards. Clawing at the source of the agony. He turned and a blunt force crashed into his face. It melded with his skin and he immediately tasted blood. Then the car lot blackened. He passed out.

When he came to he was bound; his arms clamped to his sides, knees into his chest. He was side on. It was dark and bumpy and he could hear traffic noise. His hands scrambled to his pockets. The rope that bound him yielded slightly, so he pushed and pulled until he had some traction. Then he eased his mobile from his pocket. The charge was still good. The neon lit up the dark space. He gradually scrolled through his contacts then began tapping out a message. It was a slow process. Agonisingly so. He was two words in when the ride came to an abrupt halt. Robert waited in the darkness and listened. Then he heard footsteps and the trunk of the car he was in lifted. Light poured in and Robert pressed 'send'.

10

Campden Hill Road joins Notting Hill Gate and Kensington High Street like the central bar on the letter H. It is salubrious, well established and very expensive. A magnet for career politicians, fading rock stars, and the young *It* children of old money parents. Kendrick whistled through his teeth as the car carrying him and Varcy pulled into a crescent of fawn, stone town houses, all large with old style sash windows, turrets and balconies, and grand entrances. The crescent of houses was built on the site that once was home to the sprawling King's College campus.

A security guard stood by the pillared entrance of one of the buildings. He held himself erect as if on sentry duty, staring forwards unblinking, his dark jacket absorbing every drop of the afternoon sunshine.

Kendrick nodded towards him as the car came to a halt. 'Thought we'd pulled up outside Number 10 for a minute there.'

Varcy had been studying an eight-page file on his lap. 'Sorry?' he said.

Kendrick parked the car. 'Nothing.'

Varcy had prepared the file before leaving the office. In it was all he could find on John Scott, the man whose house this used to be and on whom Varcy now focused all his attention. Turns out John was not as everyday as his Christian name suggested.

Kendrick wrenched up the handbrake. 'Ready?' he said, heaving himself out.

Varcy nodded and pushed open his door.

John Scott was in fact Lord John Scott, a Liberal working peer who had served in the House of Lords under the title of Lord Scott of Cranleigh and Elsemere. Varcy shook his head. Ridiculous name, although not uncommon. A lot of these Lordy types had similar monikers. Varcy seemed to remember Jeffery Archer had an equally absurd title. He flipped open the passenger door and got out.

'What was Jeffery Archer's title in the House of Lords?' he asked.

Kendrick had moved towards the entrance of the house. He was studying a high balcony above him. 'Who?'

'Jeffery Archer, the novelist.'

'Haven't got a clue.'

Varcy turned his attention back to the Scott file. Lord Scott no longer served in the House of Lords. In fact he didn't do much of anything any more. Six months ago he had been found murdered in his office. His murder had come to Varcy's attention about two hours ago when Cole had given him the details. He – Cole – had run the circumstances of Barry Townsend's murder through HOLMES and got a hit. HOLMES was an acronym for Home Office Large and Major Enquiry System. On it was all the information gathered in the course of an investigation as either evidence or as intelligence. If the statement readers are on song, HOLMES will throw up patterns, coincidences and inconsistencies.

'It's got the same crucial elements of Townsend's,' Cole had said back in the office.

'Namely?' Varcy had asked.

Cole began counting his fingers. 'One, a non-life threatening stab wound – in this case to the shoulder – two, a longitudinal knife wound to the right forearm, and three, a bucket was discovered next to the body with blood in it.'

Varcy had almost jumped out of his seat when Cole told him this. He had then asked Cole to arrange an urgent visit. This was the reason they were here. Lord Scott's son had kept the house on, and the housekeeper who found the body was still employed by him. That was who Varcy wanted to talk to.

The door was opened by Cole, who ushered the men into the entrance hall and through it to a corridor that ran adjacent to the stairs. The clack-clack of three sets of feet on the wooden flooring echoed around the high ceilings and bounced off the stone walls. Varcy admired the large, framed paintings that hung in rows on much of the wall space. They all seemed to be – to his amateur eyes at least – originals and all of them depicted the sea in one form or another. Pure sea-scapes snuck in between studies of ocean-going vessels, yachts and small row boats. Varcy could certainly relate. Much of his childhood was spent on Sheerness beach where his dad had a catamaran, and where he would spend hours on the old sea wall, watching the yachts cut through the mouth of the Thames on their way out to sea.

'Any resistance to us coming out?' Varcy asked Cole as they walked.

'No. The opposite in fact,' said Cole. 'They seemed pleased that the Met were taking fresh interest.'

Varcy nodded.

The investigation into Lord Scott's murder had hit the proverbial brick wall. Although not part of it, Varcy understood why. There were no witnesses, almost no forensics, and of course no suspects either.

'In here,' said Cole, showing them into an office. In the centre was an imposing rosewood desk; it set the tone of the whole room. On it was a wafer thin computer terminal and a framed photograph. Varcy glanced at it. It showed a slim, middle-aged woman with her arms around a dark-haired young man of about eighteen. He was smiling broadly, leaning into the woman slightly.

To the left of the desk was a set of French doors. They were open and the net curtains swayed in the breeze. Varcy moved towards them and peered out into a perfectly tended garden. About twelve feet square, it was walled, private and quiet. It had a manicured circle of lawn at the centre. This was surrounded by a bed of flowers. Varcy didn't know the names of any of them. He did recognise the roses, though. The unseasonable May sunshine had brought them on. They were pink and tight and beautiful. He leaned out to smell the one nearest to him. It had a soft, sweet aroma. Calming and delicious.

'What's the other side of that wall?' he asked Cole, who had fallen in a few steps behind him.

'The back of the mews. An alleyway that leads out to Campden Hill Road.'

Varcy nodded.

Back inside his attention was taken by a bookcase. Built to fit the room, it filled the whole side of the wall facing the desk. Varcy noticed the books. Political biographies, large tomes about history, politics and business. Varcy looked for some light reading. A novel perhaps. Something that would let him in. Let him feel Scott's emotion. But nothing fitted the bill.

'Okay,' said Varcy.

'The housekeeper's in her room,' Cole said, 'I'll go and get her if you're ready.'

'As I'll ever be,' said Varcy.

Cole moved away and Varcy and Kendrick each took a seat either side of the desk.

'Impressed?' asked Kendrick, nodding at the opulent surroundings.

'Very much,' said Varcy, balancing the thick Scott file on his lap.

'Beats my flat in Mile End hands down,' said Kendrick, adjusting his jacket. 'No doubt about that.'

Varcy flipped open the pages and scanned them once again. He had included the statement taken at the time from the housekeeper, which he reviewed quickly before moving on to the photographs. Lord

Scott was found in a leather chair, not unlike the one in which Varcy was currently sitting. A thick band of duct tape had been wrapped around both his chest and the back of the seat to keep him from slumping forwards. His head was tilted to one side and his grey hair hung forwards in strands. Varcy noted the scatter of liver spots on his right temple and checked the file for his age. Sixty-eight years old. The second of the three photographs showed a view of the shoulder wound. Almost certainly caused by a knife, thrust near the top of the scapular, puncturing the fabric of his clothing and penetrating – according to the information Varcy had – to a depth of two inches. The third and final photograph showed the arm wound. There was no doubting the similarities with Barry Townsend's injuries. In this case, the slash began near the bicep insertion and continued until it hit Lord Scott's middle finger. This digit, according to the report, was so badly damaged it was barely attached.

A light knock at the door distracted Varcy from his reading. Cole brought two people into the room. One a lady – the housekeeper. She was short, rather plump, with a mound of grey hair piled high on her head. Varcy put her age at around sixty. With her was an elderly gentleman, about ten years her senior. He wore a thick outdoor coat and workman's boots.

'This is Mrs Jenkins,' said Cole gesturing to the lady. 'And this is Mr Cairy. Mrs Jenkins thought it would be useful to bring Mr Cairy along too because he was with her when she discovered the body.'

Varcy rose from his chair and shook hands with each of them. 'Thank you for seeing us,' he said. 'This is my colleague, Detective Inspector Kendrick and I'm Detective Chief Inspector Terry Varcy.'

'Yes,' said Mrs Jenkins nodding. 'Your friend told us who you were.'

Kendrick dragged a couple of chairs from the edge of the room to the centre.

'Please, Mrs Jenkins, Mr Cairy, have a seat.'

'Call me Florrie,' said Mrs Jenkins, 'everyone else does.'

'And I'm Reg,' said Mr Cairy nodding benignly. 'I was his Lordship's gardener.'

'Fine,' said Varcy settling back into his seat. 'Would you mind if we asked you a few questions about Lord Scott? I know you've been asked before, because I've got the transcripts here in his file. But there has been a new development in this case and so I wanted to hear it from you in person.'

Florrie nodded eagerly. 'What do you want to know?'

'Well, why don't we start with what happened the morning you found his body?'

'It was a Thursday,' she said shifting in her seat. 'I'd made his Lordship his breakfast. He always had the same thing – cereal and tea – and he liked to take it here in his study. He was happy for me to leave it on his desk ready for when he came down. So I'd leave a tray with everything on it and a tea cosy on the pot to keep it fresh. Then I'd get on with my duties.'

'What were your duties that day?' asked Varcy.

'On Thursdays I clean the guest bedroom and the two bathrooms upstairs. Then I come down and clean this study. I came back down here around eleven to start on it.'

'And that's when you discovered him?'

'Yes. The door to the study was shut and I couldn't get it open. I had a key, but that was no use because something was preventing me from opening it. There was a small gap where the door had opened slightly, so I went to fetch a yard broom to wedge it open, but I wasn't strong enough to do it. That's when I went to get Reg.'

Reg cleared his throat and said, 'I was working out the back. Florrie came running out and seemed a bit panicky, so I ran in to help.'

'So you suspected something was wrong right away?' asked Varcy.

'Yes, I think I did,' said Florrie, looking up at the ceiling for a moment. 'It seemed unusual, I suppose.'

'I tried to prize the door open with the broom but it snapped,' said Reg.

'That's when you went off to get the oar, didn't you, Reg?' said Florrie.

Varcy checked back at the notes in the file. 'Oh yes, I read about that.'

'It was in the shed,' said Reg. 'Belonged with a rowing boat at one time. I don't know where that ended up. Anyway, I forced it in the space between the door and the architrave and pulled. That did the trick.'

'What happened then?' asked Varcy softly.

Reg looked at Florrie.

'Well …' she said shaking her head. 'He was just sitting there, wasn't he, Reg?'

Reg nodded gravely.

'There was some tape around him and blood. Blood everywhere. On the wall, the floor, on the desk. I screamed and don't remember much after that. I've never seen anything like it in my life.'

'I had to pull her away,' said Reg. 'That's when we called the police.'

Varcy flipped through the papers on his lap and pulled out the page he was looking for. 'It says here that those French doors were open when you entered. Is that true?'

'Yes, they were,' said Reg. 'It was breezy and the drapes were blowing in and out of the room as we came in.'

'Do those doors have a key?' he asked.

'Yes,' said Florrie. 'When it's fine, like today, and the doors are open, the key stays in the lock, like it is now.'

'And when the weather is poor?' asked Varcy.

'They're kept in the top drawer of the desk,' she said.

'Do you remember what the weather was like on that Thursday?' asked Varcy.

'Cold,' said Reg. 'I had thick gloves on when Florrie came to get me.'

'Yet the doors were open.'

They nodded.

'Did the keys ever go missing at all to your knowledge? Were they lost for a short time, for example?'

Florrie shook her head. 'Not that I knew of.'

'And the door you prized open,' said Varcy, pointing behind him. 'What was preventing you opening it?'

'A chair,' said Reg. 'It was tipped up and wedged under the handle.'

'I see,' said Varcy, scanning the files checking all this information. When satisfied he looked up and said, 'One final question. It's about the plastic bucket found next to Lord Scott's body. Do you remember that?'

Florrie's hands wrung tightly together. 'I do,' she said. 'A green one.'

'Did you recognise it?' Varcy asked. 'Was it something that belonged in the house?'

She shook her head. 'I'd not seen it before.'

'It wasn't stored in the loft or out in the shed?'

Reg shook his head. 'Not in the shed. I'd have seen it if it was.'

There was a moment of silence.

'Pity,' said Varcy, thoughtfully.

Florrie shifted in her seat again. 'You said there had been a new development,' she asked. 'What's happened?'

'A young man was murdered earlier today over at Bloomsbury. He was killed in the same way Lord Scott was.'

Florrie's hand shot up to her mouth.

Varcy rose from his chair. 'Okay,' he said. 'That's all. No need to worry.'

After Cole had led the couple out, Kendrick turned to Varcy, a grin on his face.

'What is it?' Varcy said.

'I can't believe people like that still exist,' he replied shaking his head.

'People like what?'

'*That*,' said Kendrick. 'I felt like I was in a Poirot movie.'

Varcy smiled and began stacking the papers back in the file. He ensured the edges lined up evenly before easing them back into a green, A4 wallet and folding the flap inwards to ensure they were secure. He tucked the folder under his arm and said, 'I think our killer has made a mistake. A small mistake. But enough to give me some encouragement.'

'Tell me,' said Kendrick.

Varcy moved around Lord John's desk and said, 'A repeat.'

'In English?' said Kendrick.

Varcy wiggled the mouse next to Lord John's computer and squinted at the screen. 'Barry Townsend's murder is a repeat of this one.'

'I know,' said Kendrick. 'The MO's the same. That's why we're here.'

'Ah,' said Varcy clicking the mouse a couple of times. 'But this one was deliberate. Barry Townsend's wasn't. At least I don't think it was.'

'What are you talking about?'

'It was unplanned.'

'What was unplanned?'

'Barry Townsend's murder.'

'How do you know?'

'I don't,' said Varcy.

Kendrick pushed both hands into his pockets. 'So what are you on to?'

Varcy leaned towards Lord John's computer screen until his nose was just a few inches from it. 'He had email, I assume?'

'I expect so.'

'I want access to it.'

Kendrick nodded. 'I'll sort it. Now come on, what's going on? Let me in.'

Varcy stood up straight. 'The Swiss Army knife that was lying by young Barry's bed.'

'What about it?' asked Kendrick.

'It shouldn't have been there.'

11

I move slowly, and deliberately. There is no need to rush. This is a day of pleasure not of pain, a day to reflect and learn. Granted I had a setback this morning. A challenge I did not anticipate, but since then I have had a breakthrough. A fortunate discovery.

As part of my research I made an enquiry about the safe in the laboratory where Rita Sidhu works. Apparently it is protected by two retinal scans. Hers and her boss's.

I had no idea! That piece of information has governed what my next move will be.

I cross the bridge from Mile End Park over the Regent Canal to Meath Gardens. The air, normally thick with the city's dirt and grime, is clear and fresh today as if blown clean by some great wind. I fill my lungs with it and enjoy the slight heady rush it gives me. Walking here, especially on this piece of ground gives me freedom. It eases my mind in a way I cannot get anywhere else.

I played on this ground when I was a kid. I know the smell of it. I remember the taste of the air hitting my throat when I ran, the exhilaration of being free and having energy to burn. I've tried to recreate moments like those as an adult, but I can't.

They are lost.

Time is blurred in this place.

I don't know if it is a gateway to the future or a route back to the past.

I come here to think through my strategies. I mentally check them off one by one. The arena I enter when I'm fully engaged in my work must be left as though I'd never been near. No trace, no trail and no clues.

I am a ghost.

That takes meticulous planning and careful execution. Suffice to say, I allow for all eventualities and on this occasion I took full advantage of my fact-finding.

I take a seat on the same park bench I sit on each time I visit. My back is towards the flats built where the Devonshire Street Railway depot once stood. The sun warms my face and I watch a group of children playing on the grass. They run uninhibitedly just as I used to do. There are four girls turning a skipping rope. One at each end and two jumping at the centre. They sing a tune; a pop song I think, although I'm not familiar with it. They stay apart from the boys who are playing a boisterous game of tag. My eyes settle on one boy. His hair is mousy brown and it sticks up at the back. He wears scuffed shoes and cheap spectacles. I am drawn to him because of his size – he is smaller than his friends – and because he blinks nervously behind the thick lenses. I know he is frightened of the rough game. He is on the edge of their group, wanting to join in, but afraid of being hurt.

He puts me in mind of another child I once knew.

One of the larger boys knocks into him and he flies forwards and scrapes his face in the dirt. I watch the shock take him. His body shakes and then the first sob escapes. I leave my seat and move forwards. I want to pick him up and grasp him to my chest. To shield him from the hurt. Then a woman appears – his mother probably – and yanks him up. His spectacles are broken, but he tries to put them back on. They sit on his face at an awkward angle. He presses his hand against his cheek and against his tears.

The woman yells, 'Stop being a cry baby!'

He gazes up at her helplessly and something about him connects with me as surely as if he'd spoken my name.

My eyes burn into the woman's back. I want to tear the skin from her bones.

She doesn't understand how precious the little boy is. How transient his life can be.

I do.

Little kids like him ensure I can never forget.

12

Rita slumped on a stool and stared past Meg to a place on the wall that was plain and empty. In one hand was a lit cigarette, in the other a glass ashtray with four dog-ends squashed at the bottom. The last time she had smoked, she had been a student at Durham celebrating the end of year exams. The relief of surviving exam week was nothing like the devastation she felt right now. She took another drag and hoped the dizzy hit of nicotine would help numb the horror.

It didn't.

After the detective's call, she had stumbled back to the table and fallen into Meg's arms. That was three hours ago. Since then time had passed in a blur of thoughts and images.

A policeman had met her at the entrance to Jungle Café. He was polite but distant. He had driven her to the Bishopsgate station where she had been offered coffee and biscuits and placed in an office. Through the glass partition she could see rows of desks where police staff were beavering away at keyboards and scrawling earnestly onto ledgers and short forms. A few had looked up from their work and nodded or smiled when she walked through, but most had not noticed her at all.

The office was sparse. There was a three-tier, grey filing cabinet in one corner and a black formica desk in front. A two-tier shelf on the far wall was home to six lever arch files of various colours. The air smelled faintly of paint. She took a seat opposite the desk and waited. Within a few moments the door had opened and Detective Chief Inspector Terry Varcy introduced himself and took a seat behind the desk. Rita guessed he was in his late thirties. He had dark receding hair combed back off his face, a slight swarthiness to his skin and deep rings under his eyes. Not a handsome man by any means, but kindly and strong.

'I'm sorry to have been the bearer of such bad news,' he began, clasping his hands together on top of the desk.

'Not a nice job for you,' she whispered.

'No, indeed it wasn't,' said Varcy fixing her with a benign gaze. 'I assume the young man was your boyfriend?'

'For six months,' Rita nodded.

'May I ask you a few questions about him?'

She nodded once again. 'Whatever you want.'

The questions were simple, polite and not too intrusive. The matter of Barry's death was handled sensitively and an offer of help – some kind of counselling, Rita imagined – proffered. She had refused. At some point she had been asked whether she would be able to identify Barry's body. Barry's mother was on her way but was in no fit state to do it. She agreed and regretted it almost immediately. At Durham she had joined the medical students for dissection class where a cadaver was systematically taken apart in the name of anatomy. She hated those sessions. Her reaction to the formaldehyde was visceral. It smelled of rotten flesh. Other students were not affected in the same way. She'd had a constant compulsion to gag.

By the time they had arrived at the morgue in St Mary's Hospital, the thought of what she was about to do had started to cause the same reaction. The cold, air-conditioned breeze that blew towards them as they picked their way, she and Varcy, along a dimly lit corridor and into a white, cube-shaped room, did nothing to alleviate her symptoms. The room was windowless. It had a large extractor in the ceiling above and red, ceramic tiles on the floor. There was a stainless steel counter that stretched the length of the back wall. A white tile splash back was laid behind this and a sink about half way along. In front of the sink, his arms folded across his chest, was a man in a white medic's coat. Before him was a trolley, on which was a long, rippled mound hidden under a white sheet. Varcy introduced Rita to the white coat man. The man nodded and then he and Varcy began to speak to each other quietly. Rita heard the voices but she didn't listen to them. She could not pull her eyes away from the hidden shape. It was a body, no question. Barry's body. She recalled the first time she had seen him. He was full of life, tall, confident – just what she'd needed back then. The lump under the sheet couldn't be that same man.

The lab coat man nodded his head and began talking to her directly. His words came into focus for a moment and she moved towards the trolley. He peeled back the white sheet and Barry's face stared upwards, his skin drained of all colour. His mouth turned back to reveal milky gums, the teeth small and white. His eyes were half open, enough to suggest life. That made it harder. More real. The horror propelled her backwards. The smell of chemicals and dead flesh crawled into her nostrils. Barry kept staring. Then it came: a gasp so low and breathy that it seemed to originate from the pit of her stomach. She covered her mouth to try and stifle it. Finally she turned away, covered her face and vomited.

13

Meg sat opposite Rita, a cup of steaming coffee pressed to her lips, her face drawn and pale as she listened to her horror story. The kids were in the front room. Meg had settled them with a *Monster's University* DVD. Aside from the ashtray, the breakfast table was strewn with eaten-up paper tissues, scrunched and scattered and discarded. A box of fresh ones was open and ready for use. Rita sucked hard at the cigarettes as Barry's gasping face kept looming into view.

'You should have seen him,' she heard herself say. 'It was like someone had ripped out his inside.'

Meg took another sip of coffee. 'Try not to think of it.'

Rita shot her a look.

'Okay, stupid thing to say, I know, you can't. It was too terrible.'

'He had injuries, Meg, but I couldn't get any further than the face. And the smell of that place. It made me sick.'

'Drink your coffee,' said Meg pushing the mug towards her.

Rita nodded and drew on her cigarette once more.

'What about Barry's family?' asked Meg softly. 'Have they been told?'

'His mother was there, I think,' said Rita. 'They said she was in a terrible state. He's got a brother who lives in the US, but I've never met him.'

'And what about the police? Do they know what happened?'

Rita shook her head. 'Nothing's been taken from the flat so burglary's not the motive. The place wasn't damaged or messed up. They think that the … ' Rita paused and brought the cigarette back to her lips before she spoke the next word – '… the *murderer* came in the front door. There's no evidence of a forced entry. The locks aren't damaged. Maybe Barry knew him and let him in. Or he managed to get hold of a key. They're not sure about any of that. That's what their questions were all about. They thought I might know.'

'And do you?'

Rita's eyes snapped quickly onto her friend. 'Of course not! If I did I'd tell them.'

Meg nodded quickly. 'Yes, yes I know you would. So what happens now?'

Rita gave out a sigh. 'There will be more questions. The guy in charge was fine. He said he'd stop by tomorrow to check how I'm doing.'

Rita stubbed out the cigarette in an ashtray. 'You know what bothers me most of all? The thing I can't get my head around? The detective thinks that Barry was tortured before he was killed. *Tortured.* Can you believe that? I keep thinking of him in my bedroom, begging for mercy, probably in terrible pain while this … this … *person* did God knows what to him.'

She felt the tears again now. They welled quickly and cascaded down her cheeks. She didn't try to wipe them away. She didn't sob or wail either.

Meg leapt from her seat and hugged her close. 'Don't cry,' she said.

14

Varcy sat at his desk and sipped hot tea. It was strong, but with plenty of milk and one sugar. He had drunk it that way for as long as he could remember. The sugar would have to go, he accepted that. His expanding waistline meant sooner rather than later. The tea, however, would not. Not at all.

He pored over the papers he had compiled on John Scott. The file he had taken to his house earlier that day had now doubled in size. Varcy had got Cole to download almost everything inputted into HOLMES about the Scott case. He wanted something physical he could touch and interact with. Computer files displayed on a screen didn't give him the same feeling as hard copies, and Varcy loved to *feel*. To connect. To know.

The lead on the Scott case had been a DI called Monroe. Varcy knew him vaguely. Over the years they had attended the same formal training days, interdepartmental briefings and social gatherings. About the same age as Varcy, Monroe had joined the Met from the military. Or at least Varcy thought he had. That was not uncommon. Police work was similar to military work. Or it seemed to be from the outside. Monroe had developed a good reputation. Varcy knew that much. He pressed the right buttons and was highly regarded by those whose opinions mattered.

The initial 999 call had been made by Reginald Cairy, the gardener, at 10.43am on Thursday, the sixteenth day of the previous November. Six months ago. The transcript of the call was in the file and Varcy had read it numerous times. It was straightforward enough. Or as straightforward as reporting the murder of your boss can be. Reg was a good witness, giving clear instructions to the operator. The ambulance had arrived on the scene within fifteen minutes and, because of the nature of the call, the police were automatically alerted and arrived exactly six minutes after the ambulance. Usual procedures were followed.

Forensics had revealed nothing. At least nothing of use to Monroe. There were no prints, or any organic debris that did not cross check with either Scott himself or those who worked in the house. Because of this, Monroe had briefly focused on the household. Specifically, those who had matches in Scott's study. That included Florrie and Reg, a part-time cook called Mary Fletcher and a twenty-seven-year-old man, Matt Singer, who came into the house from time to time to fix things, paint things, and generally maintain the property. Singer was dismissed quickly because he was nowhere near Kensington on the morning of the 16th November. He had been working on a building site in North London. A dozen or so of his co-workers vouched for his whereabouts on the day. Monroe dismissed

Florrie, Reg and Mary Fletcher as suspects soon after talking to them, which left the remote possibility that someone – a neighbour or passer-by – might have happened to witness something on the morning of the 16th. A few weeks of appeals, house-to-house enquiries and *Did You See* flyers proved that not to be the case.

What was certain were the murderer's entry and exit points. Monroe knew that on cold days, the French doors in Scott's study were kept closed and the key stored in his desk. According to the meteorological office, the temperature on the 16th November had been five degrees. Coldish. Cold enough to ensure the French doors remained shut. Yet when Monroe arrived at the house they were wide open. Reg, the gardener, told him they had been open when he entered the study, and Monroe had no reason to disbelieve him.

Given how well the job had been executed, there had been a plan. A careful one. A careful plan that involved the murderer knowing the doors would be open that morning, which meant he had an accomplice on the inside, Scott knew who he was and let him in, or the murderer had managed to get a copy of the key and open them himself. This meant that Reg, Florrie, Mary Fletcher and Singer were temporarily back in the frame. Monroe had fed all four of them into the system once more for another lap or two of questions, interviews and assessment. But it revealed nothing.

Varcy peered at a map of the area beyond Scott's walled garden. Assuming the murderer had exited by climbing the wall, which was about six feet high, he would have emerged into a small, crescent-shaped road – imaginatively called Crescent Road – and from there out to Campden Hill Road. Varcy assumed the murderer would have headed for Kensington High Street, a few hundred feet south of Crescent Road. There the murderer would merge with the crowd and disappear.

The whole thing was clean, ordered and neat. A professional job, clearly. Professionals do sometimes make mistakes. But not this time. Varcy took a deep sip of his tea and pulled a yellow legal pad from his desk. On it he had drafted what Kendrick had come to call Varcy's 'dump list'. Varcy compiled a dump list on every case he was assigned to. It was no big deal, he just dumped onto it whatever occurred to him. He didn't edit what he was writing, he splurged it down quickly and in no sensible order. He'd read once about free association. It was surprising what came out. He scanned the dump list now for the solid stuff: the logical things, the practical tasks that had to be accomplished, the to-dos, the lines of enquiry he had felt Monroe might have pursued more fully. The email account, for instance. Another round of questions with Matt Singer was another task. Varcy also wanted a list of meetings, telephone calls and social calls that Scott had made in the six months prior to his death. Monroe had made a sweep but had found nothing unusual. There were a thousand different avenues that needed chasing, resolving and referencing against what Monroe had done six months earlier.

Varcy ticked them off mentally one by one. Each of them had either been assigned to a team member or they were waiting to be assigned.

So he had the hard facts but he had the gut feel too. He studied the hunches, the feelings and the emotions. He read what he had written after looking at the photographs of Lord Scott's tortured and lifeless body. Three words only: *resigned, accepting, doubtless*. That was it. He tried to feel the emotion again. To connect in some way. Maybe there were more feelings to mine. He concentrated for a few minutes but felt nothing.

He took two more swallows of tea and flipped the legal pad forward a few pages to Barry Townsend's dump list. The similarity with the Scott murder was beyond doubt. The MO was the same. A smaller wound followed by the fatal slash to the arm. According to the medical report, Scott had bled to death, and although yet to be confirmed, Varcy was sure Townsend had too. Nothing had been taken from the flat. Whoever it was hadn't come to take anything except Barry's life. The entry and exit point was similar too. He'd come in through a door. In this case the front door. Not a window or a skylight. Like the Scott case, the door was untouched. They had a locksmith confirm it. So Varcy faced the same dilemma as Monroe had: was there someone inside to let the killer in or had the victims let him in themselves?

But there were differences too. It didn't feel the same as the Scott case. Something about it was rushed. Not as well planned as the first. The feel

Varcy had for Townsend was different also. He wasn't resigned like Scott was, he was surprised. Incredulous even. Disbelieving of what was taking place. Varcy had felt that especially when he was in the bedroom with Townsend's corpse. But he could be wrong. It was an impression that's all. Nothing factual. Except one thing. The Swiss Army knife. That was factual and it should not have been there. It made no sense to leave it. Two murders in, Varcy felt he knew enough about this operator to be sure he would not have left it by choice. So what had happened? Why was it there?

He finished the now warm tea with three swallows and left a quarter of an inch at the bottom. Then he heard a light tap on his door and Kendrick walked in.

15

Kendrick was jacket-less, the sleeves of his white shirt pulled up to his elbows. There were two ashtray-sized patches of sweat under each arm. A flap of shirt had come free from his belt line and spilled onto his right hip. He took a seat opposite Varcy and twizzled a silver 'K' ring around his pinky finger.

'You okay?' asked Varcy, looking up from his dump lists.

'I'm confused,' he said.

'Oh?'

'About Rita Sidhu.'

'Okay,' said Varcy.

Kendrick leaned forwards and rested his elbows on his knees. 'The usual checks come back clean. Cleaner than clean even. She's never been in trouble, never been late on a bill, she doesn't have loans or credit cards and her current account has never been overdrawn. She runs her life very tidily indeed.'

Varcy nodded. 'I'm not surprised. She's what psychologists call *a closed brooder*.'

'What?'

'It's a profiling tool,' said Varcy. 'Doesn't matter. Carry on.'

'So it's easy to follow her paper-wise. Then three years into her past she disappears and we hit a brick wall.'

Varcy cupped his chin in his palm. 'What are you talking about?'

'The trail ends,' Kendrick shrugged. 'Rita Sidhu doesn't exist before three years ago, *Ritnan Shannon* does.' He sat back in his seat. 'At twenty-one years old she changed her name. She used to be called Shannon. Ritnan Shannon. Then she appears as Sidhu. Rita Sidhu.'

'By deed poll?'

'So it seems,' said Kendrick. 'And that's what was confusing us. Everything changed on the official records. Bank details, telephone numbers, addresses. She had a small loan in her old name but that was paid off just before the change. The only common thing left is her NI number and date of birth.'

'Anything significant about the name she's chosen?'

'Shannon was her dad's name,' Kendrick said. 'Her parents were divorced when she was eight I think. Eight or nine. Sidhu is her mother's maiden name.'

Varcy spread his fingers out on the desk. 'Interesting,' he said.

'Glad you think so,' said Kendrick. 'We've been messing around with this all morning.'

Varcy smiled and yanked out a drawer in his desk. From it he pulled out his Optrex box. He opened it carefully and prized out the small plastic bottle. He used his index finger to dip the lower lid of his left eye, then squeezed the bottle gently. A dollop of fluid clipped the lid and ran down his cheek. He repositioned and repeated the process. This time he got a full dose. The cool liquid sloshed around his eyeball and Varcy dabbed away the excess with the back of his hand.

'Still bothering you?' asked Kendrick.

'Somewhat,' he said, screwing the lid on again and placing the bottle back into its box. He closed the flaps neatly at the top and replaced the box in his desk drawer. 'The question is why?' Varcy said at last. 'Why would a young woman of twenty-one want to change her name?'

There was a long moment of silence.

'Loads of reasons,' said Kendrick eventually.

'Name some,' said Varcy.

Kendrick shrugged. 'She dislikes the surname Shannon, or she dislikes her dad and doesn't want to be associated with his name.'

Varcy nodded.

'She feels for her mum,' Kendrick went on. 'She's closer to her. Feels she's been hard done by. Or maybe it's got nothing to do with that. Maybe she wanted to break free of the person she was. She was bullied at school, for instance. She had braces and spots and the other kids got stuck in. Shannon reminds her of all that.'

Varcy nodded again. 'But a deed poll change indicates a very deep desire to recreate herself, don't you think? She would have to be highly motivated to go to the bother.'

'Maybe she would,' said Kendrick, 'but unhappy kids have killed themselves for less than that. They're plenty motivated. There's loads of reasons to go to the trouble of changing a name.'

Varcy stood up and grabbed his tea mug. 'I need more fuel.'

Kendrick eased himself out of his seat. 'Right behind you.'

They moved out of Varcy's small office and into the larger, open plan space. The noise level here was a lot higher than in Varcy's office. According to the last internal audit, there were forty-three individuals working in this space. Police officers of varying rank, statement readers, administration clerks, assistants of assorted shades. Each had a workstation, each a computer. The tangle of wires from one computer to the next travelled to common printers, fax machines and scanners. Telephones rang, people talked, moved about, used photo-copiers and tapped at keyboards. There were half-eaten sandwiches and discarded crisp packets on desks, chocolate bar wrappers in the trash, and steaming drinks on blue, insignia-embossed coasters.

A four-foot snake of corridor hugged the east and north walls. It fed five offices of various sizes, a small kitchen, a WC beyond this and an exit that led to a single lift and a flight of stairs. The stairs led down to the holding cells and interview rooms.

Varcy and Kendrick stepped into the kitchen. It was narrow, and had a solitary window opposite the frosted door. Below the window was a stainless steel sink and a two-foot wide wooden counter that ran around the three walls.

Varcy rinsed his mug in the sink and grabbed another from a dozen or so draining next to it.

'There's an important reason – at least to her – why she changed her name,' Varcy said. 'Question is, did she do it for a "normal" reason like those you've suggested or was there something else to it?'

'Something like what?' asked Kendrick.

Varcy flipped the kettle on and plopped two tea bags into the mugs. He turned and leaned on the sink. 'I don't know.'

Kendrick said nothing.

'I'll talk to her and find out,' said Varcy.

'You want me to bring her in?'

Varcy shook his head. 'I'll go to her. She's staying at her friend's flat. It'll be good to speak to her in an environment she's familiar with.'

The kettle boiled and shut off. Varcy filled the two mugs with the water. Kendrick crouched down and pulled a bottle of milk from a fridge tucked under the counter. Varcy poured a slug into each mug.

'On another matter,' said Kendrick. 'We've accessed John Scott's email accounts. He had three. Two of them were dormant, the third is a Google account which he used every day.'

Varcy chased the teabags with a spoon.

'There are thousands of email exchanges to go through,' said Kendrick. 'Do you know what you're looking for?'

Varcy handed Kendrick a mug and took a full sip of his own. 'Something that connects Lord Scott with Barry Townsend. Something vague.'

'It's going to take time,' said Kendrick.

'I know,' said Varcy, 'but I'm convinced there's something that binds these two together.'

'Why so sure?' asked Kendrick. 'We might be looking at a serial where there's nothing to connect them except the opportunity to kill.'

'We might,' said Varcy, 'but I'm assuming a theme. A thread. It'll be a tenuous one but it will connect the two victims. Even madmen have a thread running through their killing sprees – women, prostitutes, authority figures. This will be the same. Except it'll be different too. This guy isn't a madman.'

'Townsend and Scott might give you an argument about that,' said Kendrick.

'They might,' said Varcy. 'But the madmen I'm thinking of do it for pleasure. This one doesn't. I don't mean he doesn't get any enjoyment from it at all. I'm sure he does. But it's the same pleasure you might get from a job well done, like mending a fence or painting a wall. He's not sick. Not ordinary sick at least.'

Kendrick took a slurp of tea.

'First, he's focused,' said Varcy. 'He plans. He follows the plan. He isn't angry. The two corpses have two wounds only. Nothing is touched. The property's not trashed. Nothing is stolen. The bodies are not defiled in any way. There's no sexual element to it. He does what he needs to then he leaves.'

'Motive?'

'Not emotional,' said Varcy, 'something cerebral. Something logical.'

'Money perhaps?' said Kendrick.

Varcy nodded. 'Possibly, but if he were paid to kill these two he'd have shot them in the head and left. You're an AFO, how long would that take?'

Kendrick shrugged. 'Seconds.'

'Nice and quick,' said Varcy. 'But he didn't, he killed them in a way that took longer than it needed to. Much longer. That means he wanted something from them.'

'And badly,' said Kendrick.

'I'm sure of it,' Varcy smiled.

Kendrick turned out of the kitchen still clutching his mug. 'I'll work the emails,' he said.

16

She was on a red leather couch, her legs tucked under her knees and a mug of coffee in her hands. The hands were pulled close to her chest. She wore grey sweat pants, a blue gym top and white trainer socks. Her dark hair was pulled into a pony tail.

Varcy watched her. She sipped and stared downwards. To Varcy's left on an upright chair was her friend. Varcy glanced down at his log to remind himself of the name. *Meg*. Meg Stanley. She was the opposite of Rita in looks. Rita was dark with a coffee-coloured skin, Meg was pale and redheaded. Meg had high cheek bones and full lips. Switched on. Diligent. Keen eyes. Efficient use of language. She too watched Rita, but she also watched Varcy.

He cleared his throat. 'Is there anything you need?' he asked softly. 'I mean anything I can do to help?'

Rita shook her head. 'I'm okay.'

'We're taking things slowly,' said Meg.

'There are people you can talk to, you know that,' said Varcy.

'Yes, you told me yesterday,' she said. 'I don't want to talk to anyone.'

He nodded. 'If you change your mind I'll be happy to fix it.'

'She's okay for now,' said Meg.

Varcy shifted in his seat. 'Yesterday was a horrible day,' he began. 'A terrible shock. But I need to ask more questions. I hope you don't mind.'

'What sort of questions?' asked Meg.

'The general sort,' Varcy replied.

'You asked a whole lot of general questions yesterday,' said Meg. 'Rita spent close on four hours with you.'

Varcy nodded indulgently. 'There's been a murder. It was committed in Rita's flat. That means we have questions. Lots of them.'

'I really don't mind,' said Rita softly. 'Go ahead. Please.'

Varcy flipped through his decision log and unclipped the cap of a plastic biro. 'I wanted to start with Barry,' he said. 'Yesterday we spoke about enemies Barry might have had. Did you get a chance to think any more about that?'

Rita sipped her drink. 'I've thought of little else. I can't think of anyone. At least no one who would be prepared to do this.'

'Who were his friends?' Varcy asked.

'Barry was born in Leeds,' she said. 'Most of his good friends were up there. People he'd known since schooldays. His mother still lives there.'

'Do you know any of them?'

'Not really,' she replied. 'I met a couple of them when we were first going out. They came down to London and we met them at a bar.'

'What about friends in London?' Varcy asked.

'He had colleagues at work,' she said. 'They'd go

for a drink in the evenings sometimes.'

'Do you know them?'

She shook her head. 'I've never met any of them.'

'Was he out with them the night before he died?' he asked.

'He wasn't working,' Meg interrupted. 'He hadn't had a job in six months.'

'He was job hunting,' said Rita.

Varcy made a note in his decision log. 'So he was spending most of his time in your flat?' Varcy said.

'No,' said Rita. 'He has a house-share in Dalston,' she said. 'He was thinking of giving it up to live with me.'

'Do you know the address of this place?'

She nodded. '1a Kingsland Road.'

Varcy nodded and jotted down a note. 'How was Barry behaving in recent times?' he asked. 'Was he different in any way? Anxious, aggressive, pre-occupied maybe?'

'You asked me that yesterday,' she said. 'If he was, I didn't notice it. He was a bit frustrated, I suppose, at not finding work. But nothing out of the ordinary.'

Meg sucked her teeth and sat back in her seat. Varcy glanced up from his notes and watched her for a moment.

'What did Barry do when he was working?'

'He worked in the backroom of a trading desk,' Rita answered.

'Where was he last employed?'

'NatWest markets.'

'In Bishopsgate?' he asked.

She nodded.

'I know it,' he said. 'Was he sacked?'

'He was made redundant. They were stream-lining. He hadn't been there long, so he was one of the first to go.'

Varcy nodded. 'What about Barry's finances? What was he living on?'

'He had the small NatWest pay-off,' she replied, 'and a savings account. I've no idea how much was in it.'

'Any debts?' he asked.

She shook her head. 'Not that I know of.'

'No one he owed money to?'

'No.'

Varcy scribbled into his decision log. 'Okay,' he said at last. 'Anything else you think I should know about Barry?'

Rita clasped her mug tightly and sipped. Meg folded her arms across her stomach. Varcy said nothing and waited.

'Are you going to tell him?' said Meg after a long moment.

Rita glanced up from the floor. 'Tell him what?'

'About Barry's friend,' she said, emphasising the last word.

'Oh, that,' said Rita. 'You tell him.'

Meg turned to Varcy. 'Barry had an affair,' she said, 'with a girl he met in The Coffee Bean while "job hunting".'

She made speech marks with her fingers.

'He was job hunting in a coffee house?' said Varcy.

'They have WiFi,' said Rita. 'He was surfing job sites on his laptop. She worked there as a barista.'

Varcy made a note. 'How long ago?'

'About three months,' said Rita.

Varcy continued to write and said, 'Do you know the girl's name?'

Rita shook her head.

'Can you describe her?'

'Blond,' said Rita. 'Tall.'

'Polish,' said Meg.

'Where is this place?' asked Varcy.

'Drury Lane,' said Rita. 'On the corner of Parker Street.'

Varcy nodded. 'I know it. This relationship was over before Barry died?'

'He told me it was,' said Rita.

'Did you believe him?' asked Varcy.

'I had no reason not to,' she said.

Varcy glanced at Meg. 'And you?'

Meg shrugged. 'Who knows?'

Rita set her mug down on the floor and adjusted her position on the couch. She pulled her hair off her face, widened the pony tail band at the back and eased a palmful of hair into the space. She executed it smoothly, without effort. Varcy admired her elegance. Her beauty.

He closed the decision log carefully, sat back in his seat and watched her. She adjusted her Calvin Klein's and looked back at him.

'Can I ask you a personal question?' he asked suddenly.

She nodded.

'It may be something I should ask you in private,' he said, glancing at Meg.

Meg took the hint and got up from her seat. 'I'll go and make more drinks,' she said.

'No, don't do that,' said Rita. 'I'd rather you stayed.'

'Are you sure?' asked Meg.

'Yes. Stay, please.'

Varcy waited for a long moment and then said, 'I wanted to ask you about your past.'

'Okay,' she said softly.

'You changed your name,' he said. 'You used to be called Shannon. Ritnan Shannon. I wanted to know why you changed it.'

Rita looked him in the eye for a moment. Then she glanced at Meg. 'What does this have to do with Barry?' she asked.

'I don't know,' said Varcy. 'Probably nothing.'

'Then why do you want to know?' interrupted Meg.

'Because this is a murder investigation,' said Varcy. 'And I'm curious about everything. You don't have to answer. I'll understand.'

He slid the biro into the top pocket of his jacket and eased the decision log into the pocket inside. Brushing out his trousers, he stood up from his chair.

'I will answer your question,' said Rita suddenly. 'I don't mind. I was surprised you asked it, that's all.'

Varcy waited a beat then hitched his trousers and perched once again on the chair.

'It was because of my dad,' she said. 'He was never home when I was growing up. He drank quite a bit. He was in and out of work. My mum brought us up on her own. She had two jobs, two kids and never-ending work. Just after I finished uni I decided to change my name. It seemed like a pivotal moment to do it. It was like starting a new life. I owed so much to my mum and almost nothing to my dad. I wanted to recognise mum's effort. So I changed my surname to the name she had before she was married.'

'What about your first name?' said Varcy.

She shrugged. 'I never liked Ritnan. It was too ethnic. Rita suited me much better.'

'How did you cope with the practicalities of it?' he said. 'Asking friends and family to call you something different, I mean. That must have been difficult.'

'Not really,' she said. 'Many of them called me Reet anyway so the shortening of my new name was no different. I became Rita with no trouble at all.'

Varcy nodded. 'Was it cathartic?' he asked.

She stared ahead for a long moment and said, 'Yes it was.'

'Do you regret it?'

She shook her head. 'Not at all. Why do you ask?'

'No reason,' he said, standing up.

He adjusted the buttons on his jacket. 'There will be more questions no doubt, but I'm finished asking for today.'

'Can I go back to work?' Rita asked. 'I need to keep my mind busy.'

Varcy thought for a moment. 'On Saturday?'

'I've always got stuff I can be getting on with,' she said.

He shrugged. 'I don't see why not if that's what you want to do. But please stay contactable. I may need to get hold of you.'

Meg stood up and showed him to the door. They exchanged a look as he left. Her's full of distrust. Or dislike.

Varcy took the stairs down to ground level and checked his log. The Coffee Bean on Drury Lane was just a few minutes' walk away. He decided to go there next.

17

Varcy blinked against the May sunshine and took out his battered cell phone. It was vibrating violently in his jacket pocket.

Kendrick said, 'Where are you, Gov'nor?'

'Holborn. Why?' Varcy replied.

'I wanted to run something past you.'

'What is it?'

'I might have a link between Lord Scott and Barry Townsend.'

'That was quick.'

'I know,' said Kendrick, 'I got lucky.'

'How strong is the link?' asked Varcy.

'Weak,' said Kendrick. 'So it can wait until you get back.'

'I'll be about an hour,' said Varcy.

'Okay, I'll find you when you get in.'

Varcy rang off and hurried south towards Parker Street. Parker Street was a narrow rat-run from Holborn to Covent Garden. As a younger man, Varcy would use it to stagger half-cut from the Punch and Judy at Covent Garden back to the tube at Holborn. This afternoon, Parker Street was empty except for a small crowd outside The New Connaught Rooms. Men in dinner suits. Women in puffy dresses. They were laughing and talking. There were fancy cars decorated with white bunting, and a couple of chauffeurs with formal grey jackets and peak caps. Then a white Rolls pulled up. It was hung with pink ribbon and white roses. The driver, with the same garb as the rest of his colleagues, leapt from his seat and hurried to the passenger side to open the door. He smiled broadly as the bride and her groom emerged. A loud cheer went up from the crowd.

Varcy pushed on towards Drury Lane and The Coffee Bean.

The place was busy when he arrived. There were few tables to be had. A line of customers were waiting at the counter. The two young men making the drinks were working full out. There was hissing and bubbling from the milk steamer. The noise blocked out an Ella Fitzgerald track playing on the sound system. He scanned around for someone free to talk to and spotted a young woman at the back of the store who was cleaning a table, a tray balanced in her hand. He checked her hair colour: blond. That was promising.

'Excuse me, Miss,' he said, approaching her.

She looked up and smiled.

'May I have a word with you?' he asked.

Her smile faded slightly. 'What about?'

'I'm trying to find a young lady who works here or used to work here,' he said. 'Trouble is, I don't know her name. But she looks a bit like you. Are you Polish?'

The girl laughed out loud. 'I'm from Hackney,' she said. 'But Marcianna is Polish, I think. She's got a funny accent anyway.'

'What did you say her name is?' Varcy asked.

'Marcianna.'

'M-a-r-c-i-a-n-n-a,' said Varcy, opening his decision log and spelling the word out loud. 'Yes, that must be her.'

'Why do you want her?' asked the girl, glancing at the notebook.

'I'm a police officer,' said Varcy, underlining Marcianna's name in his book. 'I need to ask her some questions.'

'Oh,' she said quickly. 'I didn't realise.'

'It's okay,' said Varcy, realising the girl's dilemma. 'She's not in any trouble. I just need to talk to her, that's all.'

'You'd better see the manager,' said the girl, backing away slightly.

'That's okay,' said Varcy. 'I'll wait here.'

He sat at the same table the girl had just cleared. It was against the back wall with a view of the whole of the café. The girl scurried away to a door marked PRIVATE and Varcy waited, watching the diners drink coffee and talk and read newspapers. He debated whether to order a tea himself. The prospect was appealing but the wait was not. The queue was backed up to the end of the serving aisle. He decided to wait until he got back to Bishopsgate. To fill in some time he opened his decision log and went over the notes he made during the interview with Rita Sidhu. He checked his entries line by line. The relationship between the two women was interesting. It had a mother-daughter feel to him, with the friend, Meg, taking the role of the parent.

Natural perhaps, given the circumstances. She was looking out for her mate, after all.

Rita was interesting in her own right, though. She was quiet. Contained even. And she was smart. Beautiful too. The change of name story was weird. He had written the word 'fable?' in the margin of the log as soon as she had told him about her poor mum and her drunk dad who was never around. It just didn't feel right. He'd have to look at that.

He read the name of the Polish girl again. Marcianna. Nice name. Looking back towards the main body of the café, he listened to the music. Frank Sinatra was singing *Summer Wind*. Varcy smiled. His dad was Frank's biggest fan.

Frank sounds great, doesn't he, Terry? he would say whenever the radio played his music.

Always does, Dad, Varcy would reply.

Then his dad would nod and carry on with whatever he was talking about. Varcy enjoyed the memory.

The girl reappeared and smiled shyly at him. 'The manager will be out in a moment,' she said.

'Thanks,' said Varcy.

She moved to the front of the restaurant and began to work another table. It was littered with the usual café debris. He shifted in his seat and watched steam rise from the coffee machine on the barista station, drift towards the cooler air coming from the outside and settle as mist on the store front window. He loosened his collar.

That's when he spotted Rita Sidhu.

A swipe of steam on the store front glass was

rubbed away and a face peered through it into the café. Rita had a baseball hat pulled low over her face but there was no doubt who it was. Varcy squinted into the light and wondered if she had come in search of him. Then he wondered if she was searching for the same person he was. He pushed his body against the back wall and watched. She seemed to be scanning the room. Definitely on a search, then. But why? Had his visit prompted this? He continued to watch her. She stayed pressed against the glass for a long moment then pulled her face away. Varcy debated whether to make himself known to her or at least follow her. Then the door marked PRIVATE swung open and the decision was made for him.

A young man with an off-white shirt buttoned up close to his pimply neck said, 'Hello, I'm Darren,' and held out his hand for Varcy to shake.

'Hello, Darren,' replied Varcy, gripping the young man's hand. 'I'm Terry Varcy.' He showed him his identification. 'I'm from the City Police.'

'You want to speak to Marcianna?' he said.

'If that's okay,' nodded Varcy.

'She's at lunch just now,' he said, checking his watch. 'But she'll be back in the next ten minutes or so. You can wait if you want.'

Varcy nodded. 'Sounds good.'

'Can I get you a drink?' said the young man.

'Ah,' said Varcy brightening. 'Tea would be lovely.'

The young man nodded and disappeared behind the barista station. He emerged a few moments later and deposited the drink in front of Varcy. The teabag was still in and Varcy began to steep it. He poured the milk and hesitated over the sugar. Should he wean himself off or go cold turkey? The image of himself in crime scene garb at the Sidhu apartment was persuasive. The gut would have to go, no doubt about that. He decided cold turkey. He took a sip. It was awful. Bitter and bland at the same time. He might have spat it back in the cup had it not been for the restaurant door opening and a tall, blond girl stepping through. Varcy swallowed the tea and kept his eye on her.

She was willowy. Like a half-grown tree just after planting. She wore a brown, leather jacket and oversized sunglasses which she removed almost as soon as she entered. Varcy watched her glide past him and disappear through the door marked PRIVATE.

He sipped the brew and waited.

She emerged soon after and moved slowly towards his table. She obviously knew who he was. The manager must have told her he was waiting. Varcy smiled reassuringly and stood for a moment. 'Marcianna?'

She nodded. 'Yes.'

He gestured to the seat opposite. 'Please.'

She lowered herself elegantly onto it. 'Is anything wrong?' she said.

'I've come about someone you might know,' said Varcy.

Marcianna stared at him as if transfixed.

'A young man called Barry Townsend.'

'Barry?' Her brow furrowed into a single crease. It looked as if it had been scored with a knife. Varcy studied her face. It was angled into sharp lines. The cheekbones were prominent. So was the jaw line. She wasn't manly, neither was she typically feminine. Varcy thought she looked like an athlete. Maybe a swimmer or a triathlete. Something like that. Her eyes were green and vivid. As though she was wearing contacts.

'He was murdered yesterday morning,' he said.

Her eyes bulged. 'My God,' she breathed. 'How?'

'He was in the flat he shared with his girlfriend. A neighbour found him.'

'Was he shot?' she asked.

Varcy shook his head. 'Stabbed to death,' he said.

She bit her lip and looked away.

'You knew Barry well?' asked Varcy.

She nodded gently.

'How well?'

She looked back to him. Her pale face was set hard but her eyes were suddenly wet and reddened. 'We were together,' she said, dabbing her eyes with the back of her hand.

Varcy held her gaze for a long moment. 'When was the last time you saw him?' he asked.

She swallowed and blinked a couple of times, brushing aside a tear from the ridge of her cheekbone with a flick of her finger. 'The night before last,' she said.

Varcy began writing in his decision log. He glanced up briefly after a few moments. She was staring forwards as if she was lost in thought. He could see she was struggling to keep her composure. Her fingers were interwoven and she was squeezing hard, the digits whitening as she did so. Varcy returned to his notes. Then when he was ready, he put down his pen and asked, 'How did you meet Barry?'

Marcianna had a ring on the middle finger of her right hand. She grasped it and slid it up and down like a yo-yo. 'He was a customer here,' she said. 'He came in most days and we got friendly.'

'And you had never seen him before he came in here?'

She shook her head.

'Did you know he had a girlfriend?'

'Yes,' she said. 'But their relationship was difficult. They didn't get on.'

'Did she know about your relationship?'

'She found out,' Marcianna said. 'We didn't see each other for a week or two after that. Then he came back in here and we started over again.'

Varcy nodded. 'How did you find Barry?' he asked. 'I mean was he charming? Friendly? How would you describe him?'

'Charming,' she said. 'We got on well. He had spent part of his gap year working in Zagreb so he could speak a bit of Croatian. We had lots in common.'

'I thought you were Polish.'

She shook her head. 'Croatia,' she said. 'The accent is similar.'

'Ah,' said Varcy, taking up his pen and making a

note.

She kept silent.

Varcy flip-flopped the pen between his first two fingers and continued, 'Was Barry worried about anything?'

She shrugged. 'I don't think so.'

'Was he in trouble?'

'No.'

'Did he have debts?'

'Money was tight, I think,' she said. 'He had been speaking about that recently.'

'How tight?'

'Just that he needed more money. He was job hunting.'

'Where did you and Barry go Thursday night?' Varcy asked.

'He met me here when my shift finished. Then we went on to a pub.'

'What time was this?'

'I finish at 6.30. He was here just before then.'

'And when did he leave you to go back home?'

'When the pub closed,' she said. 'About 11.30.'

Varcy nodded and made a note. He then turned the decision log to face Marcianna. 'Would you write your full name and address here?' he asked, handing her a pen. 'I have to know where to contact you if I need to.'

He watched her write. When she was done she handed back the pen and looked up at him. Her green eyes were still crimson in the whites. 'What happens now?' she asked softly. 'To Barry, I mean. Will there be a funeral?'

'Yes,' said Varcy, 'but the coroner will hold an inquest which will delay things.'

She nodded.

Varcy pocketed the pen and closed the log. He took a long look at Marcianna then said, 'I'm sorry for your loss.'

She nodded once again.

18

Twenty-two minutes after Varcy had left Meg's flat, the text had arrived. It was short and cryptic. At first Rita was unsure what to make of it. Was it for real? It had been a year since they had spoken. Within twenty minutes she had showered, dressed and was ready to go. She pulled on a King's College baseball cap and left Meg's flat. Meg wasn't happy about it – her over-protective streak was kicking in – so Rita told her she needed space to think and to come to terms with what had happened.

Meg's place was on Northampton Row. Rita walked towards High Holborn. The May sky was cloudless, with the sun not at full blast but warm enough. Spring was fading and summer was emerging. The Saturday crowd were out in force. Unlike the week-day scrum who pressed and drove and hassled, these were tourists on their way to Covent Garden or students from London University with thick tomes under their arms. Some were local. They strolled, and talked, and laughed. In no hurry to get where they were going. Content to enjoy the moment. It was still busy. Holborn always was but the insanity had gone. Rita was grateful for that. It gave her the breathing space she needed.

Once on Kingsway she turned right onto Parker Street and followed it until it hit Drury Lane. She made a left and came to The Coffee Bean where Barry had met the Polish girl. She stopped for a moment and peered through the glass. The bar seats were occupied by singles and the couches and the easy chairs by couples or groups of friends. The single counter to the left had a string of customers waiting for the two male baristas to make their drinks. Rita looked around for someone who looked like Barry's Polish girlfriend, but couldn't see anyone who fitted. She had no idea why she was looking now. She hadn't been interested while Barry was alive. She supposed it was curiosity, as if seeing this girl would bring Barry closer. A weird connection to a man she knew she no longer loved but had been an intrinsic part of her life for the last six months.

A few people at the window counter glanced up at her face looming at the glass. She began to feel self-conscious and pulled away. She moved on towards Broad Court, a narrow Dickensian street with high buildings made of dark brick and old stone. Once houses for the old rich, now luxury apartments for brokers, traders and banking professionals. Rita hurried forwards towards Covent Garden.

The restaurant was generic. An Italian chain painted green and yellow. There was a menu on a stand outside with a few tables clustered around it. Each was covered with a white tablecloth, had a glass ashtray, a sugar bowl and a thin vase with a single flower standing in it. There was an outside gas heater turned up full and a heavy-set man at one of the tables, drinking espresso from a small steelite cup and smoking a cigarette.

Rita peered into the doorway and scanned the tables inside. The restaurant was about half full; tables of family groups talking loudly and eating pasta and pizza. The aroma of Italian cooking and fresh bread wafted up at her as she stepped inside. A waiter moved towards her.

'Table for one?' he asked.

'For two,' said Rita. 'In the back if there's space.'

He nodded. 'Of course.'

She followed him to the back where the restaurant was narrower and the light more subdued. 'This okay?' he asked.

She took a seat with a view of the front of the restaurant and the waiter handed her a menu. She glanced at her wristwatch. A few minutes early. She wouldn't be eating. She hadn't been hungry since the day the detective had called her. She ordered a coffee and kept a watch on the door.

What could this be about? The agreement they had was clear. No meetings, no phone calls, no contact. Ever. She couldn't handle it any other way. She had stuck to her part of it so why was he now breaking it?

The waiter delivered the coffee and a small jug. She poured in some milk from the jug and added half a sachet of brown from the sugar bowl. She stirred the drink and took a long sip.

Then she spotted him. Standing in the doorway as if he had never been away. As if they had never been apart. He was as large as life. Larger in fact. Taller than she remembered and more athletic. His skin seemed to shine. The deep blue of his eyes sent a shimmer of electricity through her body, acting like a stimulant to her heart which began beating rapidly. She tried to take him in but couldn't. Not all at once. His eyes scanned the restaurant and she stood up and waved. He spotted her and moved towards her table. She remained standing as he approached. He stood for a moment too. They were silent and looked at each other like a couple of kids who had been introduced for the first time. Then he said: 'Hello, Rita.'

'Hello, Mark,' she whispered.

They stood awkwardly a moment longer then she sat down and he took the seat opposite.

'What are you having?' he asked.

'Just this coffee,' she replied.

'I'll have the same,' he said, calling the waiter over.

'How have you been?' she asked.

'Okay. And you?'

'Fine.'

He nodded. 'You got my text message?'

'Of course I did. That's why I'm here.'

He smiled briefly. His teeth were white against his skin. She felt another jolt of electricity. She reached for the coffee cup quickly and took a drink.

'I'm sorry I had to send it,' he said. 'It must have come as a bit of a shock.'

'A bit,' she said. 'There's been nothing for months.'

'As agreed,' he said.

'As agreed,' she nodded.

There was silence.

'I wouldn't have sent it if I hadn't thought it necessary,' he said after a moment.

'So what's happened?'

The waiter moved towards them and set down the coffee. He pushed a small milk jug towards Mark.

'My uncle is dead,' Mark said when the waiter had left.

'Mark, I'm so sorry,' she murmured.

Mark nodded. 'I think he was murdered.'

Rita gulped in a breath. 'Murdered?'

'Shh.' He put a finger to his lips.

'How?' she whispered.

'He was at home. Someone broke in.'

He poured the milk into his coffee and stirred in a sachet of white sugar. She watched him take a sip and set the cup down again. His face looked drawn. She could see it now. It hadn't been obvious from the door.

'He was deliberately targeted, Rita. I know it,' he said.

'Why?'

'Because he blackmailed someone, that's why.'

'Who?'

'You heard of Charles Pine?' he said.

'The oil guy?'

Mark nodded. 'Remember the analysis I asked you to do at the beginning of last year?'

'The hair analysis?'

He nodded. 'That was part of it.'

'That was part of what?'

He stared down at the table for a moment. 'I mean I think it was part of it. I don't know for sure.'

'What are you talking about, Mark?' she asked.

'I'm sorry,' he said softly.

She leaned forwards. Spread her hands on the table. 'You mean you had me do an analysis so that your uncle could use it for blackmail?' she said.

'Of course not,' he replied. 'I didn't know what it was for. I overheard a conversation my uncle had one morning that's all. He was on the phone in his office. I was outside. I caught a word or two and listened. It was blackmail. No question.'

'So what's the hair analysis got to do with it?'

'I'm not sure exactly. He was talking about it on the phone.'

'And you never told me?'

'What would have been the point?'

'Christ,' she said, looking away.

'I'm sorry,' he said again after a long moment.

'*Sorry?*'

'I really am,' he said.

'So why you telling me all this now?' she said.

'So you can get rid of the evidence,' he replied. 'You put it in the safe, right?'

She nodded.

'Then bin it.'

'Why should I?' she said.

'Because if Pine thinks it's still around he'll come after you too. You know how powerful he is. God knows what he's prepared to do. Just trash it and pretend you never saw it. Get on with your life.'

'What about you?' she asked. 'If the evidence exists you're implicated too.'

He shrugged.

'What's so special about a hair analysis anyway?'

He shrugged again. 'I think one of those hairs was taken from a car Charles Pine's son owned. Beyond that I really don't know. Honestly I don't. I'm just telling you what I *do* know.'

She took a sip of coffee and watched his face. Watched his eyes and his nose and his lips. A face she once loved. A face she used to dream about. 'You really are a piece of work aren't you, Mark?'

He looked up briefly and then looked away.

'After I came home and found you with that woman, I tried to defend you. Not to my friends – I didn't dare tell them – but to myself. I made excuses for you. Found reasons for it. When you called today I was … *excited*. Now you tell me this.'

'For your own good,' he said. 'That's all. I'm worried about you.'

'You're worried about yourself, Mark. That's the real reason you want this evidence destroyed.'

She replaced the cup back down on the saucer and got up from the table.

'Rita!' he shouted.

She didn't turn around.

19

Varcy had ridden the Central line from Holborn to Liverpool Street and emerged onto Bishopsgate. The sun was well established now. It glinted off the RBS glass tower and bounced off the cars and buses. If he'd owned a pair of sunglasses he would have put them on. Instead he removed his jacket and slung it over his shoulder. His office was just across the road but it could wait. First, he had a date with a plate of sausage and mash on Brushfield Street. He pulled out his cell phone and dialled Kendrick.

'I'm going for food,' he said. 'Care to join me?'

'What a good idea,' said Kendrick. 'Where?'

'Brushfield.'

'S&M?'

'Of course.'

'Give me five minutes.'

The waitress brought two oval, white plates and presented them to Varcy and Kendrick. The two men were sitting at one of the wooden tables that looked onto the pavement. The panel doors had been opened – for maybe the first time that year – and the warm breeze drifted in. Varcy was sipping a sugarless tea. It was as bland as the last time he'd had it but he sipped on regardless.

Kendrick must have noticed his distaste and said, 'I never thought I'd see the day.'

'What day?' asked Varcy.

'A bad tea day,' said Kendrick pointing to Varcy's mug.

'It hasn't got sugar in it,' Varcy said, taking another small sip.

'Give it a week,' said Kendrick.

'For what?'

'For salvation,' he said. 'After that you won't want it any other way.'

'You speak from experience?' said Varcy.

Kendrick shrugged. 'I used to take four sugars in tea and coffee. But now I'm saved. This coffee,' he said, holding his mug, 'is unsoiled.'

'I'll take your word for it,' Varcy replied, picking up his fork. On the white, oval plate was a bed of mashed potato. Three sausages were arranged in a wigwam and the lot was covered in a lake of onion gravy. Varcy scooped up a generous fork full of mash and began to eat.

'So,' he said after a few mouthfuls, 'tell me what you've got.'

Kendrick patted his mouth with a paper napkin. 'It's not much,' he said, 'and I'm not sure it's a link to anything, but Lord Scott's email contacts have at least one interesting fact.'

'Oh?' said Varcy.

'They contain an address of someone we both know well.'

'Who?' asked Varcy.

'You, Gov'nor.'

'Me?'

Kendrick nodded. 'Your private address too.'

'Me?' Varcy repeated. 'How did he get hold of that?'

'No idea,' said Kendrick, resting his elbows on the table.

'How bizarre,' said Varcy. He put his fork down and grabbed the mug of tea. 'Any mention of this on the reports Monroe filed?'

'Nothing. They missed it.'

'They weren't looking for it,' said Varcy.

'True,' said Kendrick.

Varcy sipped his brew. 'The fact he's got my address doesn't worry me. He could have gotten hold of it if he wanted to. But why? That's the thing. Why would he want it?'

Kendrick gulped some coffee. 'Maybe he read about you.'

'When?'

Kendrick shrugged. 'There was a bit of publicity after the Stichell case. Maybe he thought you could help him in some way.'

Varcy skewered a sausage and bit the top off. He chewed for a long moment then said, 'Okay. So we've dug a little and come up with a link that we didn't expect.'

Kendrick had a mouthful of food. He nodded.

'Then let's do some more comparisons between him and me.'

'Like what?'

Varcy thought for a moment. 'Check our relatives, friends, clubs, likes, dislikes. Anything that comes to mind. See if we have anything in common apart from my email address.'

'Okay,' said Kendrick.

'Also compare what you find with what we have on Rita Sidhu. Can you get access to her email account?'

'Shouldn't be a problem,' said Kendrick.

'Look at her contacts and check her activity. I want to know who she sent emails to, who she received them from and what they contained.'

'How far back do you want to go?'

Varcy thought for a moment. 'Eight months.'

'You getting interested in her?'

Varcy nodded. 'Slightly. She may have spun me a yarn today.'

'About what?'

'Her name and why she changed it.'

Kendrick chased some mash potato around his plate with a fork. 'What did she say?'

'She said it was because of her drunken father. Her mother had brought her up alone, struggled daily, never complained and so on.'

'That's why she changed her name?'

'Apparently.'

'And you don't buy it?'

Varcy shrugged and took a sip of tea.

'How did she react in the mortuary yesterday?' Kendrick asked.

'To seeing the body?' Varcy said. 'In the usual way.'

'Nothing forced? No drama?'

'Not obviously,' said Varcy.

'So they were loved-up, then?'

'I doubt it,' said Varcy. 'Barry Townsend had a lover. An Eastern European girl.'

'Nice,' said Kendrick, swallowing a forkful of mash. 'Did Sidhu know about that?'

'Yes, but she thought the affair was over. Evidently it was not.'

'Do you think she's the jealous type?'

Varcy put his fork down and said, 'Who knows? She has a motive for murder now, that's for sure, but I don't think the murder was committed by her.'

'She might have paid someone to do it.'

'She might,' Varcy agreed. 'But the murderer wanted something from Barry, I'm certain of that. If it was purely a hit he'd have shot him and left.'

The men ate in silence for a while. When Varcy had finished, he pushed his plate away, sipped more of his tea and gazed out on Brushfield Street. The lunchtime crowd were buzzing in the sunshine. Most headed for the Spitalfields mall with its bars, restaurants and bric-a-brac stalls. Varcy remembered a time when the city was deserted at weekends. That was before the regenerated East End melded with the city's financial district. Spitalfields sat between the two.

A group of young, tanned women huddled around the S&M menu on the pavement just beyond where Varcy sat. All wore sunglasses; the large kind favoured by Victoria Beckham that cover the entire face. The girl nearest reminded him of Barry Townsend's lover, Marcianna. At least as tall and just as lean. She pushed her shades onto her head which acted like a hairband and tucked the loose strands of hair behind her ears. She said something to her friends. Varcy couldn't make out what it was but her accent was local, not like Marcianna's at all which was distinctive. Eastern European, yes, but something else as well. He remembered the angles to her face and those of her voice. The way she dropped articles from her speech. Then something clicked in his memory.

Something that had been gnawing at him since his visit to the Sidhu flat.

Varcy smiled and said, 'You finished?'

Kendrick set his knife and fork together. 'What's cheered you up, Gov'nor?'

'I'll tell you later,' said Varcy. 'Come on, let's get the bill.'

20

Rita decided not to go back to Meg's flat. At least not yet. She needed time to think. There was no use getting stressed out. All of her successes in life had come from doing the opposite of that, from detaching and moving away from emotion. She needed a plan. One that made sense. She traced her steps back through Covent Garden towards Drury Lane. She passed The Coffee Bean where Barry's girlfriend worked and hesitated for a moment before deciding to go in. It wouldn't hurt and it was the perfect place to get her thoughts together. It was less busy than it had been earlier, and she quickly got a coffee and took it to a seat by the window. She glanced around at the staff. There were a couple of blond girls on duty. Both of them decent looking. She wasn't sure if either of them was the woman she had seen Barry with that afternoon. She sighed. What did it matter now anyway? Barry was dead. There was nothing anyone could do.

She reached into her bag and took out her iPhone. She scrolled through her contact list and punched Robert Fleet's number. It went to answer message. Robert's voice came on. 'Hi, this is Robert Fleet. Please leave a message and I'll get back to you as soon as I can.'

'Robert,' she said, 'it's Rita. Please get in touch when you receive this. I want to talk to you about the safe in the lab. It's urgent, so call as soon as you can.'

She rang off and drummed her fingers on the table, then dialled Meg's number. Meg answered on the second ring. 'Meg. Have you heard from Robert?'

'Nope,' she said. 'I didn't like to mention it because you had enough on your plate. But I had a weird text from him last night.'

'What did he say?'

'*Help me*,' Meg said.

'That's all?'

'I tried calling him but got no reply.'

'Me too,' said Rita.

'Where are you now?'

'In The Coffee Bean on Drury Lane. Do you want to join me?'

'Give me ten minutes. I'll round up the kids and meet you in there.'

Rita replaced the phone in her bag and pulled out her silver A4-sized diary. She flicked to the back where the blank note pages were. She fished a biro from the same bag and wrote the following:

Mark's uncle – dead

Analysis? Blackmail?

Barry – dead

Taking a sip of coffee, she re-read what she had written. What was going on? Was this a coincidence or was there a link?

She wrote: Robert Fleet – help me!!??

She pulled the cup towards her for another sip. Then she froze.

Of course there was a link. The most obvious one.

Her.

21

I check my watch. 7.34pm. I am outside the lock-up. The evening is warm and still. The wharf is quiet except for a constant trickle of river water flowing westward. I breathe deeply and mentally go through the last twenty-four hours. Checking every detail in my mind. Ensuring I have been focused and disciplined.

I allow myself a moment to reflect on how much knowledge I have acquired these past two days. Robert Fleet has given up his secrets. One of them surprised me. I never suspected there would be a retinal device fitted on the laboratory safe. One that required his and Rita Sidhu's profile before it would open. I assumed the code would be enough. I probed Robert about this and he told me that the safe contained information on a gene that he and his colleagues were working on. One with very high commercial value. That was why the extra security was deemed necessary. He offered to share the knowledge with me if I allowed him to go free. I declined. Although I admire men like Robert for their skill and knowledge, the work he is engaged in is of no interest to me.

There is something else in his laboratory safe that drives me. Something put there by Rita Sidhu. I told

Robert this and he seemed genuinely surprised and claimed not to know what it was.

I asked further questions concerning the retinal device on the safe. Retinography, it transpires, uses infrared light to map the unique pattern of blood vessels on the retina. As a person looks into the eyepiece, the blood-filled capillaries absorb more of the infrared light than the surrounding tissue. Hence a unique profile is read.

This posed a challenge. I wanted to know if the scanner would work on a dead retina. One that has not received blood-flow for an extended period. The challenge lay in the fact that there was no available data upon which to make a firm judgment.

I resolved to work from first principles. On death, blood separates into solid matter and water. This is as true for major blood vessels as it is for small capillaries. Would this phenomenon cause the scanner to misfire? I assumed it would. However, if the tissue was frozen before separation, what would happen then? Would the matter in the blood – the platelets and the immune cells – be held in solution just as they were when the retina was functioning normally? Like a snap shot caught in time? Surely the scanner would be unable to distinguish between what was alive and what was dead.

Thus the decision was made.

I turn my gaze to the lock-up. Robert Fleet is inside. I've sedated him with three 5mg pills of benzodiazepine. I have withheld food these past eighteen hours so I expect the drug to pass quickly into his bloodstream and render him unconscious.

This is good. There is no need to distress him unnecessarily.

I turn the axe over in my palm and an orange streetlamp catches the edge of the steel. The blade is wide and deep. I unlatch the hinge and push the barn-like doors of the lock-up inwards. The space is mostly empty. There is a chest freezer against the far wall. Next to this are three ten-gallon kegs of engine oil, one stacked on top of the other. To my left are the wall-mounted photographs and to my right is a matrix of shelves. These are filled with a selection of workshop tools and consumables. On the lowest shelf is a blue soldering torch that I shall need shortly. In front of me, approximately at the centre of the space, is a log of blankets. I tread softly on the concrete and listen for Robert's breath. I hear it. Deep and rhythmical. I move near and notice he is on his side with his neck and head extended slightly against a small pillow. This is fortuitous. It means I will have no need to move him. I take up a position behind his head with my feet planted a couple of feet apart. I use a two handed grip on the shaft of the axe and raise it slowly. I concentrate upon a spot on Robert's skin where I intend to deliver my blow. I bend my knees slightly and use my entire body weight to throw the axe forwards and down. It travels swiftly and hits the target with a satisfying thud. A great chunk of flesh is thrown upwards and a jet of orange, oxygenated blood is propelled forwards and outwards. I wrestle the axe free. The blade has bitten deeply. Perhaps three-quarters of the way through. I alter my stance slightly and raise it again. I throw my weight forwards and the axe falls once more, slicing through the remaining flesh. Robert's head detaches completely and rolls a single turn. His headless body neither writhes nor moves. The stream of blood from his carotid artery continues unabated. It will do so for a few more minutes yet.

I set the axe down and turn towards the wall where my tools are kept. I take down the soldering torch and ease the tap on. The hiss of escaping gas dissolves into a whoosh as I ignite the flame with a cigarette lighter. I retrace my steps and pick up Robert's head by a large tuft of his hair. I play the flame on the neck stump, then I hurry across the lock-up to the chest freezer. I open it and a haze of cold air escapes upwards. Its interior is empty and clean. I carefully place Robert's head inside and close it shut.

I check my watch: 7.56pm. All is going to plan. The clean-up can now begin. My first task will be to remove and burn all clothing on the corpse. Then I will divide the body into four separate sections. Upper torso, arms, trunk and legs. These will then be cut into manageable chunks and bagged ready for collection. Robert's blood – which is now pooling on the concrete – will be sucked into sealed containers. I've elected to subcontract the task of disposal of both flesh and blood to a trusted contact. The bags and cylinders will be taken to the coastal port of Lowestoft. From there they will be loaded onto a fishing boat and taken ten miles out to sea. The body parts will be thrown overboard and the blood emptied into the ocean.

The kegs of engine oil will be poured out onto the concrete and worked in deeply. This is insurance. Not only will it authentically colour the stone and give the space a working smell, it will corrupt any forensic analysis should it be carried out at a future date.

I take a deep breath and centre my energies. I mentally focus on the tasks before me. Then I take up the axe and continue my work.

22

Meg arrived with the kids. Max was in the buggy. Charlie was holding onto the handle. They had colouring books and a tin full of felt-tip pens. Max got up onto Rita's lap and Charlie sat next to his mum. Rita ordered a cappuccino for Meg and orange juice for the kids.

'How you doing?' asked Meg.

Rita shrugged. 'Okay.'

'Did the walk clear your head?'

'A bit,' she said.

Meg took a sip of her drink.

'Meg, I want to go to Robert's flat,' said Rita suddenly.

Meg nodded. 'Okay. When?'

'Soon. I've got a bad feeling.'

'Don't say that,' said Meg sitting forwards.

'I'm overreacting probably.'

Meg sipped her drink. 'It's understandable given what's just happened.'

'Can I see the message Robert sent you?' said Rita.

Meg groped in her jacket pocket and tossed the phone over. 'Scroll through,' she said.

Rita worked the keys and cued Robert's message: *help me …*

It was stark and clear. A cry for help. What else could it mean? Robert was an intelligent, rational man. This had to be taken seriously. He was in trouble.

'Maybe we should go to the police with this?' Rita said.

Meg shrugged. 'Sure.'

'How did Robert seem to you this last week?' asked Rita.

'On a high,' said Meg. 'We all were.'

Rita nodded and glanced down at the message again. A waitress came to clear the space next to them. She was lean and tall. Rita caught a glimpse of her blond hair which fell forwards as she worked. Her cheekbones were high and defined. She pushed the hair from her forehead and Rita saw her face clearly. She was beautiful but not in the classic sense of the word. There was a look about her that was different. She wondered if this was Barry's lover.

'Are you done?' said Meg.

Rita handed the phone back. 'Yep.'

'Come on then. Kids, finish up your drinks. We're going!'

They took a bus to Old Street. Robert lived in a converted warehouse on Eagle Wharf Road. The area was a strange mixture of new and old. Old from as early as anyone could remember. Slums, small-time manufacturing and poor families. Then in the post war years, council projects to house them. Now there was private money regeneration. Professionals moving into smart apartments.

Clean lines and pared back bricks wedged between graffiti-strewn 1950s monstrosities.

Robert's apartment was part of the regenerated sector. The warehouse conversions gave professionals a large living space within a stone's throw of the trendy part of town.

'His is the basement flat,' said Meg as they came to a high iron fence and a security gate. Rita traced her finger along the list of flat numbers until she found B for basement. There were four alternatives. 'Which one?' she asked.

'B2, I think,' said Meg.

Rita pressed the button and waited. Nothing happened. She pressed again.

'Try B3,' said Meg.

She pressed B3 and a voice responded. It was female. Young sounding.

'Hi,' said Rita. 'Sorry to trouble you but we're looking for Robert Fleet. He lives in one of the basement flats but we're not sure which one.'

'I've just moved in,' said the voice. 'I don't know my neighbours yet.'

'Oh,' said Rita.

The line went dead.

Rita tried B4 and a male voice responded. Rita repeated what she had just said.

'I know Robert,' said the voice.

'Fantastic,' said Rita. 'We work with him. We're trying to get hold of him but it's as if he's disappeared.'

'I saw him on Friday,' said the voice.

'Yes,' said Rita, 'so did we but since then we

haven't been able to reach him.'

'Have you called him?' said the voice.

'Well, yes,' said Rita. 'But he's not responding. We're worried about him. I was wondering if you'd give him a knock.'

There was a moment of silence. Then: 'Okay wait a moment.' The line went dead. Rita glanced at Meg. They waited.

Finally: 'No response, I'm afraid. Maybe he's gone away for the weekend.'

'Is there a key holder?' asked Rita. 'Someone who could check his apartment to make sure everything's okay?'

'I have a spare key,' said the voice.

'Brilliant,' said Rita. 'Would you please go in and put my mind at rest?'

Another pause. 'What's your name? I don't want Robert thinking I went into his apartment for no good reason.'

'Sure,' said Rita. 'It's Rita Sidhu.'

There was a pause. 'It'll take a few minutes.'

The line went dead again and the two women waited. Four minutes passed then the voice came back on and said, 'It's empty. Nothing to cause alarm.'

Rita let out a sigh.

There was a pause. 'Thank you for your help,' she said.

'No worries,' said the voice.

The two women turned and headed back up the path that led to the gate.

'I was certain he was going to come back screaming,' Rita said.

'Well, he didn't, thank God,' said Meg. 'So what do we do now?'

They turned back onto Eagle Wharf Road and then New North Road. Rita thought for a moment. 'You go back to the flat with the kids. I'll meet you there a bit later. I want to do something first.'

'Something like what?' asked Meg.

'Nothing to worry about,' replied Rita.

'I am worried, Reet. Very worried.'

Rita smiled gently and pulled her friend into a hug. She held her tight. 'Thanks for being such a great pal,' she said softly.

'You're too secretive,' said Meg. 'It drives me crazy.'

'I know,' nodded Rita. 'I won't be long. Honest.'

23

Varcy was back at his desk. He had fresh tea steaming in a mug by his elbow and a preliminary report from Barry Townsend's autopsy in his hands. According to the coroner, there was nothing remarkable to find. Assuming that bleeding out into a bucket is an unremarkable thing. There was no evidence of drug usage, organ damage or other irregularities. Varcy set the sheet down and leaned back in his office chair. He thought about Barry Townsend. A young life snuffed out and for what? Varcy flipped open a file on his desk and removed the photographs taken at Barry's bedside. A corpse staring outwards from a bed. A peaceful place where he had slept before. A cradle that had nurtured him. Now a cradle of death. *A Cradle of Death*. Something about that was familiar. Varcy tossed it around for a beat and then something came to his mind. He wiggled the mouse by the terminal on his desk and Googled the title of a book he'd once read. The name, Brian Keenan, came up as the author. The book was called *An Evil Cradling*. Brian Keenan was the Lebanon hostage held with John McCarthy in the 1980s and 90s. Varcy remembered the crisis well and the explosion of press interest when they were released. He sat back in his seat once again. These men were tortured. Barry was tortured too.

Varcy got up from his desk and crossed the room to a grey, lockable cabinet that sat in the far corner. At the bottom was a yellow ring binder folder. Varcy had received this folder during a talk he had attended a couple of years ago. He reached for it now and began to flick through the hand-out sheets and notes he had kept inside. He came to a small section towards the end of the notes and jabbed his finger to mark the place. He took the folder over to his desk and sitting back on the office chair, he studied what he'd written. The seminar had been given by a military officer. An ex special forces man who had served in the first Iraq war and then in Yugoslavia. The Met employed him as a consultant. His talk concerned the crossover between military operations and those of the police. What the military see today, the police are liable to see tomorrow and so on. He had dozens of examples of how this worked and, as far as Varcy could remember, the two hours spent with him had been informative and enjoyable.

The part of his lecture near the end was what was getting Varcy's attention. The girl with the blond hair outside the S&M had reminded him of it. At least she had reminded him of Marcianna who reminded him of it.

Varcy had written in bold letters on the hand-out sheet, CONTROL WOUND, and circled it several times. He remembered now. A phenomenon that was recognised by frontline military personnel during the height of the Bosnian war. Used by

Serbian forces to extract information from captured personnel, it rendered the victim passive, terror-stricken and compliant.

There was a light knock on Varcy's door and Kendrick breezed in. He held a reporter's notepad in his hand and had a pencil clenched between his teeth. He removed the pencil and said, 'Bad time, Gov'nor?'

'No, it's fine,' said Varcy, looking up briefly, rubbing his left eye with the back of his hand.

'What's that?' said Kendrick, pointing to the folder.

Varcy opened the top drawer of his desk and groped inside for his anti-bacterial eyedrops. 'An answer to something I've been puzzling over since we saw Barry Townsend's body in the Sidhu flat,' he said, flipping open the small box and easing the bottle out.

'Sounds interesting,' said Kendrick.

Varcy unscrewed the bottle's lid. 'The knife wound in Barry Townsend's thigh and the one on Lord Scott's shoulder? I think I know why they were inflicted.'

Kendrick pulled up a seat opposite while Varcy suspended the bottle above his eyeball and squeezed the dropper.

'Tell me,' said Kendrick.

Varcy blinked against the liquid and pushed the seminar file across the desk. 'They are control wounds,' he said.

'Control wounds?' said Kendrick. 'I've never heard of them.'

'Used by Serbian forces in the 1990s during the Bosnian war to extract information from captured prisoners.'

Kendrick read the two-year-old seminar notes.

'A control wound,' Varcy went on, 'was used as a prelude to torture.'

He screwed the lid on the dropper bottle and placed it back in its box. 'Those notes came from a special forces officer. He was on the ground – literally – during the conflict. Apparently there is a sequence of events in which the control wound becomes very useful.'

'I don't doubt it,' said Kendrick. 'But that's war. Desperate times and all that. This is the city of London.'

'The method used to handle both Barry Townsend and Sir John Scott is very similar.' Varcy jabbed his finger on the sheets in the file. 'Look at that sequence of events this military guy was going on about. I've written it there. *Surprise – normality – violence – passivity*.'

Varcy pulled the file back to his side of the desk and began reading his notes. 'Surprise is obvious,' he said. 'You are captured, set upon, attacked unexpectedly. You are surprised, fearful and uncertain.'

Kendrick nodded. 'Okay.'

'Then, having taken you by surprise, the attacker acts normally. Shows you he is human. He offers you a drink. A cigarette perhaps. He jokes with you. You are starting to calm down. Things are not as bad as they seemed. You start to think rationally again. This is normality.'

Varcy moved his finger down the page. 'Then he does something very violent indeed. He stabs you. There is no reason for it. It might be in the leg, in the arm or in the shoulder. The pain is intense. Shock floods your system. The shred of calm you might have felt is immediately dispelled. You are paralysed with fear. What did you do wrong? You are desperate to get back to friendly terms again. You become passive. The control wound renders you docile. The attacker then moves the nightmare on and extracts information. In the Barry Townsend and the Scott case, a lethal cut was inflicted. They both had the time it took them to bleed out to part with their secrets.'

There was a long moment of silence before Kendrick flipped open the reporter's pad and said, 'All right. Let's give it a go. You got a profile in mind?'

'Military,' said Varcy. 'Special forces maybe. Active service a distinct possibility.'

'Rank?'

'Goodness knows,' said Varcy.

'I'll run it past the profilers,' said Kendrick. 'Nationality?'

'British probably,' said Varcy.

'Not Eastern European?' asked Kendrick.

An image of Marcianna bounced around Varcy's brain. He blew out his cheeks. 'I hadn't considered that,' he said.

'We agree he's a professional?'

Varcy nodded. 'A madman but not in the usual

sense,' he said. 'Not a danger to the public is what I mean.'

'Agreed,' said Kendrick. 'To his target, yes. But not to the rest of us.'

Varcy nodded again.

'Disposition?'

Varcy ran his hands through his hair. 'Ice cold,' he said.

'Not sunny or bubbly or big hearted?' Kendrick asked.

Varcy grabbed his mug of tea and took three swallows. 'Probably not.'

'What's the name of the special forces guy?' asked Kendrick. 'I'll have him study the photographs. Get an opinion.'

Varcy thumbed through the notes. 'Andy Stevens,' he said, squinting at his own handwriting. 'I've got no rank or department written down. He was working as a police consultant at the time. Ask HR. They'll have his details.'

Kendrick nodded again. 'I'll get on to it,' he said and shoved the pencil back between his teeth.

'Did you want something?' asked Varcy. 'You looked as though you wanted something when you came in.'

Kendrick pulled out the pencil. 'I was going to ask you about Whitechapel House.'

Varcy frowned and four deep lines creased his forehead. 'Never heard of it.'

'It's a private members club,' said Kendrick. 'Cole was going through Scott's desk diary and there was an entry on …' Kendrick flipped over a few pages of the reporter's pad and began to read – 'the 6th of November which says, "*Arrange a meeting with TV at Whitechapel House*".'

'TV?'

'Your initials, Gov'nor,' said Kendrick.

'When was the date?' asked Varcy.

'The 6th November. Two weeks before Scott's death,' said Kendrick.

Varcy massaged his forehead. 'Bit lame though, isn't it?' said Varcy.

'Probably, but it's a link of sorts,' said Kendrick.

'I knew nothing about it.'

'Checked your email?' asked Kendrick.

'I would have remembered him sending it to me.'

'Check the spam filter. He may have sent you mail you didn't get.'

Varcy pulled his office chair forward and grabbed the mouse. 'I'll do that now,' he said.

24

Functionality over style is how Rita always thought of the Guildhall Library. She noticed the grey stones and rectangular slabs of glass as she approached. The angular arches and a wide concourse laid with beige and slate slabs. It was old but had the characterless feel of a 1970s' building. She had visited the library a number of times since coming to London. Always to seek out something relevant to her work. An obscure science journal perhaps or a reference to a long since out of print biological text. Now she had come for something much more straightforward.

During the last fifteen minutes, she had covered the ground between Old Street and London Wall. She needed to move at a pace to do it. But the urgency ensured that she hardly felt the strain. City Road and Moorgate were eaten up quickly. She entered London Wall and traversed the warren of back streets to Aldermanbury. She heard the clack-clack of her footfalls echo off the concourse paving as she approached the entrance.

The microfiche facility was on the first floor. She had used the machines often and knew how they worked. She stopped and asked the photocopy assistant about the newspapers they kept on them.

It turned out they didn't. Thanks to NEWSPLAN they were now on a website database which she was able to access from one of the terminals outside the Clock Room.

She knew the newspaper she wanted and the issue date. *The London Evening Standard* almost three years ago. She keyed in the information and found the copy. She hardly had to scroll through. The article was on page one, first column in. There was a picture of a young woman with dark, wavy hair, and an oval face with a small, thin nose. She wore spectacles. Not geeky but sophisticated. She smiled broadly, relaxed, her eyes gleaming in the photograph. Rita read the article.

```
POLICE have confirmed they have
launched a murder investigation
following the death of the
parliamentary assistant, Kimberley
Westfield.
    The post-mortem has revealed that
the twenty-four-year-old died as a
result of strangulation.
    Kimberley's body was found in
woodland near Green Park on 19th
April.
    Detective Chief Inspector Andrew
Lane from The Metropolitan Police says
the post-mortem was made difficult due
to the fact that her body had been
left in the wood for what they believe
was a number of days.
```

It was found fully clothed, although officers say they are keeping an open mind as to whether there was a sexual assault.

Det. Chief Ins. Lane also added that he was open to the possibility that Kimberley's murder could be linked to other such cases.

Her family visited the spot where Kimberley's body was found yesterday, to lay flowers in tribute to her.

Rita sent the article to print. Then, on a whim, she typed another name into the NEWSPLAN database.

A man's name.

She got a hit. *The Evening Standard* was thrown up once again. The reference was much more recent. She read the article. This time it was not a murder but a suicide.

25

Varcy poked his head out of the door of the Bishopsgate police building. The sun was still warm. He decided he could leave his jacket back in the office and walk east in shirt sleeves. The traffic on Bishopsgate was backing up towards Norton Folgate and Great Eastern Street. A bus had broken down and was banked up on the curb, its driver out on the road directing traffic. A patrol car had pulled up behind the bus and a young policeman was getting out. He walked towards the driver who began to gesticulate, explaining what had gone wrong. The young police officer was nodding. Listening to his anxious frustration. Varcy smiled. He had done that job himself when he was fresh out of Hendon. It was okay. Boring but okay.

He pushed on towards Bethnal Green Road. Whitechapel House was on the corner of Ebor Street. It was tall and narrow and made of red brick. The location meant it once had some industrial purpose. Manufacturing or storage. Certainly not a private club where wealthy, fee paying members relaxed, drank and made business deals. Not in this part of town. Not back then. There was a brass sign outside the entrance and a heavy double door that allowed access. Varcy pushed it inwards and entered a lobby. It was full of cool air and soft carpet. Windowless and quiet. Varcy noticed a lift in the far corner and a sign detailing what was on the upper floors. Restaurants, bars, wet facilities and private function suites. It spoke of the kind of exclusivity normally associated with Kensington or Chelsea.

Varcy smiled at the front desk girl and showed his badge. Then he asked his questions. The girl called her manager and he came down in the lift from one of the floors above. He held Varcy's badge in his long fingers and studied his credentials. Then Varcy took over. He wanted to know if Scott was a member of the club. The manager accessed the database and confirmed that he was. Varcy asked if he came to the club often. The manager had that information too. Yes, he was a regular visitor. Once or twice a week on average but he'd not visited for about six months.

'He's dead,' said Varcy. 'That's why.'

'Ah,' said the manager, unleashing a burst of keyboard staccato. 'Yes,' he said, nodding his head in confirmation, 'his direct debit payment has been cancelled.'

The fact was presented without emotion or irony.

Varcy wanted to know about Scott's activities in the club. What time he came in, what facilities he used, who he met. The manager didn't have the answers but thought that he knew a man who might. His name was Philip and he worked the Square Bar. Varcy was invited upstairs. The manager showed him into the lift and rode with him to the fifth floor. They walked into a thickly carpeted brown room with leather brass-studded couches and tub seats carefully positioned around it. The windows to Varcy's right were tall and narrow and the sunlight dissolved into lines of straw as it hit the rich interior. Ahead of him was the bar, which was covered in a panel of polished copper.

The manager showed Varcy to a seat next to one of the windows and offered him a drink. He asked for tea before taking out his decision log and running through the scribbled notes he had made back in the office. A trawl through his email's spam folder earlier had indeed thrown up something. Lord Scott had sent an email to Varcy some six weeks prior to his death. His email came with the crown and gate House of Lords insignia. In it he introduced himself and asked if he could meet with Varcy on a private matter. He suggested Whitechapel House. The reason Varcy hadn't seen the email was bothering him. He asked one of the IT technicians at central office why it had been spammed. There were a number of explanations. The most likely was that Lord Scott's email account was set to HTML rather than rich text, and that's why Varcy's spam filter grabbed it. He had no idea why this would make any difference but he had accepted it.

The manager came back with a small pot of tea on a tray which he placed on the table. Varcy checked his notebook again. The email that got spammed did not specify when they might meet. He took a sip of tea and felt his mobile phone vibrating in his pocket. He answered.

'Inspector Varcy?'

He recognised Rita Sidhu's voice at once. 'Yes, speaking. Hello, Rita.'

'Hello,' she said. 'Do you have a moment?'

'Yes, of course.'

'I wanted to ask you about my flat,' she said.

'Okay,' said Varcy.

'When can I go back?' she asked.

Varcy didn't know specifically. He knew it wouldn't be for a while. 'Not yet,' he said, 'there's a lot of work still to be done. Are you okay at your friend's house?'

'Yes and no,' said Rita. 'I love Meg to death but I need my own space.'

'I understand,' said Varcy. 'I'll get our team to arrange something for you. It might be a private address or even a hotel. You okay with that?'

'Sounds fine,' said Rita. 'Will I be able to get some of my things from the flat first?'

'Shouldn't be a problem,' said Varcy. 'Send over a list of what you want and I'll arrange it.'

'Thanks,' she said and rang off.

The manager approached. He had with him a young man with short gelled hair who was drying his hands on a checked tea towel. He wore a white dress shirt buttoned up to his neck and a black clip-on bow tie. He had a round, chubby face with wispy tufts of facial hair over his top lip.

'This is Philip,' said the manager.

Varcy rose and shook the young man's hand.

The manager gestured to Varcy and said, 'This is Detective Chief Inspector Varcy.'

Philip smiled.

'Philip works all the bars here,' the manager said. 'He may be able to help you.'

Philip perched on the edge of one of the tub chairs.

'I wanted to ask about someone who was a member here,' said Varcy.

'John Scott,' said Philip. 'Or Lord Scott, I should say. My manager just told me. I remember him, yes. Though I didn't realise he was a Lord. We all called him John.'

'What was he like?' asked Varcy.

'Nice bloke,' said Philip. 'Not stuck up. He introduced himself to me when I first started working here and was always friendly.'

'Which facilities did he use?' asked Varcy.

'This bar a lot,' said Philip. 'The restaurants. I think he went up to the pool sometimes.'

'Did he come here alone or with others?'

'Alone usually. He would drink coffee and read. Documents, papers, that kind of thing. I'd sometimes see him talking to other members. He was very friendly.'

'Were there any occasions when he did come with someone else?'

'One time towards the end,' he said. 'He came in with a bloke I knew wasn't a member. They sat over there.' He gestured with his hand to a circular table with two tub chairs either side of it. 'They drank coffee for a while and then the other guy left. I remember it because John didn't seem his usual self afterwards. It was one of the last times I saw him.'

'How would you describe his behaviour afterwards?' said Varcy.

'Upset,' said Philip. 'He left soon after.'

'And you'd not seen this other person before?'

'Only in the newspapers,' said Philip.

'A celebrity?'

Philip shook his head. 'The oil guy.' He flicked his fingers trying to bring his name to mind. 'He's on TV a bit. The bloke that owned the football club for a while.'

'Charles Pine?' said Varcy.

'That's him,' nodded Philip. 'Charles Pine.'

'And you'd not seen Charles Pine in here before then?'

Philip shook his head.

Varcy made a note in his decision log.

Philip fiddled with the tea cloth.

'Do you think that occasion might have been the last time you saw him?'

Philip shrugged. 'Maybe.'

'Did you ever see Lord Scott with other famous people?'

'There are famous people here all the time. Soap stars, models. He would talk to them. As I say, he was very friendly.'

'Of course,' said Varcy.

Philip wrung the tea cloth some more and cleared his throat softly. 'I hope you catch whoever did this to him,' he said. 'John … Lord Scott was …' He paused while searching for the word. 'He was a nice bloke, you know? Quiet. He didn't deserve what happened.'

'No, indeed,' said Varcy. 'Very few do, I'm afraid. I shall do my very best.'

Philip nodded and looked down.

'One last thing,' said Varcy. 'Did he ever talk to you about worries he might have had? Things in his life that were bothering him?'

Philip shook his head. 'No. We'd talk about football mostly. He was a Leyton Orient fan. On the board I think. I'm from Southend and used to go to watch them with my dad when I was a kid. Our teams were always in trouble in the lower leagues so we had a lot in common.' Philip smiled at the memory. Then he said, 'Do you like football?'

Varcy shook his head. 'Not really.'

Philip looked back at the floor. 'Is there anything else?' he asked.

Varcy shook his head again. 'I don't think so.'

Philip nodded. 'I'd better get back then.' He rose from his seat.

Varcy shook his hand. 'Thanks for talking to me.'

Philip smiled and walked out of the bar.

Varcy took out his mobile and called the office. He wanted to speak to Hooper. He knew she was thorough. She liked detail and could drill down deep. She came on the line.

Varcy said, 'Kate, please get me what you can on Charles Pine.'

'Charles Pine, the oil guy?' she asked.

'Uh-huh,' Varcy said.

'By when?'

'We're meeting this evening, aren't we?'

'We are,' she said.

'Can you get something by then?'

'I'll bring what I can.'

26

At the intersection of two streets – Brushfield and Crispen – is a pub called The Gun. Thirty odd years ago it catered to market porters, cart minders and those who worked in the exchange when the fruit market was booming. It now serviced the needs of the expanding city and the pale, care-worn executives working there. It was also handy for most of the police crowd in the Bishopsgate station. Varcy's crew called it 'the other office'. Varcy would go in on a weekend after his shift had ended. He did so today and got his usual table in his usual alcove. Out of the way and semi-private with enough room to fit in half a dozen people. He ordered a Guinness and had it delivered. He watched as the barmaid set it down. Half a pint. Stem glass. Extra cold and as black as tar. He watched the condensation run down the side of the glass. It reminded him of rain. The soft kind that soaks you through.

Kendrick came in, took off his jacket and hung it over the back of the chair. Varcy looked up and said, 'I ordered yours.'

Kendrick nodded and went to the bar to collect a pint of Stella.

Varcy went back to watching the glass. The drift of the rivulets depended on a small white crown embossed on the side of the glass. If they hit it left they ran left. If they hit it right they ran right.

'You staring into the future, Gov'nor?' Kendrick said, setting down his drink.

Varcy moved his glass to a spot just in front of him. 'I'm thinking,' he said, looking up, 'that's all.'

Kendrick pulled up his chair. 'So what's on your mind?' he said.

'I'm thinking about John Scott,' said Varcy. 'I went to Whitechapel House today.'

'And?'

Varcy took a sip from his glass. 'Do you remember me saying how I thought Scott was resigned to his fate? Like he was almost expecting it?'

'Yes.'

'I got the same feeling while I was at the club today.'

Kendrick took a gulp from his pint glass. 'He had a death wish?'

Varcy shook his head. 'Not exactly, but he was up to something. Something dangerous. That's why he emailed me. He wanted help with it. To offload perhaps.'

'And you got all this from visiting a club?'

Varcy smiled. 'There's more to it than that.'

Varcy touched the base of his glass. It was cold and damp. 'It goes back to the torture he suffered before he died,' he said.

'The control wound thing?' asked Kendrick.

Varcy nodded. 'Scott was tortured for information,' said Varcy. 'We agree on that. Information he had either just acquired or something he had known for a long time. If he knew this information for a long time, which is what I'm leaning towards, then something happened to trigger the attack.'

'Something like what?' asked Kendrick.

'Like the attacker suddenly becoming aware that he had it. Scott tells someone, he phones someone, he does something that makes the attacker suspicious. Perhaps it's an inadvertent slip or perhaps it is deliberate. I think it was deliberate. He's lived with this for a long time and feels the burden. The attacker is compelled to take action. What information would someone kill for do you suppose?'

Kendrick took another long swallow of beer. He replaced the glass back onto the table and finger counted. 'Let's see. Information about money, power, fame,' he suggested.

'What else?'

Kendrick watched the ceiling for a moment then said, 'Information that leads to a blackmailer, or information that will save a loved one, or set you free, or save your religion, or your cause, or your sex.'

Varcy smiled. 'Okay, okay.'

'I'm on a roll,' said Kendrick.

'I can see that.'

'Shall I go on?'

'No,' said Varcy.

'Sure?'

'Positive,' Varcy replied. 'I just want to find the *thing*. The spark that started the killings. It has to be something highly emotive.'

Kendrick took another swallow of beer as Katz and Cole came in. They took off their jackets. 'Evening, Gov'nor,' they said.

'Gentlemen,' nodded Varcy.

They glanced at Kendrick who gave them a wink.

Varcy studied Katz's face. He looked healthier than he had yesterday. He was still pale, that was usual for him, but he didn't look ill the way he did at Barry Townsend's murder scene. Cole on the other hand always looked healthy, hair cropped close and clean-shaven, although the shadow along his jaw was starting to show.

'I've got a tab at the bar,' said Varcy, waving at the barmaid. 'Order what you want.' The barmaid came over and Katz and Cole ordered a pint each.

'Where's Hooper?' said Varcy.

'She's coming,' replied Cole.

'Okay,' said Varcy, looking around the table. 'Let's start without her. Progress?' He addressed the comment at Kendrick who flipped open his decision log.

'First up,' said Kendrick, 'I've tracked down the SAS guy. He's looking at both the Scott and Townsend photographs right now. I'm waiting for an opinion.'

Varcy nodded.

'Next: Lord Scott's relatives,' said Kendrick. 'He has a wife. Younger than him by about thirty years. She spends most of her time in the south of France. He also has a stepson, the child from her first marriage. I've talked to both of them. Same questions Monroe asked. Nothing comes up. I've checked against what Monroe found. It is boringly consistent. I've put the report in your file.'

Varcy nodded again.

Kendrick gestured to Cole. 'Coley has spent some time with Barry Townsend's mother.'

Cole cleared his throat and glanced at his decision log. 'She's in a state, Gov'nor,' he said. 'They've sedated her. I can't get anything from her. Nothing that helps us anyway.'

'What about Townsend's friends?' asked Varcy.

'I followed the leads that Sidhu gave us. Spoke to two of his colleagues at NatWest. They say he was a regular bloke. Nothing sinister. Nothing off. He was popular. His friends in Leeds say the same thing. I've been in email contact with his best mate. Again nothing significant.'

'Report?' asked Varcy.

'I've filed it,' said Cole.

Varcy turned his attention to Katz.

Katz took a quick sip of beer and said, 'I've been working with the IT guys. One of them spotted spyware on Scott's computer system. Not the regular software you can buy online but much more advanced. A long complex programme code. It must have taken a specialist to knock it together.'

'What's the significance?' asked Varcy.

'His computer activity was being monitored,' said Katz. 'Everything he did on it was watched.'

Varcy took a sip of Guinness. 'Does that mean the email he sent me was monitored too?'

'Probably,' said Katz.

Varcy whistled through his teeth. 'How does it work?' he asked.

'It's an advanced version of the key-logger programme.'

'What's that?' said Varcy.

'It's similar to the software they sell to parents to monitor the computer activity of their kids, but this is much more sophisticated. Every keystroke is recorded, translated and sent to the stalker. It means the stalker can watch what's happening on the target computer in real time. Because it's advanced, detection by the target computer is difficult.'

Varcy watched his glass again. He studied the embossed crown and considered a scenario. A scenario involving Scott. One in which Scott sends an email. An email requesting a meeting with a senior police officer. An email that eventually hit the police officer's spam filter. What was the significance of that to the stalker?

Hooper arrived. She was flushed as if she'd been running, red spots of colour high on her cheeks. She raked her dark hair off her face with long, pale fingers. Varcy noticed her bitten down nails.

'Sorry I'm late,' she said, removing her jacket and pulling up a short stool.

Varcy turned to Cole. 'Order her a drink, please. Use my tab.'

'I'll have a vodka and tonic,' said Hooper. 'Thanks, Gov'nor.'

'We're updating,' said Varcy.

Hooper nodded.

He turned back to Katz. 'Can we track the source of the programme?'

'It's difficult,' answered Katz, 'but not impossible. Our guys are working on it.'

'Good,' said Varcy, now looking at Hooper. 'How did you get on with Charles Pine?'

She flipped open her log and pushed a strand of hair behind an ear. She leaned forwards on her elbows. Varcy watched her thin and wiry frame. She had the physique of a marathon runner. Fit for sure. But something else too. She was hard like marble.

Hooper read her notes: 'Charles Pine. Fifty-eight years old, entrepreneur, businessman, philanthropist. *Forbes* puts his wealth at 500 million. Business interests include oil, media, property and retail. Parent company, Amonto Oil, is listed on the FTSE and traded actively.'

'Any criminal activity?' asked Varcy.

'Nothing he's been charged for,' said Hooper. 'There's been a couple of lawsuits against his oil company – spills, environment damage, compensation – that sort of thing. His property company had a big tax investigation a couple of years ago. There were some "inconsistencies".' She drew speech marks with her fingers. 'The company had to pay 1.3 million quid to HMRC. Beyond that nothing.'

'Over a million quids' worth of nothing,' said Kendrick.

'Personal life?' asked Varcy.

'Wife of thirty-five years,' Hooper replied. 'They live in Surrey.'

'Mistress?'

Hooper creased her brow. 'Not sure. I can find out.'

'Please do,' said Varcy. 'Go on.'

'One daughter and two sons,' Hooper continued. 'Daughter is thirty-four years old and married. The eldest son, Luke, is thirty-one. Unmarried. Works for his father. The youngest, James, is deceased.'

'Deceased?' Varcy asked.

She nodded. 'Suicide. Hung himself a month ago.'

'A month?'

'Just over,' said Hooper. 'Twenty-eight years old.'

Varcy thought about a twenty-eight-year-old man swinging from a beam. Neck contorted. Blue face. Swollen. His body limp. Swinging gently. Then Varcy thought about John Scott. His frail body slumped in the chair. Age spots scattered on his forehead. Raw flesh exposed along his arm. A plastic bucket at his feet. His own blood sloshing into it. Sloshing gently.

There was a roar of laughter from a group near the door. Five men stood in a circle, pints resting on their bellies. One of them held the attention of the others. He was the storyteller, his face pulled back. An impression of someone they all knew. He was nearing the punchline. The men were giggling like school kids.

'What you thinking, Gov'nor?' asked Kendrick, taking a long pull on his pint.

'I'm thinking Scott and Charles Pine met at Whitechapel House,' he said. 'According to the barman, it was one of the last times he was at the club.'

Varcy turned back to Hooper. 'Anything else?' he asked.

Hooper shook her head. 'That's all I have.'

'Do you have the address of Amonto Oil?'

'It's in the file but I can email it to you.'

'Please do,' said Varcy. 'And continue digging around Pine.'

'Will do,' said Hooper.

Varcy stood up and brushed his jacket down.

Kendrick asked, 'Are you going?'

Varcy nodded.

'Where to?'

'Somewhere to think.'

27

I am travelling on the top deck of a number 8 double-decker bus. It is empty except for an elderly woman who occupies the very front seat. She wears a woollen hat and a heavy coat. Spread on the seat beside her are six plastic supermarket bags of various sizes. She grips them tightly with one hand and holds the upright bar next to her seat with the other. The bus has taken us both from the market end of Roman Road. It will drop me where Brick Lane meets Bethnal Green Road. I do not drive. It is not that I am unable to do so. I just choose not to. I have my reasons. Cupped in my hand is a photograph. It is worn at the edges because I have held it so often before. It is a precious thing. It is the *only thing*. I focus my attention on it now and the image burns into my brain. I mentally reach for it with a longing that will never be eased.

The bus hits a bump and my concentration is temporarily broken. I check progress and notice my stop some two hundred yards ahead. I carefully replace the photograph into my jacket's inside pocket. As I do so, my hand brushes the holster that fits over my shoulder. In it is a type 67 silenced pistol. A Chinese export. It is light, versatile and perfect for the use I intend for it. I get to my feet and use the handrail to steady myself on the descent to the lower deck. The bus pulls to a stop and I hop onto the pavement.

I stand still for a moment to rearrange my jacket and to tap down my back pocket to check for the stub knife I always carry there. All is in order so I walk the one hundred yards westward. The evening is warm for the time of year. I pass a couple of winos sitting in a disused doorway. They are drinking Tennents Extra and muttering in a language I don't understand.

The Bagel Stop on Brick Lane is open twenty-four hours a day. According to my watch, it is 10.38pm and it's lively. I am early for my meeting so I take my place in the queue behind a short, fat man with a tangled beard. He has a sour body odour and shuffles forward as the queue diminishes. When my turn comes, I order a chopped herring bagel and a black coffee. The order is dispatched by the first server, who bags the bagel and pushes it along to her colleague who has already poured the coffee into a styrofoam cup and clamped on a plastic lid.

I take my food to a corner. This is a no-seat establishment, so I stand. That suits me fine. There is a foot-deep counter that runs along a single wall and cuts into the alcove where I am standing. This position affords me a complete view of the front of the shop and the pavement beyond it. I lean against the counter and begin to eat. I have just over ten minutes before they arrive, which will be plenty of time.

I see them a lot sooner than they see me. There are two of them. I have never met either one but I know the type. One is tall and thickset. His face is broad, the bridge of his nose wide and deep. A white scar snakes along the left side of his cheek. His head is balding. What hair he does possess is buzzed close to his scalp. Beside him is a smaller man with jet black hair and a thick neck. His hands are thrust deep inside a dark spitz jacket. He is calm. They approach the entrance to the shop and their eyes sweep the interior. They assess the clientele. The tall one spots me in the corner and they both move into the shop. There is a change of energy as they enter. A few customers in the line are from out of town. Most are local. The locals know who these men are. The out of town folk might have heard their names, but the locals recognise their faces. There is a shift. Fear mixed with a strange kind of admiration. The admiration that surrounds violent men. And these men are violent. They are gangsters. East End hard men. I don't know their names – Mad Kenny or Pretty Boy Dave or some other moniker – but they define what it is to be dangerous and cool.

But – and I feel I have to stress this – neither one of them has killed in the way I have done. Or been tortured as I have. Or been shot in the head. Or faced a machine gun nest and run it down. Nor strangled an opponent while frozen and half-delirious from lack of food. They haven't knifed or maimed or gouged or destroyed as I have done. Their bodies are well fed. They are muscular and slow.

I am none of these things.

The taller one looks me in the eye and holds the stare. The smaller one remains distant. I am passive.

I look back at them but I am not aggressive. I hold a certain expression on my face that I have perfected well. It is non-threatening and docile.

'He's been spotted,' says the larger of the two men. 'You were deadlined.'

It was true. I did have a deadline. A man they wanted hit – or at least their boss wanted hit – was still alive. I had initially agreed to the job. The degree of difficulty was minimal and the pay was good. But I changed my mind at the eleventh hour.

'You've taken a payment,' says the taller one.

That was true also. But the payment was not for the full amount. It was a deposit only. In return I had scoped out the target. His terrain, his routine. I had purchased the weapon. I spent long hours planning and legislating. The careful forethought that goes into my work is the most expensive part. Then something happened. A small gesture is all. I was following him home. The last time before I would make the kill. He was on the roadside waiting for a break in the traffic before crossing. A young mother approached the curb next to him. She too wanted to cross. She was pushing a stroller and holding the hand of a young child who was perhaps five years old. He was excitable and lost in a game of his own making. He kept gesturing with his arms. Folding them into an 'X'. He was a superhero or a magic man or a Kung-Fu master. The baby in the stroller stirred and began to cry. The mother briefly let go of the toddler's hand to attend to her baby. Free from her grip, the youngster charged into the road. The young woman's maternal response kicked in quickly. She let go a high-pitched scream and lurched forwards just as a Volvo X90 loomed into view. The target grabbed the toddler's shoulder and yanked him back onto the pavement, a split second before the X90 sped past. The toddler ran to his mother crying. The mother cuddled him close. I could see the relief and the gratitude on her face. She spoke to the target briefly. The target smiled. He then crossed the road and went on his way.

I stood entranced for a long moment. Stunned at what had taken place. Trying to find meaning in it. When I came to, I aborted all my plans for him.

'I'll keep the deposit,' I say to them both. 'But I won't allow the hit.'

The two men exchange glances. The taller one says, 'You serious?'

I nod my head. I rarely joke about anything.

The smaller man speaks for the first time. He says simply, 'You are fucked.'

They both turn and leave the shop. I expect them to do this. I have planned for it. This setting is too public to do what they want. But I know they will act soon. There is a third man on the road outside. I spotted him earlier. He wears a small earpiece and is hooked up to a mic. His job is to follow me out of the shop and keep the other two informed of my movements.

The two men cross Brick Lane and are moving towards Bacon Street where they will get into a parked black Ford Mondeo. Once inside, they will liaise with the third man who will follow me. His commentary will guide them in their car. They will hit me when I arrive home or, if I happen to stray into a location that suits them before then, they will complete the action on the street.

I know this because my due diligence is exhaustive.

I know also that they will complete twenty-five strides before they reach the top of Bacon Street. Then another twenty until they reach the car. I count the strides and will make my move on the fifteenth.

Meanwhile the third man moves to the right of the shop. He watches the other two and waits. They reach stride eleven. I move to The Bagel Shop's window. I glance past the third man who is now leaning against a wall. I'm interested in Cheshire Street that lies two hundred and twenty feet south of the shop. It runs east where it joins Chiltern Street, then turns north and finally joins Bacon Street that leads back to the black Ford Mondeo.

A complete square.

They hit stride twelve. I slip a pair of nylon gloves out of my jacket and pull them on. I pull the stub knife out of my back pocket and move to the entrance of the shop. They make stride thirteen and then fourteen. I take a deep, long breath and stand completely still. Fifteen. I slip out of the shop, put my head down and run south. I'm at full tilt. I do not make eye contact with the third man. He is confused. Unsure what I'm up to. But that doesn't last long. I come up adjacent to him and lash out with the knife. The blade rips the flesh of his neck near where the ear-piece is stuck in. He crumples. There is no sound. I continue to sprint and soon turn east on Cheshire Street. I have covered two hundred feet in less than ten seconds. Back on Brick Lane the two men will have completed another ten strides. That means they are some fifteen strides from the car. I run the length of Cheshire Street and then turn north on Chiltern Street. I run hard until I reach the Bacon Street junction and turn east once again. I have travelled another three hundred and fifty feet and sixteen seconds have passed. The two men have completed the remaining fifteen strides of their journey and I watch from the rear as they duck inside the black Mondeo. They will take a second or two to realise the third man is not responding. That will generate confusion. I grip the type 67 and remove it from its holster. The Mondeo is some one hundred and fifty feet ahead of me and I sprint the first hundred. Then walk the final fifty. The car looms up on my left. I see the silhouettes of both men in the back seat. They are looking forwards toward Brick Lane. There is another man in the front seat. The driver. That means three altogether. I will need to be sharp. Surprise will, of course, be the key. I calculate the nearside door will be unlocked. I grip it now and wait a tiny beat. I pull it quickly. It opens and I swing into their view. They turn towards me in tandem. The type 67 is already at the head of the smaller man nearest me. He sits the same way he stood. With his hands thrust into his jacket. His eyes bulge with surprise for a fraction of a second. I pull the trigger. His skull rips open and a red cloud bursts forwards. My arm immediately arcs right to where the taller man sits.

His hand has disappeared into his jacket where he gropes. I pull again. His head erupts and he crashes against the far side passenger door. I swing my arm another forty-five degrees to find the driver. He has slumped down behind his seat. Because of the time delay, he will be the most difficult kill. I duck inside the Mondeo further. A dangerous move. His hand appears between the two front seats and I get a brief look at him. He is a black man with a shaved head. It shines with skin-balm and sweat. He is clutching a handgun – a Glock, I think – and lets one off just as I swing away. The shot clips the top of my shoulder. The torture is familiar. A raw flame burning into my flesh. I get two off into the back of his seat. I hear him moan. But that could be a bluff. I back out and close the door. I hunch down and grab the handle on the front passenger's door. I snatch at it and it swings open. There is silence. I hold my position for a moment than I spring forwards, keeping low. I get off a shot and roll away. The shot misses but he is out of it anyway. He is hunched down and bleeding in the footwell. The two I put into the back seat found their mark. I finish him with a final round into the back of his neck and close the door. I replace the type 67 and check my watch. The encounter has taken less than fifteen seconds. I check the locality. Nothing of note to concern me. I check my injury. I bleed front and back. A good sign. The bullet has passed straight through. I walk briskly towards Brick Lane and then turn north towards Bethnal Green Road.

28

The hotel was off Tottenham Court Road. It was decent. Neither high or low end. A family run place with chintzy curtains at the bedroom windows and white cloths on the tables in the dining hall. Rita's room was on the third floor. It was a twenty-foot square with a single bed, an en-suite bath and a desk under the window with a large, white phone on it. In the first drawer of the desk was a pad of branded notepaper and a large brown envelope stuffed with tourist flyers. The carpet was orange with swirls of dark ochre. From her window she could see the top of Centrepoint.

The call had come a couple of hours ago. Chief Inspector Varcy had been as good as his word. The arrangements were made swiftly. Meg had travelled with her and helped her unpack her half-empty luggage case. All the clothes inside it had been bought by the police support officers on the afternoon of Barry's death. They were generic and cheap, but usable and she was grateful for that.

Meg hugged her at the door. 'I'll text when I get back,' she said.

'Thanks for being so kind,' Rita replied.

'No worries,' said Meg. 'Are you going in tomorrow?'

Rita nodded. 'I want to talk to Robert.'

'Me too,' said Meg.

The women embraced again and Meg left. Rita was on her own.

She locked the door of her room. The clunk of the bolt hitting home was a comforting sound. A signal to shut out all the madness. She felt safe. Finally able to breathe. She kicked off her trainers and opened the sash window. Bedford Avenue was several storeys below. It was narrow and quiet. The muted sounds of Tottenham Court Road drifted upwards. The rhythm of the city. She sat on the edge of the bed and removed her socks. Padding out to the bathroom in bare feet, she set the shower going. She undressed quickly, got under the spray and savoured the hot gush as it soaked her skin. She tried to relax. Back in the Guildhall Library, she had entered a man's name into the database expecting to find nothing of significance. But it threw up the article about his suicide, and that in turn threw up a whole slew of bad memories.

The man's name was James Pine. He was the son of Charles Pine.

Rita had been silent for much of the time at Meg's. Preoccupied and distant. She had a lot to think about. The meeting with Mark had made her face something she would rather have forgotten. Something that would now have to be faced.

Rita emerged from the bathroom and got into a robe hanging on the back of the door. She went to the phone, dialled room service and ordered a tray of ham sandwiches and a half bottle of white wine.

She unpacked her case quickly and folded the clothes. Then she took out a manila envelope she had tucked into a pocket at the bottom of the case. She pulled it free and opened the flap. Inside, folded neatly, were the two NEWSPLAN articles she had downloaded at the library. She re-read the report about James Pine. His picture was placed next to the article. He was thick set with light hair. A rugged sort of man. Good looking with a wide neck and shoulders. Found hanged in the apartment bought for him by his father. The apartment, said the report, was untouched. There had been no forced entry. Nothing was stolen or destroyed.

The coroner had found some trace amounts of the drug ephedrine in Pine's system. But the dose was not enough to blow his mind or render him incapacitated. A straight case of suicide, then. Under normal circumstances, Rita might have been relieved at the news. After all, it was the evidence taken from James Pine's car that she had hidden these past two years. But she was not relieved at all.

She looked again at the article featuring the young woman called Kimberley Westfield. Something about her she couldn't let go of. A deep connection. Or a deep responsibility.

There was a quiet knock on the door. Rita opened it a few inches.

'Room service,' said a young male voice.

She opened it wide and a tall, bony youth tiptoed in. He had pale skin and wore a brown jacket at least a size too short for him. He placed the order on the desk and Rita fished out a pound coin from her purse and handed it to him. He nodded quickly and hurried out.

The sandwiches were okay but the wine was delicious. Ice cold and as dry as a bone – just the way she liked it. She took the glass to the window and sipped. The air was warm. Summer was just around the corner. A young couple appeared at the top of Tottenham Court Road and walked towards her hotel. They passed under her window, holding hands and giggling. They were bathed in the light from a street lamp as they passed below. It bleached out the man's hair and tinged it with red. It reminded her of James Pine's photograph. She took another sip of the wine.

James Pine.

A month ago, James Pine had died. That should have been it. But it was not. Mark's uncle had been murdered and now Barry too. There had to be a connection. Rita gazed eastward towards Charing Cross Road and considered her options. She herself and the analysis she'd performed were the link. Mark as good as said so. She had to find out why.

Placing the wine glass back on the desk, she checked her watch. Then she made a decision. She moved towards the bed and pulled on a fresh pair of jeans and a clean tee-shirt. She got back into her trainers, and pulled on a light jacket. She unlocked the hotel door, slipped out of the room and took the stairs down to ground level. From there, she turned towards Tottenham Court Road and the tube station.

* * *

Canary Wharf is an enigma. Isolated east of the city, but as much a part of it as any corner of the square mile. Developed in the 1980s from a dockland slum to an oasis of corporate luxury, it's home to some of the world's biggest and best companies. With so much money slopping about in a relatively small space, property developers had created high-end apartments along the wharf. That move brought in retail, restaurants and bars.

James Pine lived in Redden Court. His penthouse apartment was front line Canary Wharf. West of the tower. It had panoramic views of the Thames as it snaked from the O2 down towards the Isle of Dogs.

Rita checked her watch. 11.00pm. It had been a spur of the moment decision to come here. She was not sure what she wanted from the visit except that she felt she had to do something. Find out something. Anything. Redden Court had two brick pillars at the entrance and a steel gate that was closed shut. The ubiquitous silver buttons on the squawk box mounted on the right pillar were the only means of entry. Rita scanned the options and noticed the abbreviation, PH, beside one of the buttons. She assumed this stood for penthouse. She pressed it and waited. She had no idea what she would say if someone answered. There was a long silence and then someone did answer. A male voice. Mature. Deep with well rounded vowels. An educated man probably. There was something else too. He sounded familiar.

'Hello,' he said.

'Hello,' Rita stammered. 'I was wondering …'

'I can't hear you,' the voice interrupted. 'Who is this?'

'Sorry,' said Rita, clearing her throat. 'I am calling because … because …' She desperately tried to think of something to say. '… Because I was James Pine's girlfriend,' she blurted out. It was a lie but it was out before she could edit it.

There was silence.

'Did you know him by any chance?' she added.

'James?' the voice said.

'Yes. James Pine.'

There was another moment of silence. Then: 'Yes, I knew James.'

Rita stumbled on. 'I was wondering if I might ask you some questions about him?'

There was another short silence. Then the voice said: 'Come up.'

The squawk box buzzed and Rita heard a click as the locks on both the gate and the front entrance door disengaged. She pushed open the entrance door inwards and arrived in a small hallway. It was about ten-foot square and smelled of varnished wood. The floor was covered with a brown, spiky matting, and Rita rubbed the soles of her trainers clean before pushing a glass double door and emerging into the main lobby. The lobby was classy with oak-panelled walls and a stone floor. It was softly lit. There was a small reception desk to the right of the door where a porter in a parsley green jacket sat flipping a pen between his fingers. He smiled.

'The penthouse?' Rita asked.

'The lift will take you right there,' he said, pointing with the pen.

The elevator was buried in an alcove. Rita stepped inside and pressed the 'P' at the head of a column of chrome buttons. It deposited her at the top of the building and into another lobby. This one was a replica of the one downstairs except it was much smaller. It had nothing in it but a dark wooden door directly opposite the lift with a spy hole three-quarters of the way up it. It was fitted with an ornate knocker. Rita was about to use it when the door opened. The man that stood there was in his late fifties and had light, sandy-coloured hair and a face full of freckles. His ruddy, windblown skin spoke of the outdoors. He was medium height, certainly no more than six feet, and wore a white polo shirt and dark trousers. His eyes were his most striking feature. Milky blue. Slightly reptilian. Then he spoke, and the combination of face and voice together made it completely clear who he was.

'Welcome,' he said, stepping back and gesturing inside.

Rita smiled and moved into the apartment. It was glorious. Expansive and light. The far wall was glass. The view of the river during the day must have been spectacular. Inside was a mixture of white and beige. The sofa was low and the carpets deep and spotless. There was a raised platform which acted as a dining area on which an eight-place dining table was laid out. Beyond this a kitchen. Rita could see the marble hardware and chrome fittings.

The man closed the door and introduced himself. 'My name is Charles Pine. James' father.'

'Yes, I know,' said Rita. 'I'm Rita Sidhu.'

'Have we met?' he asked.

She shook her head. 'No, but I recognise your face from a photo James showed me once.'

There was a moment of silence.

'Can I get you a drink?' he asked.

'No,' said Rita. 'I'm good.'

Pine nodded and gestured to the sofa. 'Have a seat.'

Rita moved towards the sofa and perched on the end. Pine sat opposite.

'So,' he began, 'you said you had some questions?'

Rita nodded and desperately tried to think of one. 'I've not been myself since James passed away,' she began slowly. 'I don't know why. Well, I do. Grief is difficult ...'

She paused for a long moment. 'It's just ... the police say he committed suicide but I keep wondering if there was something else to it, you know?'

Pine cupped his chin in his hand. 'Something like what?'

'I don't know,' she said. 'That's the trouble. Maybe he was worried about things. Things he never told me.'

'What kind of things?' Pine asked.

She shook her head. 'As I say, I don't know. It's just I find suicide hard to accept, that's all.'

Pine stared at her for a long moment but said nothing.

'He had everything to live for,' she added. 'Why would he do it?'

Pine leaned back into the sofa. He folded his arms across his chest and said, 'Why do *you* believe he did it?'

She swallowed hard. 'That's the point. I don't think he did,' she said. 'I think he may have been murdered.'

'Murdered?' said Pine.

She nodded.

Pine shifted in his seat and leaned forwards. He rubbed his palms together gently as if he was rolling a plasticine sausage.

'I wish you were right,' he said at last. 'That might make it a bit easier to bear. But unfortunately you are not. James did have worries,' he said. 'Deep worries.'

'What were they?' asked Rita.

Pine took a deep breath then waited for a moment. He continued to roll his palms. 'He had been set up,' he said at last. 'Set up to take the blame for a crime he didn't commit.'

Rita felt her face flush. 'What crime?' she stammered.

'A serious one,' Pine replied.

There was a long moment of silence.

'Who was trying to set him up?' Rita asked softly.

Pine half smiled. 'I'm in the process of finding out.'

'Why would anyone want to do it?' she asked.

Pine's eyes fixed on hers. 'Jealousy, revenge. Money.'

The last word was spat out.

'Blackmail?' she said.

'Of course blackmail,' he replied.

His anger had started to make her feel uncomfortable.

Rita nodded again. 'Of course.'

Pine stood up and walked towards the kitchen. 'You sure you won't have a drink?' he asked.

'No. I really should go,' she replied.

Pine ignored the comment. He disappeared into the kitchen and reappeared a moment later with a bottle of beer. He took a long swig. Then he sat directly opposite her and fixed her with a watery blue stare. He took another long swig. Then he said, 'And so, Miss Sidhu, now it's my turn to ask you a couple of questions.'

Rita shifted in her seat. She didn't like the feel of this at all. 'Of course,' she heard herself say.

'Why did you come here?' he asked.

The question was direct and wrong footed her for a moment. 'Like I said,' Rita began, 'I came –'

'I know what you said,' Pine interrupted. 'You said you were James' girlfriend. But I have never met you. You were not at his funeral. Megan – his real girlfriend – was. You come here at,' he checked is watch, 'at 11.10pm and begin asking questions about something that happened nearly five weeks ago. You have not shown the least bit of interest up to this point. You say you think James might have been murdered but have no evidence to support your suggestion except some vague feelings. Nor have you any idea who might have murdered him or why. I'll tell you what I think, Miss Sidhu. I think you are fishing and I want to know why. So I'll ask you again. Who are you and why have you come?'

Rita's mind raced. She tried to quell it. What was she thinking coming here anyway? This was the lions' den and she had walked right into it. Her mouth felt dry. 'James and I were dating,' she whispered. 'He may not have told you about it but that doesn't make it untrue. I knew about his other girlfriend. I didn't know her name – I didn't ask – but James told me the truth about her. I couldn't turn up at the funeral. How would it have looked?' She glanced up and then added, 'He was about to leave her anyway.'

At once she regretted saying it. It sounded clichéd and hollow. She tried desperately to think of a way to get herself out it. 'I know how that must sound,' she persisted. 'Our relationship was new, that much is true. Neither of us knew where it was going. I understand how you feel about me coming here but as the weeks have gone on, I've found it more and more difficult to let go.'

Rita searched Pine's face. Hoping for a chink of softness. There was none. She felt flustered. Blood rushed to her neck. It was hot and clammy. She tried to control it. 'I've outstayed my welcome,' she said quickly. 'I'd better go.'

Pine took another swig of beer. 'Where do you live?' he asked suddenly.

'Why do you want to know?' Rita said, flushing once more.

'I'll call you a taxi,' he said. 'It's late and you shouldn't be walking the streets alone.'

Rita took a deep breath. 'I'm a grown woman,' she said. 'I got myself here and I can get myself back.'

'Where is back?' he asked. The smile appeared again. His eyes burned into hers. It gave Rita the creeps.

'I'm over at Bloomsbury,' she replied. 'Not far from Holborn tube.'

He nodded slowly. 'I know the area well,' he said. 'Whereabouts in Bloomsbury?'

'Near Theobalds Road,' she said vaguely.

'I know Theobalds Road. Where exactly?'

Giving him her address was the last thing she wanted. She considered her options, but couldn't think of any alternatives. So she gave him the address of her flat. Pine waited for a long moment, then got off the sofa and walked to the front door. He held it open.

She stepped through, then stopped. 'I came here out of genuine concern for your son,' she lied. 'I'm sorry if I have upset you.'

Pine said nothing.

Rita walked to the lift and called it. It pinged open immediately. She stepped in and pressed the ground floor button. Turning, she saw Pine staring at her. His eyes were cold and blue and sent a tingle of fear across the back of her neck. The doors closed, and the lift dropped. Rita covered her face and burst into tears.

29

Varcy scrunched his eyes closed and rubbed them both with the heel of his hands. The left eye was still catching. He pulled the upper lid over the lower and blinked a few times.

'What time is it?' he asked.

Kendrick checked his watch. '1.15am.'

They were sitting in a dark blue BMW. It was standard police issue and unmarked. The interior was black leather. The radio was set to LBC and turned down low. Cristo was talking about overbearing parents and how they affected the lives of their children. The city's insomniacs had plenty to say. A woman from Fulham had married the wrong man, then divorced him. She now took Prozac every day of her life and blamed it all on her mother.

'You had enough?' asked Kendrick.

Varcy peered through the windshield and squinted. 'Is there any tea left in the flask?'

Kendrick grabbed the chrome jug perched on the dashboard and shook it. 'A dribble,' he said, holding it to his ear.

'A dribble will do,' said Varcy.

Kendrick unscrewed the cap and poured the tea into a plastic mug. He handed it to Varcy who downed it in one hit.

Kendrick's cell phone pinged with a solitary trill. He fished it out of his pocket and pushed a key. The text was from Katz. It simply said: 'Home.'

He showed it to Varcy who nodded and handed back the mug.

The BMW was parked at the south-west end of Morwell Street. It had been there for three and a half hours. The position allowed a good view of the hotel in which Rita Sidhu had been placed. She had been back inside the hotel for exactly twenty-one minutes after leaving two hours ago and travelling – followed by Katz – to an address in Canary Wharf. She had stayed inside the Canary Wharf property for thirty minutes then gone back to the hotel. Katz had sent the address to Varcy who had phoned it through and was now waiting for a name.

Kendrick shifted position and the seat leather squeaked out a protest. London's Biggest Conversation continued with a man from Battersea who had been dominated by his arrogant father. Cristo was sympathetic. The man started to choke up. It had plagued his whole adult life. He was shy. He didn't go out much.

Varcy blocked out the chatter. Balanced on his lap were the two dump lists he had compiled on Friday. One for Barry Townsend, the other for Scott. He checked for common traits between the two. Things that were similar. Things that were odd. He had practised this routine in dozens of cases. It was a meditation. A groove of thought that he could slip into and ride. The thought was not random or inconsequential. It was structured and targeted. He did it now and it felt good. Images and sounds drifted through his brain. Tastes and scents settled on the back of his tongue.

His cell phone sprang to life. He killed the generic ring tone and answered.

'I have a name for that address,' said the voice.

'Good. Go ahead.'

'Mr Charles Pine,' the voice said.

'Pine?' repeated Varcy.

'Yep.'

'Hmm,' Varcy said.

'Anything else?'

'No. That's fine. Thanks for getting back so quickly.'

'No worries.'

Varcy rang off and glanced at Kendrick.

'Did I hear right?' Kendrick asked.

Varcy nodded. 'The apartment is registered to Charles Pine,' he said.

Kendrick asked, 'Can I borrow your pad?'

Varcy flipped the pages until he came to a fresh one. He handed it to Kendrick who pulled a biro out from behind his ear and scribbled:

John Scott (dead)

Barry Townsend (dead)

James Pine (dead).

He showed the list to Varcy. 'Let me get this fixed in my brain,' he said. 'All of them die within the last month or so and his father,' he circled James Pine's name, 'has a meeting with Scott at Whitechapel House some time before Scott's death.'

Varcy nodded. 'According to the barman.'

'Now tonight, Barry's girlfriend,' he circled Barry Townsend's name, 'visits a flat owned by James Pine's father, Charles.'

Varcy nodded.

'To meet with him,' said Kendrick. 'Or to meet someone else. Didn't Hooper say Charles Pine lived in Surrey?'

'True,' said Varcy.

Kendrick held up his cell phone and waved it. 'Want to phone Katz back?'

Varcy chewed his lip. The last thing he wanted to do was send Katz out again. He'd just got home after all. But Varcy needed to know who was in Pine's apartment. He nodded. 'Ring him.'

Kendrick speed-dialled Katz's number. Varcy looked back at his dump lists. The connection had been made, but what did it mean?

'Sorry mate,' Varcy heard Kendrick say. 'I need you back at Canary Wharf.'

There was a pause.

'Right now … yes. It'll be an all-nighter.'

Another pause.

'We need to know who leaves the apartment you saw Sidhu go into. Yep, take whatever you need.'

Katz had a young wife and a small daughter. He would have to leave them again. Varcy thought about that. You either loved this job or you plain didn't. If you didn't you got out. Katz loved it. Varcy knew that much. He was a bright lad too. He'd do fine. Varcy concentrated on the lists again.

The link then – the one between James Pine and Scott – was found. The link was Charles Pine. Varcy had a link between Barry Townsend and Charles Pine also. That link was Rita Sidhu. What he did not have was a link between Townsend and Scott. At least not directly. A direct link may not exist, of course, but Varcy felt it probably did. Somewhere just below the surface.

Kendrick rang off and said, 'Katz is going back.'

Varcy nodded. 'Good.' Then he glanced up at Sidhu's hotel room window and said, 'Let's go. I've got things to do.'

30

Rita Sidhu was out of the bed she had got into fifty-five minutes earlier. She had tossed around in it for a while and then left it to sit at the desk in her hotel room. She was thinking about Kimberley Westfield. The parliamentary assistant who had been murdered two years before. The article Rita had downloaded was laid out in front of her. She read it several times over.

The facts were the same as they had been the first time she had read them two years before. Nothing had changed. Sidhu picked up her iPhone and tapped the Safari icon. She Googled Westfield's full name. A Wikipedia page was offered and she chose it. It was an account of what had happened on the night of her disappearance. Unlike the NEWSPLAN article, this one had the benefit of two years' worth of hindsight. Rita read through quickly.

At around 7.00am on 6th March – two years before – a dog walker had found Westfield's body in woodland on the edge of Green Park. Sidhu's fingers raked her hair off of her face. Okay, that much she knew.

Westfield's flat mate, Joanna Strait, was due to meet her on the evening of 5th March in a restaurant in Bayswater at 8.45pm. When she didn't arrive, Strait called Westfield's mobile and got her recorded message. Returning to their flat at 10.00pm, Strait waited until around midnight and then, when Westfield failed to turn up, she called the police to report her missing. Rita vaguely remembered that too.

Investigators determined that Westfield had spent the early evening of the 5th March with colleagues at a pub called The Lion, Praed Street, leaving around 8.00pm to make the twenty-minute walk to Bayswater Road, where she had been due to meet Strait. Westfield was spotted on CCTV at around 8.10pm in a Co-op supermarket where she purchased ten menthol cigarettes. She then phoned her ex-boyfriend, Richard Lester, at 8.20pm to arrange a meeting the following week. The last known whereabouts of Westfield was recorded by a CCTV camera outside a BP petrol station that she passed at 8.40pm the same evening.

Westfield's killer had not been found and so the case remained unsolved.

Sidhu scrolled down the article. It mentioned that Westfield's parents lived in Canterbury, Kent. The name of her father was hyperlinked. Rita hit the link and was taken to a fresh Wikipedia page. It was short – just a couple of paragraphs – and gave basic information only. Peter Westfield was the father of the murdered parliamentary assistant, Kimberley Westfield. He had died of heart failure two years after his daughter's murder. He was survived by his wife and the mother of Kimberley, Violet Westfield.

Sidhu drummed her fingers on the desk in front

of her. She Googled Violet Westfield's name along with the town of Canterbury. She got a hit. She read the web page and then pressed the home button on her iPhone. Tapping the message icon, she scrolled through her contacts until she came to Meg's name. She sent a text. *Won't be in tomorrow. I'll see you on Tuesday. x*

31

Amonto Oil's head office was at the west end of Tottenham Court Road at the junction with Maple Street. Varcy pushed through a revolving door and scanned the reception space. It was mostly white marble with dark veins and distressed edges. It had reflective metal at the edges which were chrome or stainless steel.

The reception desk was wide and arc shaped. Behind it was an auburn-haired woman in a cream tunic. Her make up was applied sparingly. Not too heavy, not too light either. Behind her was the Amonto logo. It was big and bold and stretched across most of the back wall. The whole place was understated. Varcy could sense wealth but it was hidden. Money at ease with itself – not trying too hard. His footfall clacked against the stone and the receptionist made eye contact with him. She smiled and her teeth were white and even.

'Good morning,' she said when he reached the arc, 'how are you?'

'Very well,' Varcy said, placing his brief case between his feet. He leaned forwards and tried to establish the origins of her accent. It sounded Australian or New Zealand. 'I have an appointment with Charles Pine,' he said.

She nodded as though expecting this response. 'Detective Chief Inspector Terry Varcy?' she asked, tapping a few keys on a flat screen mounted off to her left.

'Yes,' he said.

She nodded, satisfied. She hit a few more keys and a printer whirred from somewhere behind the desk. She waited for it to finish then tore off a chunk of paper along a perforated line. She folded it in two and eased it into a square plastic cover. The cover had a red lanyard attached to it. She showed it to Varcy and said, 'Here's your identity pass for security purposes.' She pulled the lanyard apart and held it open. Varcy bowed his head and she looped it over his neck like an Olympic medal.

'Mr Pine will be available very shortly,' she said. 'Will you take a seat?' She gestured to one of the leather sofas.

Varcy moved to a sofa positioned at right angles to the outside road. He undid the buttons on his jacket and lowered himself into the soft leather. Balancing his briefcase on his lap, he got his new bearings. To his right, making up the entire wall, was glass. It was dark and reflective. He peered out onto Tottenham Court Road and his eyes followed a number 24 bus as it crawled north towards Euston Road. Then he fiddled with the brass locks on the edge of the briefcase and pinged open the spring. He lifted the lid and retrieved a square cut folder. Shutting the case, he placed it next to him on the sofa. The folder was stuffed with papers and photographs. Everything he thought relevant to this meeting with Pine. He tidied the pages as the receptionist appeared from behind the arc. Her stiletto heels clacked on the marble. Now that she was completely visible he saw she was wearing a skirt. Tight and contoured. Legs slim and long, shoes high and black. She might have been an air hostess on a TV ad. Almost too good to be true. *Very* attractive. She fiddled with a perspex stand which was displaying glossy company brochures. Tidied them, then walked elegantly back to the arc. Varcy returned his attention to the folder and pulled out the first sheet. On it were the points he wanted to bring up. He went through each one in turn and re-familiarised himself with them. He flipped through the other sheets. They contained background information on Pine and his family, including his deceased son. The team had worked through the night to get it ready for this morning. He had work-ups on John Scott and Barry Townsend. He also had photographs and a short biography of Rita Sidhu. Much of it he wouldn't use – at least not yet – but he wanted to have it to hand all the same.

The receptionist appeared again smiling broadly. 'Mr Pine will see you now,' she said. Varcy slid the file back into his briefcase and got to his feet.

'This way,' she said.

She led him to an elevator on the south side of the lobby and pressed the call button. 'He's on floor twelve. Madeline will meet you when you get off.'

The lift pinged open and Varcy stepped in. There was carpet on the floor and on both sidewalls, but the back of the lift was mirrored. The receptionist leaned in and pressed button twelve on a panel just inside the door. She smiled again. 'Have a great meeting,' she said as the doors closed.

Madeline did indeed meet him. She shared the same low key good-looks as her colleague downstairs. Varcy wondered if this was an essential requirement at Amonto. She welcomed him with enthusiasm, introduced herself as Charles Pine's PA, asked after his health and spoke about the early summer the city was having. She led him through a series of corridors with open office areas on both sides. People sat at desks, some on the phone or busy on their computers, a few were photocopying documents. They continued to walk until they came to a suite of meeting rooms. Each was separated from the corridor by glass. The spaces were standard. A long, buff-coloured meeting table at the centre, various white boards screwed to the walls, a flat screen TV at one end and a couple of flip charts. Two out of the four were occupied. Men and women talking, listening and making notes on pads.

They passed through a set of double doors and immediately the white noise died behind them. This area was carpeted with a deep red pile. It ran at ninety degrees to their entry point. Varcy counted three doors. One away to the left, one in the centre and one to the right. Each was heavy and constructed from wood. All were polished to a high shine.

Madeline moved off to the left and rapped

sharply on the first door. There was no response but she pushed it inwards anyway. She stepped back and the room was revealed. It felt like a library in a country house. To the left was a bookshelf that rose from the floor and finished at the ceiling. To the right a portrait of a middle aged man. His clothes looked 1920s. He stood erect and stared off into the distance. The centre of the room was dominated by a wide desk. It too was formed from the same dark wood as everything else. Behind it, getting to his feet and moving to the front, was a man whom Varcy recognised as Charles Pine.

'Inspector,' he said, extending his hand.

Varcy shook Pine's hand and replied, 'Mr Pine, a great pleasure to meet you.'

Pine gestured to an office chair opposite the desk and Varcy sat down. Pine walked back to his own. He leaned forwards and rested his hands on the desk. Smiling broadly, he held Varcy's gaze for a long moment.

'Well now,' he began, 'to what do I owe this unexpected pleasure?'

Varcy balanced his briefcase on his knees and pinged the lock. He removed the folder once again and placed the briefcase on the floor. 'Well, first of all,' he said, 'thank you for seeing me at such short notice. I know how busy you must be.'

Pine inclined his head in acknowledgement.

'The main reason for my visit is to see if you might be able to help me in a rather delicate matter.'

Pine laced his fingers together and nodded. 'My

PA said that's why you wanted to come. Of course I will if I can.'

'Excellent,' said Varcy, opening the folder. He flicked through and removed a photograph of Barry Townsend, a fairly recent one given to Cole by Townsend's mother. Barry was sitting outside a bar. The sun was high. It looked to be a European city. Barcelona or Milan perhaps. He held a glass of red wine in his hand and he was toasting the camera. He looked suntanned, happy and healthy. Varcy turned it around and placed it on Pine's desk. He pushed it towards him and said, 'Do you know who this young man is?'

Pine looked at the picture. Then he reached inside his jacket and pulled out a pair of tortoiseshell spectacles. He pulled them over his ears and peered at it again. He shook his head and pushed the photograph back towards Varcy. 'I'm afraid I don't. Should I?'

'Maybe not,' said Varcy, creasing his brow. He flipped through the pages again and pulled out a picture of Rita Sidhu. It was the standard bio shot from IMDB's website. Kendrick had printed it onto glossy photo paper. Varcy set it down on the desk and pushed it forwards. 'What about this woman?' he asked.

Pine peered at the photo for a long moment and then shook his head once again. 'Sorry, but no.'

Varcy shifted in his seat. 'Are you sure?' he asked.

'Of course I'm sure,' said Pine, peeling off his spectacles. 'What's this all about?'

'This young man,' said Varcy, leaning forwards and pointing to Barry Townsend's photograph, 'was found murdered last Friday over at Holborn. This woman,' he pointed to Rita's photograph, 'was his girlfriend.'

There was a moment of silence.

'So what has that got to do with me?' asked Pine.

'This woman made a visit to your Canary Wharf apartment last night,' said Varcy.

Pine frowned and snatched the photograph up again. He put the tortoiseshells back on and stared at it intently.

'I know you were there last night because we observed you leaving this morning,' said Varcy.

'You've been monitoring my house?' said Pine.

'Not really,' said Varcy. 'But last night, when this young woman visited we had to find out who she was meeting.'

'She's a suspect in her boyfriend's murder?' said Pine.

'She has yet to be eliminated,' said Varcy.

Pine drummed his fingertips on his desk. Varcy studied him carefully. He was wrestling with something. Trying to make it add together.

'So,' Varcy said, 'do you recognise her?'

Pine nodded. 'Now you have pointed it out, I do. Although she looks nothing like the woman who turned up last night.'

'You'd never met her before last night?'

'No,' said Pine.

'What did she want?'

Pine shrugged. 'She turned up uninvited and

said she was dating my son, James, before his death.'

'Was she?'

'I doubt it,' Pine said, sitting back in his chair. 'I'd never met her and I doubt if James had either.'

'So what happened?' asked Varcy.

Pine gripped the armrests on his chair and said, 'She played the grieving girlfriend. I told her James had a girlfriend – the one who attended his funeral. She said they had just started dating and that they were in love. She claimed James was about to leave his current girlfriend for her just before he died. It was a story. One I've heard – in various forms – many times before. It's an occupational hazard.'

'I don't understand,' said Varcy.

Pine pulled a face. 'She wants money, Inspector.'

Varcy sat upright. 'You think so?'

Pine nodded. 'Of course. They all want money. She won't be the first to try it and she'll not be the last.'

'Did she ask you for money directly?'

Pine shook his head. 'Not specifically. She was fishing most of the time. Testing the ground. Trying to flesh out a strategy. She's got nerve, I'll give her that much.'

Money was not on Varcy's list of possible reasons for Rita's visit. He wondered why he had not considered it.

'Having said that,' Pine went on, 'I assume you'd have to have nerve to kill your boyfriend, right?'

There was a light knock on the door.

'Come in,' Pine called.

Madeline appeared, holding a similar tray to one

Varcy had seen downstairs. 'Sorry to interrupt, gentlemen,' she said, setting down two white cups and saucers.

'Thank you,' said Varcy.

'Thanks, Madeline,' added Pine.

She picked up the tray. 'Let me know if you need anything else,' she said and turned back towards the door, closing it after her.

There was a long silence. Varcy deliberately tried not to fill it. Instead he picked up his cup and took a small sip. Then he glanced at his notes for a short spell. Finally, he decided to change his approach.

'I'm sorry about your son,' he said suddenly. 'It must have been awful.'

Pine's eyes shot to Varcy's. They exchanged something. Empathy perhaps. Something intangible. The moment passed quickly and Pine slid his eyes away.

'Do you have children of your own, Inspector?' he asked.

Varcy shook his head. 'I did – we did – my late wife and I. A baby boy many years ago. He would be thirty-three now had he lived.'

Pine nodded slowly. 'Then you have some idea of how I'm feeling.'

'Indeed I do,' said Varcy softly.

Pine gazed down at his desk.

'He was your youngest?' Varcy asked.

Pine nodded. 'My baby.'

Varcy gently leafed through his notes. The James Pine information was stapled together. There were eight pages. Varcy had read it numerous times during the previous night. James had been found by his cleaning lady. He was hanging from a steel beam in the lounge of his London apartment. Nothing in the apartment had been disturbed or taken. It had not been broken into. There was no suicide note, no sign of a struggle. The clothes on his body were neat and ordered.

There were, however, two curious facts about this case which had got Varcy's attention immediately. The first was the rope James Pine had used to hang himself. Rope per se was unusual. It is seldom used. People usually hang themselves with a belt, washing line or twine. Something to hand, that they would have around the house. This was bonafide three-strand, twisted, natural fibre rope. One-inch diameter. It was new and pristine as if it had never been used. The other curious fact – at least to Varcy – was to be found in James Pine's kitchen. A full mug of black coffee had been left on the counter. Next to it was a spoon and next to this was a small pot of sugar. Analysis had been carried out on both. The sugar was not present in the coffee. Varcy wanted to know why. Why hadn't the sugar been used in the coffee? It had been got out and placed next to the mug for that very purpose, surely. Hooper had drilled down further. The original investigation had considered this fact. It was an inconsistency that had been explained by a sudden compulsion to commit the act of suicide. Varcy tried to imagine it. Pine makes the coffee, he gets out the sugar and spoon and then abandons it. He goes into the lounge and fixes the rope to the light. Or maybe he makes it, gets distracted and forgets about it. He then kills himself some time later. Varcy had checked the report. There was no information on how long the coffee was left before it was found.

'I looked at his case file before coming over here,' said Varcy gently. 'He died in the Canary Wharf apartment.'

Pine nodded. 'That's why I spend so much of my time there. I feel closer to him.'

Varcy was silent.

'My wife won't go there,' Pine went on, 'it upsets her too much. For me it's different. It softens the blow somehow. I can almost sense him there. I know how that must sound. But there it is. I make no apology for it.'

'Nor should you,' said Varcy. 'It's perfectly understandable.'

More silence.

'May I ask you a direct question?' said Varcy suddenly.

'If you wish,' returned Pine.

'Why do you think your son took his own life?'

Pine took a deep breath and placed his hands behind his neck. His arms seemed to tighten. 'I don't know,' he said. 'I wish I did know. I'd do something about it.'

'Had he any worries? Fears you're aware of?'

'I'm sure there must have been. Why else would he have done it?'

It was a fair point. Why else do people commit suicide? But the question was not asked to elicit a direct answer.

Varcy removed his gaze and went back to his notes. He flipped some more pages and stuck his finger in the section the team had gathered on Sir John Scott. There was a photograph paper-clipped to the front of one of the sheets. Varcy eased it out. Scott was shown standing upright and smiling in a black dinner suit at a function of some kind. Varcy flipped it over. Cole had marked the approximate date in black ink. Varcy turned it the right way up and handed it to Pine.

'Do you know this man?'

Pine peered at it. 'Yes, of course. It's John Scott. I've known him for years.'

'You know he was murdered?' said Varcy.

'Yes,' said Pine.

'How well did you know him?'

Pine sat back in his seat and watched Varcy. He folded his arms across his chest. 'Why do you want to know? That's the third photograph you've shown me this morning. Two of the people in them have been murdered and the other is a suspect. When you made your appointment you said you wanted a chat. Help with a "delicate matter" you said. It feels distinctly different to that.'

'It's not meant to feel different, Mr Pine,' said Varcy. 'I'm just trying to understand a puzzling series of events, that's all.'

'Then why are you asking me about John Scott?'

'Because,' said Varcy, 'you were seen with him at Whitechapel House just before his death.'

'So what?'

'I'm curious, that's all.'

Pine pushed his chair away from the desk and stood up. Varcy watched him move towards the dark wooden bookcase. He pulled off a large, leather bound volume from the lower shelf and brought it back to the desk. On closer inspection Varcy could see it wasn't a book at all. It was a photo album made to look like one. Pine flipped the pages and Varcy saw rows of neat photographs arranged on the leaves, with small, carefully written descriptions under each one. 'Here,' said Pine, turning the album around so it faced Varcy. He tapped a photograph on the top row of the opened page. 'Nineteen eighty-eight or thereabouts,' he said. 'Do you recognise those two?'

Varcy looked at the image. Two men stood angled towards each other. They were shaking hands and beaming at the camera. They wore collar length hair. One of them had it pushed back and cut into a mullet. Varcy recognised a much younger Pine, but the other one was not as obvious. He guessed at Scott.

'Correct,' said Pine. 'This was around the time we went into business together. Did you know we were in business together, Inspector?

'No, I confess I didn't,' said Varcy.

'I thought not,' said Pine, sitting back in his chair. 'John had a company back then. Quite innovative one too, I thought. They were providing forensic services to the Cambridgeshire police force. The overspill from in-house work. Things they couldn't cope with. He knew about me through a mutual friend and asked me to help grow his company. I looked at his model and made some suggestions. He liked them and I joined the board.'

'What suggestions?'

'DNA analysis mainly,' said Pine. 'This was the eighties remember. DNA analysis was new back then. The technology was still shaky. I suggested we recruit the best we could find and develop techniques for analysing crime scene samples accurately. At least better than the local police teams could manage. Soon we had contracts with all the major forces in the UK. We expanded into Europe too. It was a big success.'

'What happened to the company?' asked Varcy.

'We sold it,' said Pine. 'For fifty-two million pounds.'

'Wow,' responded Varcy.

'Wow indeed,' Pine nodded.

Varcy looked down at the photograph again. The inscription underneath read: 'With JS at Claridges charity dinner.'

'And you were talking over old times when you met at Whitechapel House?' Varcy asked.

'Pretty much,' said Pine.

'The barman there knew Scott well,' said Varcy. 'He was a regular visitor to the club. He thought Scott looked visibly upset after speaking to you. Any idea why he would say that?'

Pine snorted. 'None whatsoever. As far as I remember we were speaking about his charity work and the upcoming session in the Lords. He was in good spirits.'

Varcy nodded. 'You're aware of the circumstances of his murder?'

Pine took back the photograph album and snapped it shut. 'I know he was murdered, Inspector. That's all I want to know.'

Varcy said, 'It was brutal.'

'All murders are brutal, I imagine,' said Pine.

'They are indeed,' replied Varcy.

Pine rose from his seat and moved back towards the bookcase. He replaced the photograph album.

'Do you have any idea why he was murdered?' Varcy asked.

'None at all,' answered Pine.

'Did he have enemies? Business enemies perhaps?'

'John hadn't been in business since we sold the company,' said Pine. 'So I doubt it.'

Varcy flicked through the notes and pulled out a copy of the email Scott had sent him. The one his computer had spammed. 'He wanted to meet me,' Varcy remarked, handing it over. 'This was sent to me before he died. He suggested we meet at Whitechapel House.'

Pine glanced at it and asked, 'What did he want?'

'I don't know,' said Varcy. 'I never received it so I never met him. I'm wondering why he would request a meeting with a police officer so shortly before his death.'

Pine was silent.

Varcy replaced the sheet into the stack on his lap.

He patted the edges together and slid them back into the folder. He glanced up at Pine who was sitting forwards again with his hands clamped together securely on the desk top. Varcy watched him for a short moment. There was an uncomfortable silence.

Varcy smiled. 'Well now,' he said, 'I think I'm all out of questions.'

32

I have worked throughout the night. Lack of sleep is a small price to pay. I have to be thorough in my work. I have to be perfect.

I check the field dressing. It is tight and secure against my shoulder. I stitched the wound myself and have applied a topical antibiotic. It will heal nicely. I'm a good healer. I have proven it many times over.

I make myself comfortable on the floor and stare at the photograph. The same one I carry with me at all times. The one I have had enlarged and mounted on the wall of the lock-up. I connect with it on such a deep level. It keeps me on track. It is with me always.

It was with me when they told me what happened.

I remember that feeling of detachment and free-fall when the news permeated my brain. As if I were spiralling inwards. Collapsing in on myself. I imagine it now. The dust coats my tongue. Then it fills my whole mouth. Dry and choking. Leeching out all the moisture. It is in my hair and caked onto my skin. It is on my clothes and in my shoes. Sometimes I think it has infiltrated my brain. I hear the voices in the distance. Chattering. Someone trying to get my attention. I look beyond the voices and stare into a space far away. There is a yellow sun and dappled sunlight. The chatter is gone and I hear a child's laughter. I am drawn towards it. Then I see the thing that has never left me. A scene steeped with deep colour. The child is squatting down, his blond hair is tangled and sticks up at the crown. His pale chest and legs are covered in sun block. He is talking to himself just like he always does. Then he laughs out loud. A joke perhaps or a funny scene playing in his imagination. Something known only to him. He shovels the sand into a green bucket and turns out oddly-shaped castles. I watch him make one after the other. The scene is very peaceful and in that moment I know what is important and what is not. I know that all is not lost. More sand goes in and another castle is produced. Then another and another. The bucket is tipped again and again. I have finally come home.

Then I feel the water rush into my mouth. It clears the dust and the grime. It is cool and I have a strongest urge to drink it. But I'm afraid if I do I'll be taken away. My head lifts. More water is administered and I drink. I can't help it. Immediately the image begins to fade. I try to hold onto it. I focus on the bucket. It is tipped once again then righted. Tipped then righted. The scene shrinks smaller and smaller. Finally the movement of the bucket is all that remains. I focus on its green colour for as long as I can. Then it is gone and I come back. They have turned me over and I squint my eyes against the strong sun.

I weep.

33

Rita Sidhu was up early. She had checked the times of the trains the night before and decided on the 7.30am out of London Bridge. She wanted to arrive early. She had showered and dressed in the jeans she wore last night. She pulled on a fresh tee-shirt from the police stock and tied her hair back with a red hairband. She pulled on a light jacket and walked briskly to Tottenham Court Road tube. She rode the Central line to Bank then the Northern line to London Bridge.

The concourse at London Bridge was wide and dimly lit. Lamps were fixed to a matrix of steel girders in the roof space. The mall was cream stone. Around it were dozens of vendors selling food, coffee and magazines. It was busy. Hundreds of commuters hung around watching TV monitors, waiting for their train. They carried bags or briefcases, some had rucksacks. All were switched off. They looked frustrated and bored.

Rita bought a croissant and coffee and made her way to her train. She surveyed the carriage. There were only a few people in it. The bulk of the crowd had left. They were travelling into the city while she was leaving it. She checked her watch. It read 7.14am. She unwrapped the croissant, took the top off it and thought about what she would do when she got there. How to play it. She didn't know. She was operating on instinct. On feeling. She had nothing concrete to base the feeling on – at least not yet. She would have to wait and see.

Last night when she Googled the name Violet Westfield together with the word Canterbury, she got a hit. It was the website of a florist shop in Canterbury, Kent. One of the items on the website's news page focused on the owner, Violet Westfield. There was a short interview with a local newspaper, which dwelt mainly on her love of flowers and how she hoped this new venture would be a great success. It spoke about the displays in her shop, the personal service clients could expect and the competitive prices she offered. A small section of the article referenced Violet's tragic past. It was brief and respectful and finished with a rallying call to the local community to help make the opening day a great success.

The article was why Rita had come.

The sun was up when she got out at Canterbury East. She had never been to the town so she waited at the cab rank and jumped into the first one available. She had scribbled the florist's address onto a scrap of paper. The cab driver nodded, crunched the gears and hit the accelerator after she read it out. Eight minutes later, he deposited her outside a small shop at the north end of Palace Street. It was set between two larger shops. One sold hardware, the other women's clothes. It was half the size of the other two but, unlike its neighbours, it was open. A young woman was creating a display of flowers outside. She flitted back and forth carrying pots, troughs and plastic vases. She was too young to be Violet Westfield, but Rita approached her anyway and asked if she knew where to find her.

The girl stopped and wiped her face with the back of her hand. 'She usually gets in at 9.00,' she said.

Rita checked her watch. It read 8.40am. 'I'll come back.'

The girl nodded then went back to her work.

Near the shop was an espresso bar. Rita crossed the road and perched on one of the seats outside. She took off her jacket and turned her face to the sun, savouring the warm rays. She felt calmer out of the city, as though its shackles had been released. The pressure eased and she found herself thinking about someone she had not thought about for a long time. Her name was Wilson. Or Professor Wilson to the students in Rita's study group at Durham. A matriarch figure. Protective, kind and patient with students, but intolerant of arrogant professionals. Her brain was surgical in its focus. Rita adored her. Wilson's project was Rita's first. Her group was looking at transcription factors. Rita had to determine a role for a gene called Al-1. Originally cloned by Wilson herself, Al-1 was novel, unexplored and an impossible task. Or so Rita thought.

Wood for the trees, Rita! Wood for the trees …

Wilson would repeat that every time Rita hit a road block. She was right too. The breakthrough came when Professor Wilson invited a handful of the students to spend a three-day weekend at a cottage she owned in Norfolk. They relaxed, talked and drank wine. On the Sunday morning, Rita and Wilson devised a strategy that ultimately brought the result. Rita smiled at the memory.

Wood for the trees is how things felt right now. She breathed the sunlight in, tried to relax and watched the shop. A few minutes after 9.00am, a woman appeared from Orange Street. She was short and overweight, dressed in a dark smock. Her hair was raven black and combed outwards like a privet and a ridge of red at her cheeks stood out against her pale skin. Rita watched her move inside. She waited for ten minutes, then crossed the road and went into the shop. The interior was shaded and cold. Much colder than the outside. Like the exterior, it was packed with bright-coloured foliage. Some of the flowers were in bunches, wrapped together in cellophane, others in vases and hanging baskets. The dark haired woman was standing at the rear of the shop with her back to the door. Rita watched her loop a green striped apron over her head and fasten the string at the back. She turned at the sound of Rita's footsteps and smiled.

'Violet?' Rita asked.

'Yes,' she replied.

'My name's Rita.'

'Hello, Rita,' said Violet. She smoothed down the front of the apron and smiled again. 'Have we met?'

'No,' said Rita, moving further into the shop. 'We haven't.'

'Oh,' said Violet. 'What can I help you with?' She gestured towards the floral display.

'I haven't come to buy flowers,' said Rita. 'I've come to talk.'

'About what?' asked Violet.

Rita paused trying to think of an eloquent way to proceed. She couldn't. So she said: 'About your daughter.'

* * *

At the back of Violet's shop was a small room. It was painted white. It had a sink and a draining area cut into a wooden counter. Above this was a frosted window that looked out onto a square backyard. Rita and Violet sat at a formica table pushed tight against one wall. In front of them were two mugs of coffee.

'I'm sorry to turn up unannounced,' said Rita, lifting the mug to her lips and taking a sip.

'Not at all,' said Violet. 'I'm always happy to talk about Kimberley. How well did you know her?'

Rita shook her head. 'I didn't know her at all, to be honest.'

Violet took a sip of her coffee. 'So what's the connection?'

Rita set the mug down on the table and replied, 'A man called John Scott.'

Violet shook her head. 'I don't know him.'

'He was murdered a month ago. That's the main reason I've come,' Rita said.

'I don't understand,' said Violet.

Rita fiddled with the handle of her coffee mug, nudging it back and forth so that it squeaked on the table surface. 'Nor do I,' said Rita. 'Not completely.'

There was silence.

'Sorry to be so vague,' she added.

Violet said nothing.

Rita took a deep breath. 'I was wondering if Kimberley had a boyfriend before she died.'

'Yes,' said Violet. 'Kevin. A local lad. They had been together since the last year of school.'

'They never married?'

Violet shrugged. 'They both had good careers. They were saving up for a deposit on a house. So, no, they never got around to it.'

There was another long moment of silence.

'Kevin has a couple of young children now,' Violet added softly. 'I see him out in the town sometimes.'

Rita nodded slowly. 'I'm sorry to ask this but was Kimberley seeing someone else?'

'Someone else?'

'A boyfriend, I mean. Someone secret?'

Violet's forehead folded into a fan of deep creases. 'Not that I know of. Why do you ask?'

'Because I think she could have been.'

'Someone like who?' she said.

Rita sighed. 'Does the name James Pine mean anything to you?'

'James Pine?' said Violet, searching the ceiling with her eyes. She shook her head. 'No. Should it?'

'That's the name of the guy I think Kimberley was dating.'

'Who is he? A work colleague?'

'A businessman,' Rita said.

'Good Lord,' said Violet, sitting back in her chair. 'She never spoke to me about anyone else.'

'Was she coming home late from work towards the end? Distracted maybe?'

'Not that I noticed,' said Violet. 'She was an independent woman. She came and went as she pleased. She worked late sometimes because she had a responsible job. She had friends in London. There were functions to attend. Work related things. But why are you asking now? She's been gone for two years.'

'James Pine is dead too,' Rita said. 'He committed suicide a few weeks ago. I'm wondering if the two deaths are related.'

'In what way?'

'I'm not sure. That's the problem. I'm trying to find out.'

Violet rested her elbows on the table and massaged her temples. 'How do *you* know James Pine?'

'Through a friend,' Rita replied.

'Do the police know about this?' Violet asked.

'No,' said Rita. 'I've got no proof of it. It's a hunch that's all.'

Violet sat still for a moment deep in thought. She took out a scrunched-up tissue from a pouch at the front of her apron. She dabbed her brow and pressed it to her top lip. Rita shifted in her seat. Coming out here had been a spur-of-the-moment decision. She now regretted it. It was the wrong thing to do. She watched Violet; her head drooping forwards. Rita had succeeded in worrying a widowed mother of a dead child. Violet had more than enough on her plate already and she had now given her another dollop of worry for no good reason, other than a desire to appease her own conscience.

'Look,' said Rita, sitting forwards. 'I didn't want to burden you with all this. I hoped you might know something, that's all. I'm really sorry. I'm sure the last thing you want is someone poking around in your business. Especially after all this time.'

Violet screwed up the tissue into a ball and shook her head slowly. She got up from the table and moved to a grey, metal cabinet by the door. She opened the top drawer and pulled out five framed photographs. Three of the frames had a silver floral design. The other two were plain. She laid them out on the table. They were all pictures of Kimberley. She sat back down and turned them to face Rita. In two, Kimberley wore a green uniform and a white blouse – school photos. She was smiling. In the first she would have been about six years old. Her face was round and baby-like. Her hair fell into a fringe and was cut to collar length. In the second she was about twelve. Her nose was freckled and there was a slight gap between her teeth. The others were of Kimberley in her later years. One on holiday in a bikini. Another at a table, drinking champagne from a glass flute. The last was a shot of her skiing. Her goggles were worn high on her head and she was laughing as if someone had just cracked a joke.

'I have dozens of these,' said Violet. 'They are all framed.'

'They're lovely,' said Rita softly.

'Do you have children of your own?' Violet asked.

Rita shook her head. 'I've got two godsons.'

Violet nodded. 'To lose someone close is very hard. But to lose a child is torture. That's why I can never let Kimberley go. Not ever. Not knowing what happened means there is no closure. The daily torment is what finished off my husband.'

Rita was silent.

'So I'm not at all concerned about you "poking around in my business", as you call it. I'm all for it, in fact. Whatever comes of it can't be worse than the way things are right now.'

Rita smiled. 'I'm glad,' she said, 'and relieved too.'

Violet returned her smile.

Rita cleared her throat. 'May I ask you one more difficult question?'

Violet nodded. 'Go ahead.'

'It's about the coat Kimberley was wearing when they found her. Do you still have it?'

Violet shook her head. 'They told us they would have to keep all the clothes for forensic analysis.'

34

Varcy got back to his office at 10.28am. The open workspace was buzzing, a low hum of activity that hardly ever stopped. He skirted it and headed for the kitchen. He grabbed the kettle, checked the water level and flipped on the switch. Then he plonked a mug on the counter top and tossed in a tea bag. Leaning his backside against the counter, arms folded across his chest, he mentally unpicked the meeting with Pine. The man was convincing. Genuine for the most part. However, there was something hidden that didn't sit right. The fact he did not recognise Rita Sidhu was interesting. Varcy assumed he was lying about that. It was unrealistic to accept that a woman who had spent the best part of forty minutes with him last evening, was unrecognizable to him the next morning. His explanation about John Scott was the truth. Varcy was sure of that, but probably not the whole truth. The events were edited in some way. In which way, Varcy was unsure, but he was sure there was more to discover. He would drill down a bit further and something would pop out. It always did.

Kendrick appeared at the doorway. He had a couple of sheets of paper rolled into a small scroll. He tapped them against his palm like a tennis player waiting to receive service. 'How did it go?' he asked.

'Good,' said Varcy. 'An impressive character. No doubt about that.'

'What was Sidhu doing at his apartment?' asked Kendrick.

Varcy smiled. 'She said she was dating his son before his death.'

'Was she?'

'He says not.'

'What did she want from him then? A medal?'

'Money apparently.'

'Money?' Kendrick thought for a moment. 'Possible I suppose.'

'But not probable,' said Varcy.

'Why not?' asked Kendrick.

The kettle boiled and the switch popped out. 'Do you want one?' asked Varcy, turning around to attend to it.

Kendrick shook his head. 'Nah, I've just had one.'

Varcy tipped the boiling water onto the bag. 'Sidhu's not interested in money,' he said.

'Everyone's interested in money,' Kendrick replied.

'I don't agree,' said Varcy. 'She was a bright student, she's a bright scientist. She's got brains where most of us have mush. Yet she earns twenty-eight thousand pounds a year. I checked. That's less than a bus driver. Much less. So I don't believe money is high up on her list of values.'

Kendrick leaned in the doorway. 'So why the visit, then?'

Varcy shrugged. 'There's something else

motivating her. Something that lines up with her values. Something altruistic.'

Varcy opened the fridge. He pulled out the milk, sloshed a small slug in the top of his tea and stirred the bag until it turned a dark shade of brown.

'How are you getting on without sugar?' Kendrick asked.

'It's miserable,' said Varcy.

Kendrick held up the scroll. 'Got something here to cheer you up,' he said.

'Oh?'

'Dr Daniel Nash has been at work.'

'Excellent,' said Varcy.

'He's in with the CI. I've nabbed him for a session straight after. You up for it?'

'Absolutely.'

Varcy followed Kendrick along the narrow corridor towards his office.

'I gave Nash the background,' said Kendrick. 'And the profile makes interesting reading.'

Kendrick pushed open the door and stepped inside. The room was dark and the air conditioning blew a cool rush of air into Varcy's face. He set his mug of tea on the desk and yanked at the closed Venetian blinds drawn across the wall window. They flipped outwards like ship sails and the light from the open office flooded in. Varcy took off his jacket and dropped into his seat.

'Go ahead,' said Varcy.

Kendrick sat down and unrolled the scroll. 'He's bullet-pointed it,' he said.

Varcy took a sip of tea. 'Okay.'

There was a light tap on the office door and Dr Nash stuck his head around it. 'Are you ready for me?' he asked.

Varcy got to his feet. 'Ah, Daniel,' he said. 'We were just about to go through your report. Long time no see.'

Daniel Nash stepped into the room. He was a tall lean man with pepper-pot grey hair and heavy black spectacles. His neck was long and punctuated by a conker-sized Adam's apple that bounced with every swallow. He wore a grey nylon V-neck pullover, the fabric of which clung to his arms and chest. A checked collar, done up to the top was visible at the V. He should have had an elastic bow-tie stuck in the gap, Varcy thought. That would have suited him well. But times had moved on and even Nash had observed them.

Nash wasn't a policeman. He was a criminal psychologist from King's College acting as a consultant to the Met and City Police. Varcy had worked with him many times. Nash was a gifted operator. There was no one better. He used more than his brain to get under a perpetrator's skin. He used *feel* to do it. That was uncommon, and not popular either, but Varcy could relate to it.

Varcy grasped Nash's hand and Kendrick wheeled in another chair from the pool in the open office area. Nash sat down and pulled a beaten-up, brown briefcase onto his knees. He slid a slim, blue file from the case, opened it and spread some photographs over the desk. The same ones given to him by Kendrick. The murder scene shots of Barry

Townsend and John Scott. 'I've added to your stock of photos,' he said, pulling six more from the file and arranging them on the table. 'The families of both men provided them.'

Varcy flicked his eyes over them. There were shots of both victims at different times in their lives. Moments of happiness by the look of them. Some going back to early childhood.

'I like to build a picture in my mind of the victims just as much as the perpetrator,' Nash explained. 'Faces, personalities, human needs, that sort of thing. I'm interested in any details that might give me a clue as to the psychological status of the perpetrator.'

'Are there any?' asked Varcy.

'We'll get to that,' said Nash, touching the photographs gently, almost lovingly, with the tips of his fingers as if to tune into them. 'The first thing to say is a generalised, catch-all statement. A common thread that applies in any case where there are serial killings.'

'We don't believe this is a serial killer,' said Kendrick. 'Not in the accepted sense of the word anyway.'

'I understand that,' said Nash. 'You believe he kills for money. A hired killer, however, psychologically there are definite similarities between serial killers and hit men. He – and I'm using the word deliberately – will have had a chaotic childhood, for instance. This is very common. Not that it helps you much but he will be white, likely to be in his thirties; probably late thirties. He is unlikely to be married or in any kind of intimate relationship. He will be focused and disciplined almost to the exclusion of anything else. He will have a deep desire for power. Or – and this is more likely – a deep desire for control. Control of his life and the events in it, control of his emotions and, most interestingly, control of things that might feel out of control to him. Am I making sense?'

Varcy nodded. 'You are.'

'Good. Now remember – and please don't feel I'm patronising you by saying this – killing someone and walking away without anyone raising the alarm, or without being seen or reported, takes a lot of hard work. A lot of careful and deliberate preparation. So the preparation, the act of killing the victim and the ritual of staking him out before the kill – even if it is done for money – are metaphors for the lack of control he feels in another area of his life.'

'So his taking control makes up for loss of control,' said Varcy.

'Exactly,' said Nash. 'It is a compensatory mechanism.'

'Interesting,' said Varcy.

'He feels disaffected too,' said Nash. 'Excluded in some way. Marginalised.'

'Why?' asked Varcy.

'Difficult to know,' said Nash, leaning back in his chair. 'It could be for a variety of reasons. Emotional, economic and / or social. Emotional reasons are most often found to be at the core of violent behaviour. That includes issues around self worth, abuse – both violent and sexual, or issues around abandonment.

Because of this, violent behaviour is almost always tracked back to childhood. A childhood in which the child is lonely, unpopular, highly insular and rarely interacts with the outside world, and where both the child's imagination and his intelligence are well developed. Clichéd, I know, but there you have it.'

'Okay,' said Varcy. 'So where does that take us?'

'Not very far,' said Nash. 'Unless there is a fuller and more specific explanation for his behaviour. For example, there is no record of killings similar to these beyond six months ago. Am I right?'

'Not as far as we can establish,' nodded Varcy.

'So this MO is recent.'

'It is,' said Varcy. 'Although that doesn't rule out the possibility of him killing in the past using a different MO.'

'Agreed,' said Nash. 'But an explanation that explains why he has changed MO would be useful, would it not?'

Varcy smiled softly. 'And you have such an explanation, I take it?'

'I might do,' Nash answered. 'I believe this perpetrator has experienced what I call a "camel's back" moment.'

'Camel's back?' repeated Varcy.

'As in *the straw that broke* the camel's back. It's not strictly scientific – you'll find no mention of the term in text books, for instance – but I believe it took him from wherever he was to where he is now. It was instant and it flipped him over the edge. This doesn't mean the other criteria in childhood and beyond don't apply. They almost certainly do.

However, in the camel's back scenario, the negative behaviours associated with them are suppressed until the camel's back unlocks them.'

'Examples?' said Varcy.

Nash raked the long, white fingers of one hand through his hair. 'They are diverse,' he said. 'A failure is a simple example. An inability to have done something correctly. A loss perhaps. Even something seemingly minor like the death of a pet. Injustice is another one. Again, it doesn't need to be a major deal necessarily. I know of one example in which the camel's back was a queue jumper in a burger bar. Whatever it is, it is likely to amplify his feelings of separateness and trigger a new and violent form of behaviour.'

Varcy took a sip of tea. 'We think he's ex-military. Any thoughts on that?'

Nash nodded. 'Yes, I read that in the report. I see no reason why he couldn't have operated effectively as a soldier. The qualities he has shown as a killer will be ones that may have marked him out as an outstanding soldier.'

'Is he mad?' Varcy asked.

Nash shook his head. 'As a rule, most serial killers are not mad. There are exceptions of course. Drinking the blood of victims, as one notorious killer did, because he believed death would ensue if he failed to do so, is by most definitions mad. However, in my opinion, this killer is not mad.'

'How does he live?' asked Varcy.

'Frugally,' said Nash. 'Simply. He doesn't drive. His clothes are regular and so is he. He blends in.'

'Is he angry?' asked Kendrick.

'Yes and no,' said Nash. 'Obviously the killings are highly controlled affairs. Surgical in nature. There are no overt suggestions of anger. No uncontrolled, slashing cuts, no frenzied attacks. Yet the thing that marginalises him, the thing that separates him, might well cause him to be angry.'

'Assuming he is ex-military,' said Varcy, 'did his career come to an abrupt end, do you think? Did he just drift away?'

Nash took a deep breath. He closed his eyes momentarily and then said, 'I would say his career came to an abrupt end, rather than a natural end. I could be wrong about that, of course.'

'Of course,' said Varcy.

'But I also think – and I've no tangible evidence to back this up either – that the camel's back is the thing that caused him to leave.'

'Ah,' said Varcy. 'That *is* interesting.'

Nash said nothing. Instead he returned his gaze to the photographs laid out on Varcy's table like playing cards. He began to rearrange them so that the early shots of both men were in a row at the bottom and the murder scene shots were in a row at the top. 'This green bucket is noteworthy,' Nash said, touching the photographs in which it appeared. 'In one way it's practical. It collects blood so that it doesn't seep away. But in another, it's highly symbolic. He has used it on both occasions. Same colour, same size.'

Varcy nodded and took another sip of tea. 'Any theories?' he asked.

'I've been thinking about that,' replied Nash. 'In traditional Jung theory, symbols that are receptacle-like, such as a cup or a glass or, in this case, a bucket, are thought of as feminine in nature. Womb-like. They receive and contain. These symbols are often associated – but not exclusively associated – with an over-dominant female parent, a general dislike of females or a failure to form fulfilling relationships with them. Taking the theory further and introducing the blood element – well, it gets more difficult to decipher. Blood and womb go together, of course. In the biological sense, blood leaves the womb in cycles. Here, the blood returns to the womb. The victims are male which is not usual. One would expect the victims to be female.'

'Not if he were paid to kill two male victims,' said Varcy.

'True,' said Nash, resting his elbows on the table and steepling his fingers. His eyes scanned the photographs. Flitting quickly from one to another. He let out a long breath. 'I'd say that the bucket represents something important to him. The collection of blood into it – as we've said – has a practical application. It also has a control element. The blood is contained rather than allowed to flow away. I would say the bucket is highly symbolic of this man's camel's back moment.'

There was a long silence while Varcy processed the information. He tried to build up a picture of the killer in his mind's eye. The way he looked. The way he moved. The thing that made him tick. Why he killed and who was paying him to do so.

Varcy drained the last of his tea and said, 'Can I ask you one final question?'

'Go ahead,' answered Nash.

Varcy leaned back in his seat and paused for another moment. 'Assuming this man is a hired killer, who is he working for? I mean, what type of character pays him to do what he does?'

'Ah,' said Nash, pushing his spectacles up high on his nose. 'That's a relatively easy one to answer.'

'Really?' asked Varcy.

'It hardly varies from case to case,' said Nash. 'Of the documented evidence almost all are male. Almost all are successful in terms of their career. "Over-achievers" is a good word to describe this group. They wield a lot of power within their industry. They are leaders. They are very much the boss and are used to making difficult decisions and living with the consequences of those decisions. The power they have is usually legitimately earned. Therefore they are respected, but their power can get blurred. The distinction between power in the usual sense and power in the perverted sense becomes ill-defined for them. Moving into the realm of killing, albeit indirectly, is often a last resort for these men, however, once they have made that decision they will justify it. Justification is very important to these characters. It will take the form of a higher goal being achieved. An injustice avenged. Something like that.'

Varcy nodded slowly.

'These characters are usually protective. Over-protective of anything that belongs to them. Their family, their business, the people who work in their business, that sort of thing. That's where the justification comes in. They won't let anyone threaten things and, if they do, they deserve what's coming.'

Varcy smiled.

'You have someone who fits the bill?' asked Nash.

'I might.' said Varcy.

35

I watched a documentary once about the second world war. It focused on Nazi collaborators. Those people who went unnoticed by the masses, but whose actions were absolutely vital to its growth and success. Every regime, every authority needs collaboration to flourish.

Rita Sidhu is such a collaborator.

I know now how she will die. The plan came to me fully formed when I saw her with those children. I saw the love she had for them. The bond they shared.

I know what that feels like.

I had it once.

36

Varcy was reading through Nash's profile. It went over the same facts Nash had sketched out during their meeting. Varcy was impressed with his analysis. It gave him something to work with in terms of putting flesh on this particular killer's bones. It gave him the chance to get inside his head too. By far the most interesting piece of analysis – at least to Varcy – was this thing Nash called the camel's back. That narrowed down the search criteria a bit. The team had already been searching military records for men who saw active service but were now no longer with the military – but there was little more to go on than that. No other criteria. Had he shown violent behaviour whilst in service? Had he been discharged or just drifted away? It had been impossible. However, now they were looking for someone who had suffered a trauma – a camel's back moment – during duty and left because of it. The nature of the trauma was unknown, of course, but that was okay. It narrowed the scope of the search. Varcy had asked Kendrick to revisit it.

The door of Varcy's office squeaked inwards slightly. Hooper's head emerged from behind it. Her dark hair was pulled off her face and held back with four dark clips. 'Have you got a minute, Gov'nor?' she asked.

'Of course,' said Varcy, putting down the profile. 'Come on in.'

She moved into the room. Under her arm was a stack of folders. He gestured to the seat opposite his and she dropped into it, placing the folders on her lap and starting to sort through them. Varcy watched her for a moment. The paleness of her face with a light dusting of freckles around the bridge of her nose, contrasted with her black hair, giving her an Irish look. She wore no make-up. She didn't need it. She was a nice looking young woman, but – in Varcy's opinion – the wrong side of skinny to be healthy. She appeared thinner than when she'd first arrived from Financial Investigations. That concerned him. As she flipped through the papers, he noticed her bitten down nails. Her shirtsleeves were rolled up to her elbows exposing her forearms. They were like rope. Sinewy and infused with deep veins.

'Are you okay?' he asked.

She looked up quickly. 'Yes, of course.'

Varcy smiled.

She went back to the pile of folders. 'Give me a minute, Gov'nor, I've got some photocopied sheets here I want you to see.'

'Take your time,' he said.

Varcy knew Hooper could crunch the numbers. He couldn't remember if she had been to university or not. If she had she would have studied figures. Accounting maybe. He knew she'd had a career before the police, which meant she'd joined the force later than was usual, but she was bright and focused. Her attention to the smallest detail was laser-like. He knew too that this environment could be pressurised. It was different from the other departments. It was real. Murder investigations were raw and the expectation to deliver often overwhelming. The team was driven too. They had to be. That often meant too much testosterone floating around too much of the time. Intimidating for anyone. Varcy wondered if it was affecting Hooper.

'Here,' she said, dropping a small sheaf of papers on the desk. 'Charles Pine's business deals make for interesting reading and specifically the company he shared with John Scott.'

'The forensic analysis company?'

'It was called Opus Forensic Services Ltd,' she said. 'It no longer exists because it was swallowed up by a larger firm called Fritness Holdings Ltd in 2003.'

'For fifty-two million pounds,' said Varcy. 'Pine told me how much they sold it for when I met him.'

She shook her head. 'Not necessarily true,' she said. 'This outfit, Fritness Holdings, certainly bought it, but one of its biggest shareholders is Charles Pine.'

Varcy cupped his chin in his hand. 'So he bought the forensics company from himself?'

'In a way,' she said. 'And in doing so created a big debt in his holdings company.'

Varcy sat back on his chair. 'Why?'

'Good for tax,' she said. 'This debt – the money the holding company spent to acquire Opus – hit the profits in the holding company to the tune of fifty-two million.'

'Okay,' said Varcy.

'Which reduced the profit before tax in the holding company the following year,' she said.

Varcy nodded.

'But,' said Hooper, 'and here is where it gets interesting, the debt can still get created even if no real money has been exchanged, and I don't think real money was exchanged.'

'So he never really bought it?'

'He bought it,' she said, 'but didn't pay with real money. The debt clearly appears in the accounts, but I've run a money trail and I can't see where it landed.'

'What about John Scott?' asked Varcy. 'Didn't he get any money from the deal?'

'Two million,' she said. 'I've traced that much. The rest was to be paid on an earn-out over five years based on profits. The higher the profits the bigger the earn-out percentages. Seems like a decent deal. Especially when you take a look at the performance of Opus up to this point. The earn-out would provide Scott with a great deal of money over the medium period and would ease pressure on Opus to pay out up front. However, the profits never came.' She handed him a photocopied sheet. 'These are the three sets of annual accounts for Opus post-buy out. Look at the profit column.'

Varcy studied the sheets. Deciphering a set of

accounts was not top of his talent list but Hooper had helpfully highlighted the relevant numbers. 'The profit decreases,' he said, squinting at the text.

'Exactly,' she said. 'In fact by year three the company is running at a loss. It does so for the following two years, at which point Fritness collapses it and sends it into administration with big losses.'

'So Scott never got the rest of the money?'

'Doesn't look like it,' she replied. 'But look at this.' She handed him another sheet. Another photocopy. This was a small article from *The Daily Telegraph*. 'Notice the date,' Hooper said. Varcy flicked his eyes to the top of the page: 15th July 2003. 'That's six months after Fritness acquired Opus,' continued Hooper.

The banner headline stated: '*Opus Admit Contamination Issues*'.

'The article talks about contamination problems in their lab out in Redhill. That meant the validity of hundreds of samples from police units all over the country and from all over Europe too, were affected. I've chased down dozens of other negative articles that appeared at the time and for a long time afterwards. Lawyers for those incriminated by Opus-generated evidence had a field day.'

'I bet they did,' nodded Varcy.

'The whole thing was highly damaging to Opus and they never recovered from it.'

Varcy handed back the article. 'So where does that lead us?' he asked.

'To this,' she said, handing him a thin, glossy

booklet. He took it and flipped the pages. It was a promotional brochure from a company called Minster Forensics. The pages were full of high-end shots of good-looking scientists in white coats and designer goggles at work on forensic analysis. 'This began circulating at the same time as Opus were experiencing problems. The company was formed in January of the same year. Around two years after Fritness "bought" Opus.' She made speech marks in the air. 'They're still trading to this day. Very profitably too.' She handed Varcy some more accounts. These were from Minster Forensics. They were recent too – the last three years. Again Hooper had highlighted the important figures. 'I've been doing some digging on Minster Forensics,' she went on, 'and there are three facts worth noting. First, the success of this company was built on contracts it won from Opus when its credibility was shot; second, the company laboratories are the same as those Opus used – same site, same building and probably the same equipment. Third, Minster Forensics is owned by just one shareholder – Charles Pine.'

Varcy snorted. 'Of course.'

'It stinks,' said Hooper. 'I think the problems Opus experienced were deliberately created to pave the way for Minster. In effect, Pine got control of a fifty-two-million-pound company, with all of its know-how, its infrastructure and its contacts, for just two million quid.'

'How much is that fifty-two million worth now?' asked Varcy.

Hooper blew out her cheeks. 'I know the share value of Minster. Five hundred million.'

'And John Scott?' asked Varcy.

She shrugged. 'He's dead.'

'Indeed he is.'

'I bet he was pissed at Pine, though,' said Hooper.

'I bet he was,' agreed Varcy.

'By the way,' she said, handing over a glossy six by four from the folder. 'He does have a mistress.' The photograph was taken with a telephoto lens. It was of Pine and a woman. They were on a beach somewhere hot, him in long shorts and a white vest, her in a green bikini. 'Rachael Knight,' said Hooper. 'Thirty-five years old and – wait for it – an ex fashion model. Now runs a small boutique off Mayfair selling women's clothing to the Kensington and Chelsea set. All paid for by Pine.'

'Of course she does.' Varcy smiled wide. It was so predictable.

Hooper sat back and folded her arms. Varcy watched her for a moment. 'This is outstanding work,' he said finally.

She grinned. 'Thanks.'

'It shows a lot of application.'

The grin expanded a bit more. 'Thanks, again.'

'Did you enjoy doing it?' he asked.

She nodded. 'I love getting my teeth into stuff like that.'

Varcy said, 'I can see that.'

There was another moment of silence.

'Do you want to get a tea or coffee?' he asked

suddenly.

'When?' she asked.

'Now,' he said. 'You can leave the folders on my desk and pick them up when we come back.'

'Okay,' she said.

Varcy moved to the door and pulled it wide. 'Come on then,' he said.

Varcy stopped by Kendrick's desk on the way out. Kendrick was on the phone. He had a pencil wedged between his fingers. He was flipping it back and forwards like a miniature baton. 'Hold it,' he said into the receiver.

'I'll be in AJ's if you need me.' said Varcy.

Kendrick nodded, stuck the phone back against his ear and carried on talking.

37

Meg was making a pot of coffee. Rita watched her from a bar stool in the kitchen. Meg's red hair was pulled back and held with a rubber band. She wore white, calf-cut jeans and a *super-dry* tee-shirt. On her feet were a pair of green flip-flops which clacked as she moved back and forth. Meg had been in the lab that morning, but when Robert failed to show, she had lost her appetite for work.

Meg's flat was like a second home to Rita. She and Meg had spent endless hours in it talking, laughing and planning the future. Now she was back temporarily.

'You still calling Robert's mobile?' Rita said softly.

Meg nodded and placed two mugs on the counter. 'It goes straight to answer message now. It's off. Either turned off deliberately or it's run out of battery.'

'Have you phoned the police?'

Meg nodded again. 'They're sending someone over this afternoon.'

Rita watched Meg pour the coffee powder into the filter and flip the switch. Meg leaned against the counter and folded her arms across her chest. 'So what's happened with you?' she asked.

Rita's eyes flipped up to meet hers. 'Is it that obvious?'

'To me it is,' she said.

The percolator began to moan. Meg checked that the hot coffee was passing into the pot properly. She adjusted it slightly and got a carton of milk out of the fridge. 'Go ahead,' she said. 'I'm all ears.'

Rita leaned back in her seat. 'You remember when I first arrived at IMDB?'

Meg nodded. 'Of course.'

'I was going out with Mark then.'

'You were,' Meg said.

'Do you remember his uncle?'

'The House of Lords guy?' asked Meg.

Rita nodded.

'I remember,' said Meg.

'Well, he's dead. He's been murdered.'

'My God,' said Meg.

'It happened a month ago,' Rita said. 'Mark called me and I went to see him.'

Meg pulled the band out of her hair and let it loose. She raked her fingers over her scalp and asked, 'What are the chances of two people you know getting murdered?'

'That's what's scaring me,' said Rita. 'It might not be chance. I talked to Mark. He thinks his uncle was blackmailing Charles Pine.'

'What for?'

'I don't know,' said Rita. 'But something I did has probably got a lot to do with it.'

'Something *you* did?'

'I know it sounds mad.'

Meg pulled up a stool and perched on it. 'Go on.'

'A year ago Mark asked me to do him a favour,' said Rita. 'He asked if I could run a comparison in my lab. A scientific comparison. He had a bunch of hairs he wanted matched.'

'Hairs?'

'I thought it was a peculiar request,' said Rita, 'so I asked him why. He said it was a private matter his uncle wanted sorted. He said he'd asked me because he felt he could trust me. So this type of work isn't something I do every day. It's specialised, which I told him, but the techniques were straightforward. The pay was great too. One thousand pounds for a single analysis. I was saving for the flat so I said yes. I knew I could brush up on the technology and run it one weekend when the lab was quiet.'

The spitting from the percolator began to die and Meg pulled the pot out from under it. She poured two slugs of coffee into the mugs, topped them up with milk and handed one to Rita.

'So this box arrives by courier one morning. Inside are two small eppendorf tubes and inside those are a few hairs and some cell debris. I know because I put them all under the scanning microscope.'

'All human?'

'The cell debris was human. The hair wasn't.'

'So what was it?'

'Camel hair,' she said.

'Camel hair?'

'Camel hair blended with wool to make a speciality hair fibre.'

'As in camel hair coats,' said Meg.

Rita nodded. 'I set up a couple of compound microscopes and placed a single hair from each of the eppendorfs in the same field of view.'

'And?'

'And they matched,' said Rita. 'Same length, same shape, same colour and same pigmentation. There was a peculiar white tint to all the fibres.'

'I'm impressed you knew all that,' said Meg.

'I didn't,' said Rita. 'I called up Roger Monkson at UCL. You met him at last year's inter-lab day.'

'The trichology guy?'

'He came down and confirmed it,' nodded Rita. 'The samples from both tubes matched.'

'So what?'

'Well, I called Mark and told him the hairs were from the same coat, but there was something else too. There was also human cell debris in one of the samples. I'm sure they were platelets.'

'Blood?' said Meg.

Rita nodded. 'When I told him which sample was stained with blood, he went quiet for a moment, then asked if I could store the two tubes safely. So I put them in the retinal scan safe.'

'Didn't you ask him where the hairs were from? What it meant?'

'Yes, but again he said it was for his uncle and was a private matter. He thanked me for doing it and said I'd receive the money for the work within a couple of days.'

'And did you?'

'A cheque arrived two days later,' said Rita.

'Easiest money I'd ever earned.'

Meg took a sip of coffee. 'So what happened afterwards?'

'Nothing,' said Rita, 'I continued on with my life. Then, a few months later, I was sitting in my dentist's waiting room and picked up a magazine from the rack. It was old, but in it was a report of an ongoing murder investigation.' She hopped off her stool and groped in her jeans pocket. She teased out a folded section of paper. 'Here,' she said, offering it to Meg. 'Read that.'

It was the original newspaper report of the Kimberley Westfield murder. The one she had printed from NEWSPLAN. Rita watched Meg's eyes scan the article. Then her eyebrows lifted momentarily. 'Camel hair coat?' she said.

Rita nodded. 'That's what caught my eye.'

'And you think the camel hair coat the murdered girl was wearing is *the* camel hair coat you analysed.'

'I didn't then, at least I convinced myself it couldn't be the same, but now I think that it was.'

'But you've no proof?'

'No,' said Rita, shaking her head. 'Except what Mark told me.'

'And that's why his uncle was murdered?'

Rita nodded. 'I think it could be.'

Meg took another long sip of coffee. 'Let's assume it is *the* coat. What was being matched?'

Rita took a long breath. 'I don't know. Mark says I should destroy the samples and pretend I never saw them.'

'And what do you say?'

'I say I want to find out what the hell is going on.'

'What might scare a man like Charles Pine? How could you blackmail him?' asked Meg.

'Something that would have dire consequences should it get out,' said Rita.

'Let's say there are people who will do almost anything to stop it getting out, including killing the blackmailer,' said Meg.

'Then people will die,' said Rita. 'Barry's dead. Is that why he was killed? Because I did that analysis?'

'Barry had nothing to do with that,' said Meg.

'I know he didn't,' said Meg. 'But it seems too much of a coincidence.'

'Okay,' said Meg, hopping off the stool opposite. 'Let's say it's true and you are somehow the link between the death of Barry and John Scott. What do you want to do about it?'

Rita looked down at the floor. 'There is one thing,' she said.

'What?'

'When I was in the library I read a piece on James Pine's death. They gave a bio and a life history. He was involved in a road accident with his driver a couple of years ago. It's given me an idea.'

38

AJ's was in Liverpool Street station on the upper tier. It had a rectangular, green sign out front with a yellow plate of spaghetti depicted in the centre. It was clean and bright and served decent food. Normally it was rammed during the lunchtime session and Varcy only used it for take-out. On the rare occasions he sat in it for a tea or coffee, he would get the table at the back under the TV, which was always muted and tuned to Sky News – today was no different. Opposite him was Hooper. She had ordered an Americano, tall, black and without sugar.

'Isn't that bitter?' Varcy asked as she took a sip from the glass cup.

'You get used to it,' said Hooper.

Varcy stuck with tea. Also with no sugar. He took a sip and hoped it would taste better than it had before – it didn't.

'So,' said Varcy, 'you're probably wondering why I've invited you for coffee.'

'Not really,' said Hooper.

'Oh,' said Varcy. 'I thought you'd be curious.'

'I'm joking, Gov'nor,' smiled Hooper. 'Of course I'm curious. Are you going to congratulate me on some great work?'

Varcy smiled back. 'Yes, partly I am, but partly I want to find out if you're okay, you know? If you are happy in the department.'

'I'm very happy,' she said. 'Don't you think I'm fitting in?'

'Yes,' said Varcy quickly. 'I think you're fitting in well. It's just that murder squads are different from other departments. It takes a particular type of person to work here. Sometimes our people can be intense – full-on if you like. That can be intimidating at first.'

Hooper nodded. 'I know what you mean, but it doesn't affect me.'

'Not at all?'

'Nope,' she said, shaking her head.

'Oh. Good,' said Varcy. 'I'm pleased to hear that.'

Hooper took another sip of coffee. Varcy watched her for a moment.

'May I ask you a personal question?' he said at last.

'Sure,' said Hooper.

'It's not strictly my business,' he said, 'and you can tell me to go to hell if you want to, but – and I hesitate to say it – I've noticed you've lost a bit of weight recently. Now, I would hate for you to be stressed in any way. If there's –'

'I've got Crohn's disease, Gov'nor,' Hooper interrupted.

'Sorry?'

'Crohn's disease. It's a digestive disorder. I'm allergic to a whole bunch of stuff so I've got to be careful what I eat. I had a flare up a few months

247

ago and they've put me on a strict diet to work out what's setting it off.'

'I see,' said Varcy.

'It's called an exclusion diet. You restrict the foods you eat in the beginning and then gradually re-introduce them to see what's doing it. The side effect is that you lose a lot of weight. More than I can afford to lose, if I'm honest.'

'Yes, of course,' said Varcy. 'An exclusion diet? I never thought of that.'

He watched the TV for a moment, thinking it over. Then he said, 'Scientists call that a confounding variable, you know.'

'What? Crohn's disease?'

'No, no. A conclusion that is reached based on a completely wrong set of criteria.'

'You've lost me,' she said.

'No matter. Crohn's disease … Crohn's disease …' He tossed the words around his mouth as if savouring their flavours. 'What a relief. I must look that up.'

'It makes riveting bedtime reading,' she said. 'Take it from me.'

Varcy smiled. 'Thank you for being candid with me. I was … well, I was worried, frankly. I hope you didn't mind me prying.'

'No,' she said. 'I didn't.'

'May I ask you another question?' added Varcy after a short moment. 'It's not personal this time, so don't worry. It's work related.'

'Go ahead,' smiled Hooper.

'It's about Charles Pine,' he said. 'A serious

question about him.'

'Okay,' she said.

'Is he capable of murder?'

Hooper sat back in her chair and folded her arms. 'Murder? Tough question. He's a ruthless character, that's for sure – but murder? That's a different story. I honestly don't know,' she said.

'You're not prepared to give an opinion?'

'I need more information to go on,' she replied.

'What does your gut tell you?'

She blew out her cheeks. 'He conned John Scott out of fifty million so he's *interesting,* if I can put it that way. Whether that translates to murder ...' She shook her head. 'Again, I couldn't say.'

Varcy nodded. 'Okay. I'll accept your on-the-fence response.'

'Sorry, Gov'nor,' she said, draining the last of her coffee.

'Keep digging around Pine,' said Varcy. 'I want to know anything else that's off about him. Anything at all.'

Hooper nodded. 'Of course.'

There was a long moment of silence. Varcy shifted in his seat. 'Do you like the ballet?' he asked suddenly.

Hooper smiled. 'I've never been. Why?'

Varcy shrugged. 'I used to go from time to time. It's very beautiful.'

She nodded.

'I have two tickets for La Bayadère at Covent Garden. Would you like to come?'

'When?'

'This evening.'

The door of AJ's swung open. The platform announcements from the main tannoy drifted in, along with the low hum from a frantic mix of rail passengers and city workers on the concourse outside. Kendrick appeared at the doorway and scanned the interior. Varcy waved to him and he came striding over. In his hand was a rolled up sheet of paper. He reached the table and squeezed in next to Hooper. 'May I interrupt?'

'You may,' said Varcy. 'We're just finishing up here anyway.'

He handed the rolled up sheet to Varcy. 'I've got a list I thought you might like to see. There are twelve names on there. Each are ex-military personnel.'

Varcy ran his eyes down the list. Next to each name was a single word or sentence. *Injured, depressed, breakdown, ill-disciplined* …

'We've been looking at candidates who comply with Dr Nash's profile. We've limited it to male individuals currently between thirty-four and thirty-nine years of age who were discharged from the armed forces for unusual reasons.'

'Why is *injured* on there?' asked Varcy.

'Those people were injured in the services and have subsequently tried to sue the army for compensation. We thought that constituted a bitter end to their relationship with the military.'

'Fair enough.'

'So we whittled it down to these twelve and then dug a bit deeper. One of them has subsequently died of a heart attack, three have emigrated and no longer live in the country and five of them are married and living with their spouses. If you remember, Dr Nash reckoned our man had no personal relationships of that kind.'

'I remember,' said Varcy.

'That leaves just three.'

'So?' said Varcy.

'So one of the three is wheelchair bound, but the other two are more interesting. Both have been in trouble for violent behaviour. One of them, in particular, this one,' he pointed to the name, *Paul Renton*, on the list, 'had a record of violent behaviour before military service. He was considered a decent soldier while serving, but is now on the radar of SOCA. Talking to them today, they think he's an enforcer with a drug gang operating in West London.'

Varcy flicked is eyes over to the right of Paul Renton's name. He read the letters, *CM*.

'What does *CM* mean?'

'Court martialled,' said Kendrick. 'The only one of the twelve to be discharged by that method. Now, here's the kicker. He went mad, I mean ballistic, when he found out his wife was knocking off his best friend while he was away fighting. He tore up the barracks and, according to the account given in his personnel file, it took six men to hold him down. Even then the army might have forgiven him in view of the upsetting circumstances, but a week later he attacked and broke the nose, the jaw and four ribs of a senior officer because he reminded him of his wife's lover. He was court-martialled after that and spent the best part of two years in military prison, before being dumped back on civvy street.'

Varcy took a deep breath. 'A camel's back moment then.'

'Oh, yes,' said Kendrick.

'Do SOCA suspect him of killing anyone?'

'Plenty of suspicions about this guy,' said Kendrick. 'They're more interested in watching him than arresting him at the moment, because he's so well connected. His file says he saw active service in Iraq so I'm sure he can handle himself.'

After a moment's thought, Varcy said, 'Sounds like it's worth a follow-up.'

'It is,' said Kendrick. 'Especially when I tell you about a little link we've just made.'

'Go on,' said Varcy.

'About a year ago Renton was picked up for suspected drink-driving. He was breathalised and found to be just over. They charged him and took a statement from the passenger in the car. HOLMES has the passenger's name as Marcianna Capan.'

Varcy sat up. 'She was Barry Townsend's lover.'

'Small world,' said Kendrick.

'Okay, this is the guy we'll target for the moment. I want anything we can get on him. Address, bank details, medical records, NI number, his full military record. Everything. I'll tie up with SOCA. He'll need watching and I want us to do it from now on.'

The three of them got up from the table. Kendrick surged ahead. Varcy and Hooper followed behind.

Hooper leaned towards Varcy. 'I'd love to go, Gov'nor.' she said.

39

The NEWSPLAN article on James Pine mentioned his driver's name: Frank Davies. The road accident was a serious one – a fatality – a child had been knocked down and killed. It was easy to track the driver down. Rita simply searched 192.com and his details came up. The house was ex-council and low grade. Rita wearily walked back down the small path that led from the house. She had been inside for twenty minutes, whilst Meg waited in the car. Rita strapped herself in and turned to her friend.

'Well?' Meg said.

Rita shook her head. 'Very sad,' she replied.

'Why?'

'He's a broken man,' said Rita.

'Did you show him the picture of Westfield?'

Rita nodded.

'And?'

'He's not sure. Can't say if Pine went out with her or not. He said there were many girls.'

'So useless then?'

'For establishing a link between Pine and Westfield, yes,' said Rita. 'Let's go. I need to talk to Inspector Varcy.'

40

The van was white. Unmarked and to all the world a regular Transit – but it wasn't – the inside was gutted and fitted with a bunch of telecommunication equipment. The hardware included monitors, radio equipment, listening devices, personal two-way communication kit. In the field were two officers, Katz and Cole. Varcy and Kendrick were in the van with the operator. Paul Renton had left his property fifteen minutes earlier on foot and walked west on Cable Street towards Tower Hill. From there he headed south towards the river. Katz was following and Cole was drifting in case of emergencies. In the few hours since Varcy had ordered information on Paul Renton, he had been given a dossier with reams of notes. Most of it had come from SOCA. They were reluctant to arrest because Paul Renton would lead them to all manner of goodies. Nevertheless, a murder investigation took priority and Varcy had promised to be discreet and only act when it was absolutely necessary. He had a warrant and a reason to move so, when Renton was two miles away, he and Kendrick hopped out of the van. They scanned the block of apartments Renton had vacated. The apartments were exposed at the anterior side so that the front doors of the flats were visible from the road. The block was protected by a buzz-through door that Varcy had a key to. He had a key to Renton's front door too. This thanks to the landlord – Tower Hamlets Council – who had master keys for all their properties.

The main worry for Varcy was the possibility that there would be someone else in the apartment. That would be most inconvenient and would compromise both his and SOCA's investigation. SOCA had never seen anyone else in the property and it was assumed that Renton lived alone. He was estranged from his ex-wife. He had no children. His mother had died five years before and he had no contact with his father. He did have a grandmother still living whom he visited regularly in a local care home.

Varcy checked his watch. 9.14pm. The temperature had dropped somewhat and he felt the rush of cool air assault his face as he left the van. He fixed the buttons on his jacket and turned the collar up so that it scratched his ears.

'Ready?' asked Kendrick.

'As I'll ever be,' Varcy replied.

They crossed the road and unlocked the buzz-through door. They mounted the two flights of stairs to apartment forty-nine. The air rushed up to meet them as they made their way along the exposed corridor at the front of the apartments. Kendrick checked the doors to the right and left of forty-nine. The neighbours were in. The windows of both properties burned brightly with light. Varcy peered over the balcony that looked down to Cable

Street. The white van was parked fifty yards south. He turned back to face the apartments.

'This is the one,' said Kendrick, walking back.

Varcy peered in through the window and cupped his hands around his eyes to shut out light. 'There's a light on in the back,' he said, changing his position and moving further towards the front door.

'Could be for security,' said Kendrick.

Varcy nodded. 'I can't see any movement. Can you hear anything?'

Kendrick gently lifted the letterbox and pushed his ear in the space. He waited for a minute then replaced the flap. 'Nothing,' he said.

'Okay,' said Varcy. 'Let's have a look.'

Varcy inserted the master key and pushed the door inwards. Inside was dim and warm with a sickly sweet odour.

'Cannabis,' said Kendrick immediately.

Varcy nodded. The stale smoke hung in the unaired space.

To Varcy's right was a door. He opened it cautiously and found it was a bathroom. It was white and regular, standard council fare. Kendrick moved ahead into the next room, on the left. A kitchen. It had a window to the left that overlooked the open corridor outside. Beneath this was a small, formica table. Kendrick flipped the light on. The smell of cannabis smoke was strong in here. A small electric cooker stood opposite the door. The hot plates were stained with food. The white splash-back tiles were discoloured with old grease marks. There was a sink and drainer next to this with a pile of unwashed dishes on both. On the table was a small bundle of bills. Kendrick glanced through them. There were rent demand letters, gas readings, flyers, a council tax bill and a dole card.

Varcy moved slowly to the next door along the corridor. He pushed it inwards and peered in. It was a bedroom with two single beds laid side by side. Both were made up, but not tidily so. The far bed had a small table next to it, with a glass of water and a bottle of pills on it. Varcy moved towards this and read the label on the pill bottle: *Clonidine* 0.2mg. Clonidine? He had heard of that. Heart tablets? He read the inscription on the front of the bottle: *Mrs Jean Renton*. He held the jar up to his eyes. There were a couple of dozen tablets still in the bottle. He replaced it carefully and glanced towards the other bed. This also had a table beside it but instead of pills, this one had a pile of books on it. Varcy moved around the beds and picked them up. There were four. Each was a variation on a theme. The first was entitled, *Egyptian Symbology – Hidden Meanings*; the second, *Egypt: the undiscovered truth*; the third was called, *The Power of the Pyramids*, and the fourth, *The First Pharaoh's Tomb*. Varcy flipped through them all. They were thick and filled with small print and glossy photographs. They looked too academic for an ordinary punter. At the back of each was an index giving references for the material included, and a glossary of terms. He replaced the books in the same order he had found them and scanned the room. His eyes settled on the area of wall opposite the bed. He hadn't seen it when he had first come

258

in because his attention was on the beds. It was a poster in a black frame. Roughly four feet by three, it showed the iconic image of the Great Pyramid of Giza. In the foreground was white sand. There was a small crowd of nomads riding camels off to the right. The sun was low in the sky, settling behind the top of the pyramid. The sky was clear and tinged with red.

Kendrick popped his head around the door. 'Gov'nor,' he whispered. 'In here.'

Varcy left the bedroom and followed him into the front room from where the light was coming. Specifically from a tall lamp in the far corner. It was a small space. Faded floral paper clung to the walls. The floor was laminated. There was a round, green mat in the centre of the room. It too was faded. There was a faint smell of urine. A small sofa stood against one wall, two wing-back chairs on either side of it. In one of them sat a woman who must have been at least eighty. She had a mop of curly, grey hair, a brown woollen cardigan and a grey skirt. She wore thick brown tights and a pair of grey slippers with white, fluffy trim at the instep. Her head hung to the side, mouth gaping open, breath slow and rhythmic. She slept soundly.

Varcy frowned at Kendrick and mouthed, '*His granny?*'

Kendrick shrugged.

Varcy flicked his eyes about the space. Opposite the sofa was a cheap, dark sideboard with three drawers in the front and two small cupboards at the end. On it was a photograph in a frame. Probably a young Paul Renton, although Varcy couldn't be completely sure because he had only seen photographs of him as an adult. He was standing next to a woman who had her arm around him. She looked as if she could be his grandmother. He glanced at the sleeping woman to see if there was a resemblance.

Kendrick waved at him. He was standing to the left of the wing-backed chair where there was a small, tiled fireplace. It had a wooden mantle and a three-bar electric fire. On the mantle was a box of matches, some pencils and, as Varcy saw for himself when he got over there, a red Swiss Army knife. The blade was retracted. Varcy inspected the shank to check for any similarity between it and the knife left at the Barry Townsend murder scene. He couldn't be sure the manufacturer was the same. Kendrick reached into his pocket, pulled out a plastic glove and a specimen bag. He pulled on the glove and slipped the knife into the bag.

The old woman stirred and gave a loud snore.

The two men exchanged glances.

Varcy moved back to the sideboard and searched the drawers. They were filled with the usual bric-a-brac. He didn't know what he was looking for exactly, just that he was alert to anything that stood out. He squatted to search the two cupboards. The small cupboard on the left held little interest. In it was a quarter-empty sherry bottle, a half bottle of brandy and a few small glasses. The right one proved much more interesting. It had a pile of magazines pushed towards the back. On top of this was a cube-shaped tin. Varcy eased out the magazines and sorted through them: *Woman's Own, OK, The People's Friend.*

Unusual diet for a violent man.

Varcy assumed he kept them for the old lady. He opened the lid on the tin and peered in. There was a thick roll of bank notes stored inside. Varcy pulled them out and counted each one. They were all high denominations. Fifties, twenties and tens. One thousand eight hundred and forty quid to be precise. Varcy held them up to Kendrick, who nodded.

Nice work if you could get it.

He replaced the money in the tin and returned it to the back of the cupboard.

'*Ready?*' Kendrick mouthed.

Varcy nodded.

They slipped out of the living room. Varcy glanced back at the old woman. Her breathing remained unchanged. Still very much asleep.

41

Back in the white van, the operator cracked open a thermos of coffee and poured a cup for each man. Varcy closed the back of the van and slumped onto one of the flat seats that lined the side wall. 'How are the two lads?' he said as the operator gave him the cup. He was referring to Katz and Cole.

'They've followed Renton to a pub south of the river.'

Varcy nodded. 'Okay, make sure they stay safe.'

Kendrick took a slurp of coffee. 'What was the deal with the granny?' he asked.

'I understood he lived alone,' shrugged Varcy.

'How much was in that tin?'

Varcy took a mouthful of coffee. 'Eighteen hundred and forty quid,' he said.

'He's on the dole,' said Kendrick. 'I saw the paperwork in his kitchen. Where does he get that sort of money?'

Varcy set down his coffee and rifled through his briefcase. He pulled out the folder from SOCA and flicked the pages. He stuck his finger into one of them. 'Here,' he said. 'I thought I read a paragraph about the grandmother. He visits his grandmother in a nursing home on Commercial Road. It's a council run place. She's been resident there for ten years.'

'Well, she's not there now,' said Kendrick.

Varcy had left his phone on a narrow desk at the front of the van. He snatched it up now and called enquiries. They gave him the nursing home's number. He dialled it and waited for an answer.

When he had finished, he rang off, scrolled through to voicemail and listened to a message.

'What was the outcome?' said Kendrick.

Varcy waved him down as the voice kicked in. 'Hi Inspector,' said Rita Sidhu. 'I wondered if I might have a word with you? Can you call me back when you get this.'

He hit recall immediately and waited for Sidhu to pick up. He turned to Kendrick. 'The care home signed his granny out two days ago,' he said. 'They don't expect her back until tomorrow.'

Sidhu answered.

'I've just got your message,' he said. 'You'd like to talk?'

'Yes.'

'How urgent is it?' he asked.

'Very,' she said.

'Where are you now?'

'I'm back in the hotel.'

'Okay, stay there,' he said. 'I'll come to you.'

* * *

Varcy and Kendrick arrived in an unmarked blue BMW. They breezed into the lobby and rode the elevator to the third floor. Rita was in her hotel room with Meg. Although Varcy had met both women, Kendrick hadn't, so the introductions were formal and polite. Rita and her friend perched on the bed. Varcy pulled up the chair from under the desk. Kendrick stood.

'So,' Varcy said. 'What's the problem?'

Rita glanced at her friend, took a deep breath and told him the story she had told Meg earlier in the day. She told him about the camel hair comparisons she had made a year before, about the match to James Pine's car and about her vague suspicion that the hair may have come from the coat of the dead girl, Kimberley Westfield.

'I remember that case,' said Varcy. 'Found in woodland.'

'On the edge of Green Park,' nodded Rita.

'Your ex boyfriend's uncle asked you to carry out this test,' said Varcy, making a note in his decision log. 'Who is he?'

'He's dead,' said Rita. 'That's one reason I'm telling you this now.'

'Natural causes?' asked Varcy.

Rita shook her head. 'He was murdered. I've only just found out about it.'

'What was his name?' asked Varcy.

'John Scott,' she said.

Varcy stopped writing and looked Rita full in the eye. 'What did you say?'

'John Scott,' she repeated. 'Did you know him?'

Varcy glanced at Kendrick.

'Lord Scott,' said Varcy slowly. 'Lord John Scott?'

'Yes,' said Rita. 'I didn't know him as that. He was very modest about his achievements. But, yes.'

Varcy shifted in his seat.

'What's wrong?' she said.

'He was killed by the same person that killed Barry Townsend,' replied Varcy.

Rita's eyes went wide. 'You know that for sure?'

'I'm as sure as I can be,' nodded Varcy. 'The method of killing was the same in both cases. It means there is a very strong link between both killings.'

The room went silent. No one spoke. Varcy continued to write in his decision log. Kendrick stood motionless.

'That link is me, isn't it?' Rita said at last.

'Could be,' said Varcy, looking up from his notes.

Rita slumped on the bed. Meg reached out and put her arm around her shoulders. 'Come on,' she said, 'get a grip.'

Rita stared at the floor.

'Can I back you up a little bit?' said Varcy gently. He flipped through the last couple of pages of his log to find the place. 'You said your ex-boyfriend told you about the blackmail?'

Rita nodded.

'Did he implicate Pine directly in the Westfield murder?' asked Varcy.

'No,' said Rita. 'I've no concrete proof, just a suspicion. I went to see his driver today to see if I could link him with Westfield.'

'And did you?' said Varcy.

Rita shook her head.

'Tell me about these samples,' Varcy said.

She told him the samples she had used were still stored in the retinal safe in the lab back at IMDB.

'Who else knows they are in there?' Varcy asked.

'Me and Mark,' she said.

'And why have you told me now?'

'Because Mark thought the analysis was used to blackmail Charles Pine.'

Varcy made a long note in his decision log.

'Tell him about Robert,' said Rita.

Meg rummaged in her bag and produced her mobile phone. Showed Varcy Robert Fleet's text. 'He didn't show up for work today,' she said.

Varcy glanced at Kendrick.

'Can I get access to these samples?' he asked.

'Not without Robert,' said Rita. 'The safe works on a confirmatory retinal scan before we can get access to it.'

'A what?' said Varcy.

'Basically our two retinal profiles are stored and both of them are scanned to get access.'

'Bit over the top isn't it?' said Varcy.

Rita shrugged. 'It was put in a couple of years ago after we cloned the infra-1 gene. This was a big breakthrough in cardiac science. Retnel wanted to protect their asset so they installed it.'

'So apart from the need for him to be there to get access to the safe, he had nothing to do with the analysis.'

'No,' said Rita.

Varcy nodded. 'Can the safe be overridden if one of you is not around?'

'I honestly don't know,' she said, turning to Meg.

Meg shrugged. 'We could find out.'

'Do that,' said Varcy. 'In the meantime, I'll track

down the coat Kimberley Westfield was wearing when she was murdered.'

He checked his notebook then glanced at Kendrick. 'Get on to Robert Fleet. Get access to his flat. Track him down.'

Kendrick nodded.

'Anything else?' said Varcy.

'Security in the hotel,' said Kendrick.

'Thank you, yes, ' said Varcy. 'Let's have one of your boys stationed in the corridor. No one goes in or out without him knowing.'

Kendrick nodded.

'Can we go out?' asked Rita.

'You can,' Varcy said to Meg, 'but you can't, Rita, I'm afraid.'

Rita slumped back down on the bed.

'It won't be forever,' said Varcy. 'Just a precaution.'

Meg was already putting on her coat. 'I'll have a word with Dave Adams tomorrow morning,' she said. 'He's the technical guy at IMDB. If anyone knows how to override the safe, it's him.'

Varcy nodded. 'Okay then.'

42

I followed Rita Sidhu from the address in Holborn to a hotel just off the Tottenham Court Road. During all the time I have been watching her – some two months now – she has never been here before. I wondered why she had come. Then a car drew up and parked on a double yellow outside. Two figures emerged and I was in no doubt who they were. They disappeared into the hotel's lobby. I moved towards the entrance and watched them show their badges to the girl on the reception desk, before they headed for the elevators and rode them to one of the upper floors. I watched and waited. Then I approached the receptionist and asked what room Sidhu was staying in. She gave me the information without hesitation.

I stayed around the hotel for another hour until the two figures re-emerged and got back into their car. I debated going up to the room immediately but dismissed the thought as reckless. I would execute this kill exactly as I've planned. It deserves at least that much.

I left the hotel and headed back to the lock-up.

* * *

The lock-up is a perfect place to spend time before

I go out again. It is safe and secure. All is well here. I check that nothing has been disturbed. Robert Fleet's head is still in the freezer. My things are as I left them. I flip on the spotlights. They are aimed at the large photographs hanging on the east wall. Their beauty hits my eyes afresh. I make a bed on the concrete floor with some cushions and a sleeping bag. I position it so the photographs are directly in front of where I lie.

I stare at them for a long time until my eyelids feel heavy and tired. The images fuzz slightly as I give in to the feeling of sleep. Moments pass in a gentle haze. My breath slows and I drift away.

A violent noise suddenly echoes around the lock-up.

It brings me out of my stupor immediately. I sit up quickly and listen. No sound. I rub my face vigorously to rid it of sleep. Then the noise comes again. A booming rap on the lock-up door. I am on my feet at once. I scoop up the bedclothes and store them away. I move to the metal cabinet where I keep the type 67. I hitch the holster around my body and pull on an over-jacket. The rap comes a third time. I quickly process my options and the scenarios that accompany them. The most dangerous is that the authorities have discovered my identity. I have killed numerous times now and may have been careless. I doubt this is true, but it must be considered. Alternatively, they have traced evidence back to this place. Again I struggle to accept this as credible as I have been careful to ensure there is no link. Third, this is an innocent gesture. A neighbour perhaps. The light is on after all and will be seen through the cracks in the lock-up door. I decide the last scenario is the most likely: so I move towards the door, push back the bolt and open it.

Behind it is a man. I judge he is around fifty years old. He has grey hair pushed over to make a side parting. He is short – no more than five foot six. He wears dark green step-in overalls that are smeared with grease and oil. His hands too are dark with gunk from engine parts. In his hands he plays with a torn rag stained black with the same material. I say nothing.

He smiles. 'I saw the light on,' he says, nodding towards the back of my lock-up.

I remain silent.

'I wondered who'd taken over from Jim,' he continues, 'so I thought I'd come over and introduce myself. I'm Stan Long, by the way.'

'Good to meet you,' I say.

'What line of business are you in?' he asks. 'I'm a mechanic, as you can probably tell.'

'Export,' I say.

He nods.

I say nothing.

'Export?' he repeats. 'Don't think we've had an exporter on site before. You're the first!'

I still say nothing.

'Oh, well,' he says after a long moment. 'I'll let you get on.'

'Thanks,' I say.

'If you need anything, just ask. I'm in the corner

over there,' he says, pointing to one of the lock-ups facing my own.

'I will,' I say.

He smiles again and backs away. 'I'll see you around,' he says.

I close the door and secure the bolt.

43

Hooper lived in a house-share just off Mare Street. A well connected place. Near to just about everything. Varcy jumped out of the black cab, told the driver to wait and climbed the stone steps leading to the Victorian terrace house. The evening was warm and clammy. Hooper emerged in a black off-the-shoulder dress.

Varcy's breath caught in his throat. She was elegant and pale. Her hair was worn up, her dress hugged her waist and hips. Quite a contrast from the attire he was used to.

'My goodness,' was all he could think of to say. 'You look … lovely.'

'Thanks, Gov'nor,' said Hooper closing the door behind her.

He proferred his arm.

She smiled, took it and he led her down to the waiting taxi.

The Opera House was illuminated to a perfect haze. The white stone building shimmered like a precious jewel. It was teeming with life too. Dinner-suited punters mingled with the tourists and the ticket touts on the street outside. Varcy led Hooper past the throng into the welcome area. Then past the glamorous clutch of afficianados who were chatting and laughing by the box office, up the escalator staircase to the Amphitheatre bar. Varcy grabbed a table.

'This will do,' he said. 'What will you have?'

'G and T please, Gov'nor,' said Hooper.

Varcy scuttled off to the bar and returned some time later with their drinks and a couple of programmes in hand.

'Busy up there?' she asked when he settled into the seat opposite.

'Just a tad,' he said lifting his glass. 'Cheers,' he said.

She clinked her glass against his. 'Cheers.'

'You been here before?' he asked.

'No,' she said looking about. 'Impressive place, I must say. I take it you have?'

Varcy nodded. 'A lot at one time.'

'Why did you stop?' Hooper asked.

'Oh, life got in the way, I suppose,' he said.

'It has a habit of doing that,' she nodded.

'It certainly does,' he replied sipping his drink.

'Ballet is unusual,' said Hooper. 'Most guys would rather go to a football match.'

He smiled. 'My late wife's mother was a ballet teacher,' he said. 'One of those shrill, disciplined women who taught in schools, church halls and youth clubs. She adored the ballet. Got her daughter hooked and then when we met, got me hooked too.'

'Well, I'm pleased she did,' said Hooper looking about the bar. 'Or I wouldn't have got to see this.'

'I'm pleased you came,' he said.

There was a moment of silence. Varcy took another slurp of his drink. So did Hooper.

'How did you lose your wife?' she said suddenly.

He paused for a short moment. 'Drugs,' he said. 'We lost our son during childbirth. My wife couldn't cope with it. She grieved and got very depressed. It went on and on. She became addicted to the prescription medication they kept giving her. That's what killed her in the end.'

'I'm sorry,' said Hooper.

He shook his head. 'It's been twelve years. I've come to terms with it.'

Hooper watched his face, probing his eyes. 'You still love them though don't you, Gov'nor? Your wife and boy, I mean?'

Varcy nodded slowly.

There was another moment of silence. Varcy cleared his throat and sat up straight. 'Now then, enough about me. What about you?'

'What about me?' she asked.

'I don't know you very well at all,' he said.

Hooper shrugged. 'Nothing to tell really. I'm fairly boring.'

'I don't believe that for one moment.'

'Well, maybe not *completely* boring,' she said.

Varcy smiled. 'You were in the army, weren't you?' he said.

'Cadets, when I was younger,' she replied. 'I was a real tomboy back then. Probably still am. I loved the physical side of it. Climbing, running, obstacle courses. All that stuff was great.'

'Do you have any family?' he asked.

'I was adopted,' she said. 'Both of my parents were getting on when they adopted me. They've both passed away now.'

'I'm sorry,' said Varcy.

'I was married briefly too,' she said softly.

'I didn't know.'

She shrugged again. 'These things happen,' she said.

Varcy sipped his drink.

'Do you have ambitions?' he asked.

'You mean to climb the greasy pole?' she replied.

He smiled. 'That's one way of putting it.'

She shook her head. 'Not really, I'm happy doing exactly what I'm doing.' She reached forwards to pick up one of the programmes. Flicked through. 'Right now I'm concentrating on this.' She read aloud. *'Etipa's masterpiece of passion, betrayal and redemption, culminating in the breathtaking "Kingdom of the Shades", is danced to perfection by the Bolshoi's incomparable corps de ballet.'*

Varcy laughed. 'Well, you're in for a treat.'

Just then the bar bell sounded. Varcy finished off his drink and Hooper downed what was left of hers. 'Come on,' he said. 'We don't want to miss it.'

* * *

Varcy was awake early the next morning. He had tossed and turned during the night and tried to settle. He was thinking about Hooper. The evening had passed by in a blur. He had been glancing at her during *La Bayadère* to gauge her reaction. She had seemed delighted by it. Afterwards they went for dinner at a spaghetti house on King Street. She was witty and mature and … something else.

Certain.

He liked that.

The toaster popped out a wholemeal slice. Varcy took a slurp of tea and buttered the toast. He sat at the kitchen table and chomped on it, looking around the space as he did so. It was small but modern, built by a large developer during the nineties boom years. He had traded in the Upminster semi, the house he shared with his wife. It was full of too many memories ever to be comfortable again. This flat was functional, near to his work and at the centre of every kind of amenity. Living in London felt less like being alone too. In suburbia he had felt isolated. This suited him much better. He wondered what this flat might look like through a woman's eyes. At the moment it was just a space. Functional, sparse, and without much colour or character. He understood that. He had deliberately created it that way as a defence against ever getting comfortable again.

He pulled on his jacket and drained his mug. His mobile chimed in his pocket. A text. He fished it out and read the message.

Thanks for last night Gov. I LOVE ballet! Who would've guessed? x

He smiled, then he wedged the toast in his mouth and fiddled in his pockets for his door keys. He'd eat the toast on the way in. He grabbed his briefcase and shuffled out of the front door. At street level, his mobile sprang into life again. It was Kendrick.

'I've located the Westfield coat,' he said.

'Good man,' said Varcy. 'Where was it?'

'In storage at Battersea, along with the other clothes she was wearing.'

'Arrange for a courier to collect it.'

'Already been done,' said Kendrick.

'Where are you now?'

'Bishopsgate,' replied Kendrick.

'Okay, wait for me there.'

* * *

Dave Adams worked in the basement of the IMDB building. It seemed to Meg that he was always in it. Whenever she went down there in search of help for techy problems – computer crash, PCR malfunction, faulty coffee dispenser – Dave would be in this cramped, eight by four office he shared with a metal filing cabinet and three walls crammed with photos of formula one racing cars.

Today was no different. He was at his desk, banging away at a PC. Meg stood in the open doorway and watched him for a moment. His red, curly hair flopped forwards as he worked. He had his shirt sleeves pulled up to his elbows revealing his freckly arms. He chewed on gum and stared intently into the screen.

'Can I interrupt?' Meg said.

Dave didn't react. He kept staring and tapping the keyboard. 'Just a moment,' he answered finally.

And so the ritual began.

The ritual of waiting for Dave to stop his work to give visitors like Meg some of his genius-rated time. It drove Meg nuts. Dave had built an empire. He knew it and so did everybody else who worked there. Dave knew stuff – boring technical stuff – that no one else did and he could fix it all too.

And so she waited.

He continued typing for a good two minutes, then he spun in his chair to face her.

'Finished?' she asked.

'No,' he smiled, showing tobacco stained teeth through his beard. 'But I'm all yours anyway.'

'I'm grateful.'

'That's what they all say,' said Dave.

'The retinal scanner,' said Meg.

'In lab 3467?'

She nodded.

'What about it?'

'I need access,' she said.

Dave smiled again. 'It's a retinal scanner for a reason,' he said. 'To prevent unauthorised access.' He spun back in his chair and produced a burst of staccato on the keyboard. Squinting at the screen, he said, 'Rita Sidhu and Robert Fleet are the profiles you need.'

'I know whose profiles are needed,' she said, 'but neither are here. That's why I've come to you.'

'Have you got an authorisation note?'

'No,' she said. 'I've got a police note instead.'

'Police?'

'Dave, I need access,' she said. 'I'm not prepared

to say any more than that. Please.'

He stared at her. Then he went back to his computer and typed another burst. He copied down a fifteen-digit number onto a notepad and tore it off. 'Here,' he said, 'type that into the keypad and it'll override the scans.'

'Thanks,' she said.

'You owe me,' he replied.

Meg shuddered at the thought.

44

It was called the conference room, but Varcy always thought of it as a meeting place. A functional space with MDF tables, chairs, flip charts, white boards and the like. It had stud walls and plastic trim that could be knocked down with a small hammer in one afternoon. A conference room spoke of permanence. Of quality. Of real wood and fine furniture.

At the centre of the fake pine oval table on a metal tray were eight mugs – four tea, four coffee – and a pot of sugar with a plastic spoon stuck into it. The attendees helped themselves. There was some light banter. A feeling of anticipation. The team knew there had been a breakthrough. Varcy had called the meeting to explain what had happened and to determine the next steps.

His eyes flicked around the table. Opposite him was Cole, flip-flopping a pencil between his fingers. Katz was to his right, sitting still and staring off into the distance. To Cole's left was Hooper. She wore a white, short-sleeved shirt and dark trousers. Her black hair was pulled back with a band. On her lap was a notepad. She concentrated hard on it, writing in short bursts and studying what she had written. Varcy kept glancing at her. He couldn't help it. Once or twice she caught him and smiled. Nash was to Varcy's left. His pepper-pot grey hair was uncombed. The curly mass hung limply to one side of his head. Mary Totham – a forensic scientist specialising in trichology – was to his right. She was middle-aged and portly and wore a pair of half-rimmed glasses on a chain around her neck. In front of her on the desk was a small rack with two plastic tubes sitting in it. Kendrick sat next to her, shirt unbuttoned and sleeves rolled back.

Varcy cleared his throat. 'Can we begin?'

The room went silent and Varcy said, 'We have an interesting development in the Scott and Townsend case. Last night I spoke to Rita Sidhu. She told me about a suspicion she had regarding Charles Pine's son, James.'

'The one who topped himself?' said Cole.

Varcy nodded. 'He hung himself about the same time John Scott was murdered.'

'Just over a month ago,' said Kendrick.

Varcy gave them all the details. He told them about the camel hair comparisons. He explained how Rita Sidhu came to be involved and how John Scott had refused to follow up on her suspicions.

'Then why didn't she go to the police?' asked Hooper.

'She says she's only just found out,' Varcy replied.

'You believe her?' said Hooper.

Varcy shrugged. 'No reason not to at the moment.'

'Those the samples?' asked Katz.

'The original tubes that were given to Sidhu to analyse,' said Varcy.

Mary Totham took the tubes out of the rack and handed them to Kendrick. Kendrick studied both and passed them around.

'All of you know Mary by now,' said Varcy, gesturing with his hand. 'I asked her to do some comparisons of her own this morning. Mary?'

Mary smiled. 'The tubes are labelled "car sample" and "hair sample". The "car sample" tube contains fibres taken from a car belonging to James Pine, and the tube marked "hair sample" contains a special kind of hair used for making fabric. Most usually camel hair coats. However,' Mary continued, 'the car sample contains camel coat hairs mixed with other fibres. I looked at them this morning and the other fibres are consistent with the material used in the production of seat-well matting by the car manufacturer Volkswagen AG in their Bentley Mulsanne. We know Pine owned such a model two years ago.'

'I've got the tracking bureau locating the exact car,' said Varcy. 'The Pine family don't own it any longer so it'll take a bit of time.'

'But there's more,' said Totham. 'Mixed with the camel hair and car fibres is human cell debris. Specifically blood. We are not sure whose blood it is. There's more work to do on that.'

'So what's the significance of this other tube?' asked Katz, turning it around in his fingers.

'That contains the same camel hair as is found in the "car sample",' said Mary. 'Sidhu suggested it might have come from a coat found on a murder victim called Kimberley Westfield, who was discovered dumped in woodland some time before this analysis was made. We've got hold of that coat – the one she was wearing when she was murdered – and it turns out Sidhu was right. Those hairs do match the camel hairs from the coat she was found in.'

'Was there blood on it?' asked Katz.

'Yes,' said Totham. 'But again I can't confirm yet if it matches the blood found in James Pine's car.'

'But the assumption is that it does,' said Katz.

Varcy nodded.

Cole whistled through his teeth.

'It means that James Pine has just become the prime suspect in a cold case,' said Varcy.

'Even though he's dead,' said Hooper.

Varcy nodded. 'The question that intrigues me is why he took his own life? And how does that relate to our current case?'

'He took his own life because he knew someone was on to him,' said Kendrick. 'My guess would be John Scott.'

'Who died first?' asked Cole. 'Scott or Pine?'

'Pine,' said Varcy. 'By one week.'

'Then Charles Pine has a motive for killing Scott,' said Kendrick. 'He finds out that Scott was suspicious of his son before his son hung himself. He blames Scott for both things and has him killed because of it.'

'What about Barry Townsend?' said Varcy.

'Coincidence,' said Kendrick. 'The killer's the

same, but for a different reason. If this man is active – and we know he is – his jobs come from more than one source and he used the same MO to carry out both killings.'

'People usually kill themselves because they are depressed,' said Katz. 'He had high expectations, pressure to succeed, not as good as his dad. That sort of thing.'

'I'd be pretty depressed if some bloke had me by the balls,' said Kendrick. 'And let's be clear about it, Scott had him by the balls.'

'Was he in financial trouble?' asked Cole.

'Not that we know of,' said Varcy. 'Although we should probably look at that. What about murder? What if he was murdered and didn't kill himself at all?'

'That's not what the police report says,' said Kendrick.

'I know what the report says,' said Varcy. 'But what do *we* say?'

'I say he killed himself,' said Kendrick.

'I agree,' said Cole.

Hooper and Katz nodded their agreement too.

Then Hooper said, 'Gov'nor? This might be relevant.' She reached down to the floor and heaved up a green lever arch file. 'I've been digging a bit deeper on Charles Pine and I've come up with this guy.' She eased out a black and white six by four photograph and pushed it towards Varcy. Varcy glanced at it. It was a headshot of a middle-aged man. He had a grey comb-over, a weak jaw and small, puffy eyes. 'He was a business associate of

Charles Pine about ten years ago. The two men were partners – with others – in a venture capital business. The business was eventually bought out by one of Pine's holding companies. This guy was found face down in a lake near Ashford in Kent a couple of years after that. The coroner returned an open verdict. However, in light of this conversation it might be worth looking at.'

'There you are,' said Kendrick, sipping on his tea. 'He's got form. Charles Pine has to be in the frame for the Scott murder.'

There was silence. Varcy turned to Nash. 'Thoughts?'

Nash pushed his spectacles up high onto his nose. 'Pine's character is not inconsistent with the general profile of someone who – under certain circumstances – might consider paying for a murder. That is to say he shares character traits with those who have been documented with doing just that. However, most entrepreneurial businessmen in London also share those same traits. To actually do it takes something much more than that.'

'Opportunity,' said Kendrick, finger counting, 'motive and ruthlessness. Pine fits the bill on all three. Opportunity because he knew Scott well – he knew where he lived, his routine. He even met him in Scott's club just before he died. Motive because he knew Scott had evidence Kimberley Westfield was in his son's car some time before she was murdered, and ruthlessness because you don't get to be a billionaire unless you are one ruthless bastard.'

'Is that your considered view?' asked Varcy.

'Pretty much,' said Kendrick, draining what was left in his mug.

'Anyone else?'

No one spoke. 'Okay then,' said Varcy. 'For now, Pine is our number one suspect in the Scott murder.' He glanced over at Katz and Cole. 'What's the latest with Paul Renton?'

Cole stirred in his seat. 'Spends a lot of the day in the flat. He usually leaves it at about six o'clock most evenings. He visits various places. We've followed him to pubs, clubs, he's been to a lock-up garage in Bermondsey and, of course, he wheeled his granny back to the care home yesterday.'

'What's the lock-up for?' asked Varcy.

'We're not sure,' said Katz. 'He has his own key to it so if he's meeting someone in there it's not obvious.'

'Who's he meeting in the pubs and clubs?'

'Various types,' said Cole. 'They all look dodgy. Shaved heads, tattoos, pumped up bodies. The complete opposite of him in fact. I'm not sure what that says about his character.'

'It says he can handle himself,' said Hooper. 'He doesn't need tats, pumped pecs and a shaved head to prove it.'

'Any money change hands?' said Varcy.

Katz nodded. 'Some.'

'But you're not clear what it's for?'

'Nothing over and above what SOCA know. Protection, violence, maybe a bit of drugs.'

'Is he our killer?' asked Varcy.

'He's got as much chance as anyone else given what we know about him,' said Katz.

'Have you seen him with the Croatian girl?' said Varcy checking his notes.

'Marcianna?' said Katz. 'Nope.'

'Okay,' said Varcy. 'Keep watching him.' He turned to Hooper. 'See if you can find a link – any link, I don't care how tenuous – between Paul Renton and Charles Pine.'

Hooper nodded and made a note.

'What about Robert Fleet?' said Varcy.

'Still at it,' Kendrick replied. 'Can't contact him at all. We've been in his flat, hacked into his email account. I've had the boys look at his mobile phone records.'

'And?'

'He's disappeared. No activity at all.'

Varcy nodded. 'Keep at it. Any more questions?'

The attendees shook their heads.

'Okay,' said Varcy, 'let's get to it.'

45

The act I have rehearsed so often in my head is a symbolic gesture. And symbols are things. They have meaning. They stick in the mind and stir the emotions. My symbol will reflect my loss. The act – the last act I perform – will be how I'm remembered.

I gaze at the photograph I love so much. It is beautifully shot; the colours are as vivid as I remember them. The sand is smooth and the sea a cobalt blue. I stare at the green bucket in the foreground and think back to when the photograph was taken. I smell food cooking. Fried onions and grilled sausages. It mixes with the sweet smell of candyfloss. Then the sea breeze takes it all away. I hear a child's laughter. The feelings are so clear. So alive. It's as if I'm looking at the photograph for the very first time. I lose myself in it and a chunk of time passes clean away.

46

Rita Sidhu wore a hotel-issue towelling robe. She was sitting up on the bed, a stack of pillows behind her back. On the table at the side of her bed was a pile of DVDs. On her lap was a bunch of paperback novels. Varcy sat on a chair next to the bed.

'How you feeling?' he asked.

'Bored,' she replied.

'Do you have everything you need?'

'I *need* to get out.'

'No problem. Just tell Jeff and he'll go with you.'

Jeff was the police officer stationed in the corridor outside her room.

'How long will this go on for?'

'Hopefully not too long,' said Varcy.

'I'm restless,' said Rita. 'I can't help it.'

There was a pause. Then Varcy said, 'You were right about Kimberley Westfield, by the way. The camel hair fibres you analysed definitely came from her coat. Pine was certainly with her. Whether that equates to murder is another matter. Either way we're going to open up that investigation again.'

Rita buried her face in her hands. 'Then I helped cover it up,' she said.

Varcy said nothing and watched her. Her face was covered by her hands; she stayed hidden for a long moment. 'I'm sorry,' she breathed.

Varcy said, 'Why did you suspect the coat was hers?'

Rita slowly pulled her hands from her face. Varcy could see she had been crying. She had that bunged-up sound to her voice when she spoke. He offered to get her some water but she refused. She sniffed and swallowed and blinked. Her jeans were on a hanger on the back of the bathroom door. She pointed at them. 'Please pass them over to me,' she said.

Varcy unhooked them and handed them over. She pulled the newspaper article out of the pocket. The same one she had shown Meg the day before. The one she had first seen in her dentist's waiting room. She held it out to Varcy who took it and read it.

She said, 'The camel coat just stood out for me. It was such an unusual thing that my mind immediately jumped on it.'

'Weren't you tempted to go to the police after that?' asked Varcy.

'Not then,' said Rita. 'I thought it was just a coincidence. I had no suspicion that the analysis was dodgy in any way. In all honesty, even if I did I might well have done it anyway. I'd have done almost anything for Mark at that stage. '

There was silence whilst Varcy made some notes in his decision log.

'Is there any evidence that Scott was using the analysis to blackmail Charles Pine?' she asked eventually.

'Not yet,' said Varcy shaking his head. 'But we're working on it.' He flicked through his notebook, pausing to read a note he'd made. 'You went to see Pine's driver?'

She nodded.

'What's his name?'

'Frank Davies,' she said. 'Lives in Canning Town.'

Varcy nodded and made a note.

'What about Robert?' she asked.

'Again nothing,' Varcy replied. 'We can't raise him at all.'

She flopped back onto the pillows.

'Don't worry,' he said. 'We're very persistent. We'll find him.'

'I hope so,' she said.

His mobile phone burst into life. It was Kendrick.

'Gov'nor? Guess where Cole has just followed Paul Renton to?'

'Surprise me,' said Varcy.

'The Amonto Oil building on Tottenham Court Road.'

47

Varcy, Kendrick and Cole were in Varcy's office. Nobody sat. They all stood around the desk poring over the pictures. Paul Renton had been in the Amonto building for less than five minutes. Cole had positioned himself near the entrance and watched him go in, walk to the reception desk and speak to the woman behind it. She made a call and he took a seat in the welcome area. A few minutes passed. Then he got up and went to the desk once again. He spoke to the woman some more. Then he turned and walked back across the tiled lobby towards the exit.

Cole had laid out six black and white prints on the desk which gave a visual explanation of his description. The first showed Renton at the entrance of Amonto Oil. He wore a blue bomber jacket, grey jeans and white tennis shoes. His black hair was neatly combed. He had his hands thrust into his pockets. The next four shots were taken through the Amonto building's window. They were dark and grainy. Varcy could see Renton standing at the reception desk. Just beyond him was the woman Varcy recognised from his own visit. It was impossible to make out much detail. The final shot was of him leaving the building. Cole had moved his own position by then and shot it from across the road.

'Where did he go after?' asked Varcy.

'Katz is tracking,' said Kendrick. 'I'll call him.'

'You speak to the receptionist?' asked Varcy.

Cole shook his head.

'Probably best,' said Varcy. 'I don't want Pine alerted in any way. At least not yet. Did the receptionist give him anything? A package, an envelope, a note?'

'I could only see the back of him. It's possible she did, but I didn't see it.'

Varcy thought for a moment.

Kendrick had got through to Katz. 'Renton's back in his flat,' he said, holding the phone to his chest. 'What do you want us to do?'

'We'll bring him in,' said Varcy. 'Tell Katz to do nothing until we organise it.'

Kendrick nodded, pulled the phone back to his ear and quickly filled Katz in on the details. When he was finished he said, 'What now?'

Varcy said. 'Get the paperwork sorted. Then take four of your lads and do whatever it takes. Surprise him. I want his place searched. You know the sort of thing we're looking for. Then bring him here to the station. We'll go from there.'

'You're not coming?' asked Kendrick.

Varcy shook his head. 'I'm going over to Silvertown,' he said.

'Lucky you.' replied Kendrick, smiling.

* * *

293

After they had gone, Varcy picked up the six photographs and studied each one. He turned them around and held them up to the light as if a new angle would reveal more. Something wasn't right. He couldn't think what it was, but there was a feeling about it. Something he wasn't seeing.

'Gov'nor?'

He turned round and Hooper was standing in his doorway. Her work gear – white blouse, black trousers – was light years away from the cocktail dress she wore last night.

'Hello,' he said, 'I didn't see you there.'

'You okay?' she asked.

'Yes,' he said, 'I'm lost in thought that's all.' He tossed the photographs back onto the desk. 'How are you?'

'I'm great,' she said.

They watched each other in silence for a short moment.

Varcy said, 'I … er … I really enjoyed myself last night.'

'Me too,' she smiled.

'Maybe we could do it again sometime?'

She nodded. 'I'd like that.'

More silence. Then she held up a sheet of paper. 'The Mulsanne that Pine owned?' she said. 'The tracking bureau have located it.'

'Ah,' said Varcy. 'Where?'

'West Brompton,' she replied. 'Belongs to a chiropractor.'

'Good. Have we commandeered it?'

'For a short time,' she said. 'A couple of SOCOs are there now.'

'Okay, well done.'

She nodded. 'No problem.'

'Let me know what happens.'

She nodded again.

Varcy opened his mouth as if to say something, then closed it again.

'Gov'nor?' said Hooper.

Varcy smiled awkwardly. 'I was going to ask if you were free this weekend?'

She nodded and smiled. 'I could be.'

48

Chedworth Close lay a couple of hundred yards south of the Canning Town flyover. It jutted off from the main drag and formed an inverted 'L' that wound up back towards the A13. It was full of low cost, terraced housing, with yellow brick fascias and bins full of rubbish. It had overgrown patches of grass, children's bicycles against railings and cars parked bumper to bumper at the curbside. Once the possession of the local council, most of the properties were now in the hands of tenants who'd bought them at low prices using basic-rate mortgages from the government.

One such property was owned by Frank Davies. Varcy had asked the back office to put together a report on the man. It read like a CV. It had his name, address, and a sparse record of his employment history over the last ten years. Davies had been in various jobs until he became a driver for a mini cab firm eleven years before. He moved from that into chauffeuring. He worked for a company that had a bunch of contracts with high-end service users, including embassy staff, media people and TV celebs. He was never late, was always respectful and immaculately turned out. This came to the notice of Charles Pine who was looking for a driver for his youngest son, James. Charles Pine thought Frank would be the right fit for his son. Hard-working, polite and steady – all the things James Pine wasn't.

Frank had been working for James Pine for just over a year when a tragic accident occurred. He had knocked down and killed a child on Cheapside while driving Pine's Bentley. Since that time, he had been under psychiatric care at King's College Hospital, battling post-traumatic stress issues and taking a battery of prescription pills that altered his brain's chemistry. Pills to make him feel better about life. He was unemployed and received incapacity benefit from the local dole office.

When Varcy rang the bell, a woman answered. She was pale and petite with mousey brown hair cut short. She had no make up on her face and nothing on her feet either. She had a small child with her, a girl of about three years old, who clung to the woman's leg and drank juice from a plastic cup.

'I'm looking for Frank Davies?' said Varcy.

She nodded.

'I'm Varcy,' he said. 'Terry Varcy from the Met Police.'

She still said nothing.

'Don't worry,' he said, 'it's nothing bad. I want to ask Frank some questions, that's all.'

She looked him up and down for a long moment as if debating whether to trust him. Finally she opened the door properly and said softly, 'You'd better come in.'

The woman padded across the laminate flooring of the narrow hallway and pushed open a door to the right. 'This way,' she said, leading Varcy into a small living room, oblong in shape and painted light blue. There was a TV in the furthest corner tuned to daytime television and an armchair facing it in which a man whom Varcy assumed was Frank Davies sat.

'Frank,' the woman said. 'This is a policeman.'

Frank turned slowly and glanced up at Varcy. Varcy knew Frank was thirty-eight but he looked a lot older than that. Maybe fifteen years older. His hair was thinning and his eyes were puffy in his bloated face. Pudgy arms emerged from a thin, green tee-shirt which strained hard to hold his bulging stomach. He wore knee-length shorts and a pair of plastic flip-flops. Varcy moved towards him and extended his hand. 'Hello, Frank,' he said.

Frank smiled.

Varcy glanced back at the woman. She too gave him a tired smile. 'Would you like a tea or coffee?' she asked.

'Neither,' said Varcy, shaking his head. 'Thank you all the same.'

She nodded then moved out of the room, closing the door behind her. Varcy perched on the end of the sofa and rested his briefcase between his feet. Frank looked back at him. He was passive, neither nervous nor excited, his face set in a crooked smile. Varcy thought Frank had a kind face. A face you could warm to. A face you could trust.

'Frank, I've come to ask you some questions about James Pine,' Varcy began.

Frank nodded as though this was the most normal thing in the world.

'About the time you worked for him.'

Frank nodded again.

Varcy pulled his briefcase up onto his lap. He groped inside and pulled out a coloured photograph. 'First, I'd like to know if you recognise this young lady.'

He held up a picture of Kimberley Westfield. It was one that he had discovered in her cold-case file. In it Kimberley was young, fresh faced, and best of all she was wearing the camel hair coat in which she was found murdered.

Frank nodded gently. 'I've been asked this before,' he said. 'You're the fourth one.'

'I know, 'said Varcy. 'Sorry to keep on.'

'I don't mind,' said Frank. 'I've always said that I *think* I know her, but I'm not completely certain of it. James Pine had a lot of women. I'd take him and his dates to wherever they wanted to go. There was a string of them. I think this girl was among them but I can't be one hundred per cent sure.'

Varcy nodded. 'I understand that and I'm grateful for your honesty.'

Frank smiled.

'What about this woman?' said Varcy, reaching into the briefcase again and pulling out a picture of Rita Sidhu. 'Do you recognise her?'

Frank squinted at the print. 'She came here yesterday,' he said, 'asking the same sort of questions you are. All about Pine and the girl in the picture. I told her what I've just told you.'

'And you'd not seen her before then?'

He shook his head.

'And this guy?' asked Varcy, pulling out a shot of John Scott.

'He came here too,' said Frank, taking the picture from Varcy and studying it. 'Again all about that young lady.'

'What questions did he ask?'

'Did I know her? Where was Pine on the night of her death? How was Pine acting in recent times? All sorts of stuff.'

Frank gave the photo back to Varcy.

'So you were still working for Pine when this man came to see you?' said Varcy.

Frank nodded.

'Did you tell Pine about this?'

Frank shook his head. 'He seemed genuine. A nice man. He asked if I'd keep our conversation a secret from Pine. The murder was terrible. I've got two girls of my own. I gave my word.'

Varcy put the photographs back in his briefcase. 'You mentioned the accident,' he said. 'Was that the one involving the child?'

Frank nodded. 'Philip Greenwood. That was the kid's name.'

'What happened?' asked Varcy.

Frank looked beyond him for a moment. His eyes moved rapidly, back and forth, across the wall as though he was watching a movie in his head. As though he was seeing it all again. 'I was driving Pine to a meeting,' he said slowly. 'He was angry that it was taking so long. There was some open road up by Cheapside. I accelerated into it. Not too fast. Somewhere around thirty-five I suppose. The next thing I saw was a shape. That's the best way I can describe it. It came from my left. The rest was instinct. I slammed on the breaks and heard a dull thud. I got out and the kid was on the road by the front tyre. He was lying on his side like he was sleeping. I knelt beside him and stroked his head. Then I saw the blood and clear stuff coming from his ears. Like he was bleeding from the inside. I told him it was all okay. That I was getting help. But he didn't hear me. Then his eyes fluttered and I thought he might wake up. But he didn't. I just knelt there stroking him. It seemed to go on for ages.'

'It must have been horrific,' said Varcy.

'He'd been playing with a tennis ball on the pavement,' said Frank quietly. 'It had got away from him and he charged into the road to retrieve it. He was just being a kid.'

Frank went quiet. Varcy watched the anguish in his face. The feelings must have flooded back. Feelings impossible to understand by anyone but him. His eyes went red and watery. He dabbed them with the back of his hand.

Varcy asked, 'What did Pine do when all this was going on?'

Frank sniffed and swallowed. 'Nothing,' he said, shaking his head. 'He just watched, then he walked away. I never saw him again.'

'You know what happened to him, I suppose?'

Frank nodded. 'Hanged himself.'

'Are you sorry?'

Frank shook his head slowly. 'He was a little shit. I'm not sorry at all.'

49

Today I have a feeling of liberation. A lightness in my chest that I haven't experienced for a long time. The time to finish what I started some time ago has arrived. I have three tasks to perform today before I can truly be free. The first is easy enough. It will not be a difficult thing to do. Surprise is the key. There will be a slight emotional component to this one. After all I'm human. But overcoming emotion, detaching from its clutches, is a skill I have mastered. It sets me apart and sets me free.

I am in St John's Wood. A suburb of West London. The block of low-rise flats is positioned in an arc of four. These units are occupied by young, professional men and women who work in the city of London. I have called ahead so my host is expecting me. My host is a man called Mark Fox. He was once the boyfriend of Rita Sidhu. He buzzes me through the front entrance and I bound up the two flights of stairs to the flat. I tap a couple of times and he answers.

'Hey,' he says smiling. 'Long time no see.'

'How's life?' I reply.

'Good,' he says. 'Come on in.'

He turns and walks back into the flat. I follow him over the threshold and reach into my back pocket where I keep the stub knife.

'I've got a pot of coffee on,' he says. 'Want some?'

'Sounds good,' I reply.

His back is towards me now and I fix my gaze at a spot on his neck just below the skull. This is an area of the cervical spine where the first vertebra supports the head. It's where the brain stem is thickest. A clean thrust to this area – if delivered with absolute precision – will kill in a moment. There will be no suffering if it is accurate. I centre myself quickly.

He is now several steps ahead of me.

'I didn't expect to hear from you again,' he says over his shoulder.

I spring forwards and thrust the blade upwards in a trajectory that mirrors the angle of the facet joints at the back of his spine. The steel pierces his skin easily then slips into his soft tissue and between the spinous processes. I press it in to the hilt and it punctures the spinal cord. He tips forwards like a freshly cut tree. His face smacks into the floor. I withdraw the blade and move around to the front of him. I check his pulse. It is almost gone.

I remove a plastic bag from my front pocket and place the stub knife into it. I will clean the shaft later.

I check the pulse once more. It has disappeared.

I leave the apartment and close the door behind me.

50

Kendrick was in Varcy's office. Both of them were poring over the SOCA case file on Paul Renton. There were pages and pages of it. Photographs, tracking reports, profiles. Detail enough to last a researcher hours and hours.

Renton had been in police custody for exactly one hour. Kendrick had organised the arrest. It passed off without incident. Renton was in the shower when they burst in. They had him in the back of the van within five minutes. Varcy had alerted SOCA to what had happened and they dispatched a couple of their people to Bishopsgate to take part in some of the questioning. Varcy was happy enough about that. His main objective was to establish a link between Renton and Charles Pine. They could have Renton for as long as they needed after that.

Renton had requested a solicitor as soon as he arrived at the station. He was legally aided to do so. Kendrick had already met the lawyer for the obligatory round of disclosure. Kendrick told him that Renton was part of a gang wanted in connection with drug trafficking in the West London area, a gang that was thought to be responsible for some ten million pounds of traffic over the last twelve months; that he had received and passed on stolen goods, and that there was strong evidence that he was complicit in the gangland killing of one David Keen – a man who had been found murdered out at Tilbury – three years before.

All of this was true. Kendrick did not mention the Scott and Townsend case. Varcy wanted to keep that to himself.

Katz appeared in the office doorway. He was jacketless and had his sleeves rolled to the elbows. His hair was gelled back and there was a scattering of sweat beads on his forehead. 'He's ready, Gov'nor,' he said.

Varcy nodded and, tucking the grey folder on his desk under his arm said, 'Let's go.'

They made their way through the back office towards the staircase that led to a suite of interrogation rooms below. Renton was in 1A, a featureless cube with a desk and two chairs either side. There was recording equipment on the desk, writing pads and black biros. Renton sat easily in a chair on the far side of the desk. He was with the lawyer Kendrick had spoken to earlier. Renton showed no obvious signs of stress or discomfort. His hands were snuggled in his lap and he stared down at them not looking up as Varcy and Kendrick entered. The lawyer stood and nodded a greeting.

Varcy made a big play of messing with his seat; adjusting position and ensuring it was comfortable on his back. Then he stood up again and removed his jacket which Kendrick took and lovingly hung on the back of his chair. Varcy rolled up his sleeves and checked his file. Kendrick asked if anyone wanted tea or coffee. Varcy said he'd love a tea; Renton and his lawyer declined. Kendrick went to the door and asked the custody officer to do the honours before returning and removing his own jacket. Varcy watched as he rolled up his sleeves so that they matched his own. When satisfied, Kendrick nodded to Varcy and Varcy budged his seat closer to the desk. The whole play lasted no longer than a few minutes but it was enough to break Renton's pattern. By the time Varcy and Kendrick were ready, they had his full attention.

Kendrick worked the recording equipment and stated the date, the time, the location and the parties present. Varcy opened his folder and launched into a long diatribe. It centred mainly on Renton's criminal activity with the drug gang. He had photographic evidence, witness statements, tracking information. He had facts about his movements, who he was associating with, statements from those who had known him in the past. There were months of SOCA work to go through. Renton listened but was reluctant to say anything at all. He would mumble 'no comment' or 'I don't remember' or 'it wasn't me'. His lawyer, a fat, bald man with a flushed complexion, sat nodding or shaking his head at his client depending on whether he felt an answer was appropriate or not. Varcy continued for two hours without a break. Finally, he pulled out a picture of Charles Pine and showed it to Renton.

'Do you know him?' he asked.

Renton looked at it briefly and shook his head.

'That a no?' asked Varcy.

'No,' said Renton.

'What about this?' he asked. It was a photograph of the Amonto Building on Tottenham Court Road. 'Recognise it?'

Renton said, 'No.'

Then Varcy produced the shots Cole had taken earlier that day showing Renton entering and leaving the Amonto building.

'That's you going into the building and here you are leaving it again. They were taken earlier today,' Varcy said.

Renton said nothing.

'Why did you go in there?' Varcy asked.

'I must have lost my bearings,' said Renton.

Varcy leant on the desk and cupped his chin in his hands. 'We've spoken to the receptionist. She told us you asked for Charles Pine by name. That you said you had a meeting scheduled with him.'

'I can't remember,' said Renton.

'Really?' said Varcy.

Renton remained silent.

'The more you can't remember, the longer you stay,' said Varcy, stuffing the papers into his file. He stood up and asked Kendrick to close down the session. Kendrick did so and turned the recorder off. Then he went to fetch the custody officer, whom Varcy told to take Renton back to his cell.

'We'll continue after I've had a nice long lunch,' Varcy said. 'If there's time, that is. Or maybe we'll do it tomorrow, or the day after that. There's enough good stuff in this file to keep us going for weeks. '

The custody officer moved forwards to escort Renton from the room.

'He called me,' Renton said suddenly.

Varcy glanced at Kendrick who turned the recorder back on.

'Repeat that,' said Varcy.

'He called me,' said Renton.

'Who did?' asked Varcy.

'Charles Pine,' said Renton. 'Or his people did. I've never met him so I don't know his voice.'

'When did he call?'

'This morning.'

'He called your cell phone?'

Renton nodded.

'What did he say?'

Renton shrugged. 'That he had a job he wanted me to do.'

'What sort of job?'

'He didn't say.'

'He gave you the Amonto address?'

Renton nodded.

Varcy thought for a moment. 'Where's your phone?' he asked at last.

'They took it from me when I came in,' said Renton.

Varcy thought some more. 'We'll carry on later,' he said.

51

Varcy had picked up a tuna baguette from the Pret on Bishopsgate. He sat in his office with his feet up on a low stool and munched away at it. Kendrick pushed open Varcy's door with his backside and shuffled in. He carried two mugs of steaming tea, one in each hand. Clamped in his mouth was half an uneaten ham sandwich. He set the teas on Varcy's desk, flopped into the seat opposite and tore off a slice of sandwich with his teeth.

There was food silence.

Varcy's mind began to process what had taken place. How it all fitted together and what it meant. They had checked Renton's phone and found that it had recorded the incoming call, that may or may not have come from Pine. It had been made at 8.10am that day from a cell phone. Varcy had rung it back and got a generic answer message. Then he had asked Kendrick to speak to the telecommunication geeks over at central office and organise some tracking. They were quick to come back. There was no signal emitting from it which meant it was either turned off or it had been destroyed. Kendrick then asked them to find out who the phone was registered to and how long it had been in commission. They were quick there too.

It was registered to a private company. Devflow Ltd. The phone had been registered that morning at a cell phone retailers on Roman Road in Bethnal Green. The company was fake. So was the address given for it. Kendrick dispatched one of his boys to talk to the owner of the shop. Perhaps he might remember who'd bought it.

The pressing questions in Varcy's mind were all to do with Charles Pine. He wanted to know what made this man tick. What motivated his actions. He turned his thoughts to the dump list he had compiled when he first came away from Barry Townsend's murder scene. The surprise, the feelings of disbelief he had sensed when he looked at Barry. Then the opposite reaction to Scott's death. The acceptance. The inevitability of it. Two murders with the same MO, but with a completely different reaction from the victims.

He took a bite out of the baguette and mentally joined up the dots. Formed a scenario that fitted, one that satisfied the questions. He thought of it like a square. A square of personalities. Four people connected by the lines that joined the points of the square; that came together to cause mayhem. The points of the square were the dead people. John Scott, Barry Townsend, James Pine and Kimberley Westfield. In the centre of the square sat Rita Sidhu and Charles Pine. Varcy tipped his chair forwards and laid the baguette on the desk. He reached forwards for his tea and took a long sip.

'Can I put a scenario to you?' he asked Kendrick. 'A framework that fits around this.'

Kendrick was chewing vigorously. 'Go on then.'

'It's not completely right,' said Varcy. 'There's something missing from it. Some important component I can't get to yet. However, it fits much of the criteria. It starts with Scott. I think he had seen Kimberley Westfield together with James Pine at some point. Maybe on the night of her murder or maybe a night or two before that. Either on the street or in Pine's Bentley. That isn't much of a stretch. Scott spent much of his time in Westminster, so did she. He in the House of Lords, she with her job as a researcher in the Commons. They might not have moved in the same circles, but they shared the same space – the same air. So, Scott sees Pine and Westfield together. Then Westfield is murdered and a police investigation swings into action. Time goes on and they draw a blank. Scott wonders if they've spoken to Pine. Yet he says nothing. He doesn't alert anyone. The case file never mentions Pine. The statement readers never record anything attributed to him. So he keeps quiet. However, he's not inactive. He is so convinced that Pine is involved, that he gets access to Pine's car to take samples for a forensic analysis some six weeks after she's murdered. Who does a thing like that? Why not just go to the police anonymously and tip them off? Or write to them, or email them from a phoney address? There's only one plausible answer to that. He wanted to use the information in some way. Maybe as a weapon, or a bargaining tool. God knows he had enough reason to be angry at the way Charles Pine had treated him in the past. Maybe he was planning to get his own back.'

Kendrick pushed the last of the sandwich into his mouth then snatched up his mug and took a couple of swallows. 'Go on.'

'So, it's confirmed that Westfield's camel hair coat was in Pine's car. Now he has valuable information. But he has something else too. He has accomplices. Rita Sidhu, who carried out the analysis, and his nephew – her boyfriend – who got her to do it.'

Kendrick nodded.

'Okay, so he's got the information. What then? I think he tries to blackmail Charles Pine in some way. Tells him what he has on his son and that he's prepared to use it if necessary. Maybe that's why he sent me the email I never read. Maybe he knew there was spyware on his PC and that his stalker – Pine in this scenario – would realise he was serious about using what he knew. He certainly had plenty of motive. Pine did him out of millions of pounds on a deal involving a pharmaceutical company Scott once owned.'

'But then James Pine dies,' said Kendrick.

Varcy rested the mug on his chest and continued, 'I think James Pine killing himself was a camel's back moment for his father. His golden child was gone. When I interviewed him he told me that James was *his baby*. That's how he thought of him. Then he dies. Worse still, he commits suicide. And why? Because he got wind of what Scott had on him. How is that going to make his father feel? Daniel Nash told us that people who hire killers may feel a great injustice has been done to them.

That's how they square it with their conscience. Pine senior fits the bill completely.'

'So he hires Renton to do it?' said Kendrick.

'Maybe,' said Varcy.

'What about Townsend?' asked Kendrick. 'Where does he fit in?'

Varcy shook his head. 'He was a mistake, I think. The target was Sidhu herself. If Pine knew that Scott had information on his son, it's reasonable to assume he knew where he got it from.'

Varcy leant forwards and placed his tea back on its coaster. He picked up his desk phone and dialled a number. Then he laid the handset on its side and pressed 'speaker' on the phone so that both he and Kendrick could hear what was said. The ring tone kicked in and was answered on the second round.

'Hello?' said Varcy. 'Is that you, Rita?'

'Yes,' Sidhu answered. 'Hi Inspector.'

'How are you?' he asked.

'Okay,' she replied.

'Hotel all right? Are they looking after you?'

'Yes. All okay, thanks. How are things progressing?'

'Well,' said Varcy. 'But you may be able to help me. On the morning of Barry's murder, you were in your lab, weren't you?'

'Yes,' she replied.

'What time did you get there?'

'Early,' she said. '6.30-ish. We had a sales seminar to present at 8.00. We were all in early.'

'What time did you leave the flat to make it in for then?'

'About 5.30, 5.45,' she replied.

'What time do you normally leave the flat?'

'Around 6.30. I like to get into the lab before 7.00.'

Varcy glanced at Kendrick.

'As I thought,' he said.

There was silence.

'Are you still there?' she asked.

'Yes, yes,' he said. 'That's fine. I'll speak to you later today.'

He replaced the receiver, picked up his tea again and drained it. 'So there you have it,' he said. 'The killer stakes out the flat. He knows when she leaves it and when she returns to it. He knows her pattern. He probably knows about Barry too, but I doubt if he's bothered about that. He intends to strike early at a time just before Rita leaves the flat. If he's been watching what goes on, he'll know Barry doesn't live there. What time was Barry's murder?'

'The medics say around 6.00.'

'Fits well,' said Varcy. 'The killer arrives at Rita's flat. He gets access just the way he planned – I think he must have had duplicate keys, by the way – and prepares to kill her.'

'But she's not there,' said Kendrick. 'She's left early.'

'Right,' said Varcy. 'There's no sign of her. The boyfriend is there. He's soundo in the bedroom. But not her. What's happened? The guy's been thorough. He's staked everything out. Maybe for weeks. He *knows* when she leaves. Yet on the date he commits to the job, she's gone. I think his mind goes into overdrive. He's paranoid about security. In his line of work he has to be. Did someone tip her off? If so, who? The guy who gave him the job in the first place? Or someone else? Maybe she got a phone call? Or an email? Maybe she was just told to leave early that morning and not given a reason why. He must have debated what to do. His security had been compromised. Maybe the boyfriend knows. Maybe he overheard a conversation or saw her talking to someone unusual. Maybe he knows her email address. Vital information that is essential to this man's safety. He makes the decision to find out.'

'And Barry pays the price?'

'Something like that,' said Varcy.

'So it's Pine,' said Kendrick, lacing his fingers behind his neck. 'I like it. It fits well.'

'But there's something else,' replied Varcy, shaking his head. 'Something not quite right.'

'Something like what?'

'The premise I think.'

'The what?'

'The premise,' repeated Varcy, pulling his feet off the stool and shunting his chair towards his PC. He Googled two names together. Frank Davies and Philip Greenwood. The search threw up two dozen hits. One was a local newspaper. He clicked the hyperlink and a copy of the page they ran two years before loaded. A child's face filled half of the screen. Next to this was the report. The banner read: *Tragic Death Of Young Boy on Cheapside*.

There was a knock on Varcy's door and Katz popped his head in. 'Got a minute, Gov'nor?'

'Of course,' said Varcy. 'Come on in.'

Katz looked as if he'd been running. He was flushed in the face and breathing hard.

'You okay?' asked Varcy.

'I'm fine,' he said. 'I'm a bit excited that's all. The IT techies have tracked down the source of the spyware on John Scott's computer. His stalker's UUID used a British Telecom network to log in and view Scott's machine. They traced it back from there. The machine is registered to Amonto Oil. Most of the logins hit the BT network from a location in central London.'

'Tottenham Court Road,' said Varcy.

'The last login was recorded on 15th July.'

'When was Scott murdered?' asked Varcy.

'The 16th July,' replied Kendrick.

'A day later,' said Varcy.

'Fits perfectly,' said Kendrick.

Varcy nodded.

'It's Pine,' said Kendrick. 'It's got to be. He's organised the fucking lot.'

52

Rita Sidhu is in a hotel just off Tottenham Court Road. She has been there for two days. There is a policeman on guard outside her room and one down in the lobby. The danger she is in has now been realised by all. Hardly surprising given the evidence. I was prepared for this eventuality and have a plan in place. I am on my way to the lock-up. Opposite me on the tube are Charlie and Max, two delightful boys. I have bought them ice-cream and colouring pads and we are all on a big adventure. Their mother – Rita Sidhu's friend, Meg – is back in her flat. I struck when the children were at school. I confronted their mother, told her what I intended to do and then accompanied her to collect the kids. Back in the flat, I settled the children in the living room and injected their mother with an anaesthetic. I tied and gagged her and left her laid on her side in the recovery position. Given her body weight, I calculate the drug will keep her under for thirteen hours. Ample time for what I need to do.

The children were unsure of me at first but they soon settled down. I am very good with children. It's one of my strengths. I know that these two cuties are probably the closest flesh and blood relationship Rita Sidhu has in her life. I know she will do anything for them. I understand that kind of devotion. It will be very useful to me.

53

Bringing in Charles Pine was a simple affair. Varcy and Kendrick went to the Amonto building on the off chance he would be there. Varcy wanted to keep it casual. As if they had simply dropped in. Pine was an intelligent man and would respond to a grown-up approach to all this. They spoke to the same woman at the reception – the air hostess – who told them that Pine was just about to go off to a meeting. She phoned upstairs to his office. Madeline, his PA, was less then happy about any interference with his schedule. After a twenty-minute wait in Amonto's reception area, they were permitted a small window of Pine's time. Inside his office, Pine stood behind his desk. He was getting into a jacket. He pulled it over his shoulders and tapped it down at the front. Then he fastened the top button so it hung neatly at the waist. He looked impressive. Expensive and confident.

'Inspector,' he said cheerily.

'Mr Pine,' said Varcy, moving forwards. 'A pleasure to see you again. This is my colleague, Detective Inspector Kendrick.'

Kendrick nodded curtly.

Pine eyed him for a fleeting moment, then

turned his gaze back to Varcy. 'How can I help you this time?' he said.

'Well,' answered Varcy, 'I'm hoping you'll be able to help a lot. In fact I'm banking on it.'

'Fire away,' said Pine.

'We've a lot to get through,' said Varcy. 'I'm afraid a quick-fire meeting won't do it.'

'I don't understand,' said Pine.

'We're going to have to do it all down at the station.'

'The police station?'

Varcy nodded.

Pine's brow creased into a furrow. 'Are you arresting me?'

Varcy smiled. 'I'm simply inviting you to come to the station to answer some pressing questions.'

Pine thrust his hands into his pockets. 'I asked you a question. Am I under arrest?'

'No,' said Varcy casually, 'but I can place you under arrest, if you'd prefer.'

Pine checked his watch before looking back at Varcy. He thought for a moment, then went to his chair and sat down. Leaning his elbows on the table, he clasped his fingers together. Then he rested his chin on his fingers and asked: 'Why?'

Varcy sat silent while he watched Pine. He observed his stance, his intonation. Trying to size-up what was going through his mind, how he was processing it all. Had he expected this or was it a total surprise? Guilt was almost always obvious to see. In fact, Varcy could spot it even when it was well concealed. With Pine, the signals were ill-defined.

'Because all roads lead back to you, Mr Pine,' said Varcy finally. 'Everywhere we turn, there you are. Your name appears all over this investigation. We have no choice.'

Pine remained still for a moment. Then he lifted the receiver on his desk phone. 'Madeline,' he said. 'Cancel all my appointments and call Johnston Stone. I need to talk to him urgently. He can reach me on my mobile.'

He replaced the receiver and sat back in his chair.

'Stone is your lawyer?' asked Varcy.

Pine stood up. 'The best in the business.' he said.

* * *

Johnston Stone was tall and broad. His hair was cropped tight to his skull and his face was wide, square and black. He wore a silver-grey Savile Row suit with a baby blue shirt, fastened with a Fiorio necktie. In his right hand he held a black document case. He was standing next to the water cooler in the reception of Bishopsgate police station waiting for Pine.

Varcy spotted him as soon as he walked in. Stone smiled at Pine and moved forwards, ignoring both Varcy and Kendrick who flanked his client. The two men shook hands.

'How are you feeling?' Stone asked. His voice was clear and deep.

Pine shrugged. 'I've felt better.'

'I bet,' said Stone.

He turned to Varcy and Kendrick. 'Which of you is senior?'

'I am,' said Varcy.

'I want disclosure immediately.'

Varcy nodded. 'Of course.'

Varcy led them through a set of double doors. To the left was a staircase which went to the holding cells. Kendrick glanced at Varcy briefly, but Varcy shook his head and continued through another set of doors to the open space of computers, desks and police staff beyond. Leading them into his office, he pulled the cord on the blinds and the light from the open office area gushed in.

'Take a seat, gentlemen,' said Varcy.

'We've no time to sit,' said Stone. 'Tell me why you're holding my client.'

'We're not holding him,' said Varcy. 'He's free to go any time he wishes.'

'You've not arrested him?' said Stone.

'No.'

'In that case we're leaving,' said Stone.

'Why?' asked Varcy.

'Why not?'

'Because I will then arrange to arrest him,' said Varcy. 'It will waste everyone's time and I assume Mr Pine would rather not be arrested.'

'Arrest him on what grounds?' asked Stone.

'On suspicion of murder,' said Varcy.

'Whose murder?'

'Two murders actually,' said Varcy. 'A Lord John Scott, whom your client knows well, and a Mr Barry Townsend, whom he doesn't.'

Pine snorted and shook his head.

'Evidence?' said Stone.

'I'll present it as we go,' said Varcy.

'Do you intend to do it under caution?'

'Not initially,' said Varcy. 'However, if your client cannot answer our questions satisfactorily, then we will happily do so.'

'Then you'll get nothing from my client,' said Stone.

'That's up to you,' said Varcy. 'It infers guilt in the courts.'

'Not if my client gives evidence,' said Stone.

'True,' said Varcy. 'But aren't we getting a little ahead of ourselves?'

Stone stared out of the window. Finally he said, 'Give us five minutes alone.'

Varcy nodded and glanced at Kendrick. Both men stepped out of the office and made their way to the kitchen.

'Pompous bastard,' said Kendrick.

'Stone or Pine?' asked Varcy.

Kendrick smiled. 'Both.'

Kendrick snatched a mug from the cupboard above the sink and held it under the tap until it was full. He drank it down in one hit. 'I'd like to be a fly on the wall in there,' he said.

'They're debating how to play it,' said Varcy, folding his arms across his chest. 'I'm hoping there'll be a bit of quarrelling. Stone will want to control everything. So will Pine. Stone won't want him to say anything. Pine will have difficulty with that. We haven't cautioned Pine which will relax Stone a bit, but confuse him too. He won't want to give anything away. The only benefit in talking in an interview – under caution or not – is that we might decide not to prosecute. However, Stone must assume we have some pretty compelling evidence or we wouldn't have taken this step. So non-prosecution is a remote possibility. That will make him nervous again. If I were him, I'd want a non-caution approach in return for my client doing some talking. I'd be encouraging him to talk, only in general terms. No specifics, just in case he messes up.'

'So why not caution him right now?'

'Because we'll get more out of Pine this way. I want to get under his skin a bit. Besides there's something wrong with this case.'

'You said that before,' said Kendrick.

'I know,' said Varcy, 'I can't quite put my finger on it.'

'Seems compelling enough to me.'

Varcy nodded. 'In a sense it is – but it doesn't completely add up. Besides, I bet Pine will have a watertight alibi.'

'You think?'

'I'd be surprised if he hasn't,' said Varcy. 'He's a planner. He plots strategies and implements them.'

'Then he's delusional,' said Kendrick.

Varcy shook his head. 'No. Something else completely.'

54

The lock-up is full of bright light and colour. I have decorated it with balloons and bunting and low hanging lanterns. I have a table that is covered with a white tablecloth. On it are plastic plates and cups. All of them are printed with cartoon characters. There are sandwiches and crisps and cakes arranged in swirls. There is a large jug of orange squash and bowls of coloured jelly. I have pop music turned up high and Charlie, Max and I are wearing party hats. They are eating voraciously. I fuss around them ensuring they are having the greatest fun. The party is to celebrate their first ever visit to this part of London and to take their minds off leaving their mother. It will not be for long. Children are so innocent and vulnerable. I want to make their time with me as carefree as possible.

Every so often, I glance up at the large photograph on the lock-up wall. My own child stares back at me. He is squatting in the sand. A green, plastic bucket sits between his feet and a matching plastic spade is in his hand. He shovels the sand. I took the photo myself. I called out to him a second before I depressed the shutter. His face speaks of so much. It captures his personality in a way that no other photograph has managed to do. I love it. I love him.

'May I have some more cake?' asks Charlie, breaking my train of thought.

'Of course you can,' I say, cutting him a large slice of chocolate sponge. He takes up a plastic spoon and tucks in. In many ways this is the perfect way for me to bring it all to an end. I feel I have come full circle. These two children smiling and happy while my own child stares down at us, as if he is part of the fun. For a short period I am completely immersed in the scene.

Then the alarm on my watch beeps a rhythmical beat and I check the time: 6.10pm. It is time to make the call. I leave the children and move to the corner of the lock-up. On one of my shelves is a pay-as-you-go mobile. It is fitted with a voice changer. I dial the number and she answers on the second ring.

'Rita Sidhu?' I ask.

'Yes,' she says.

'Are you listening carefully, because I won't repeat what I am about to tell you?'

'Who is this?' she asks.

I mute the phone and deactivate the voice changer. Then I call Charlie over. I hunch down so that I am level with him. 'Would you like to talk to your Auntie Rita?' I smile.

He nods.

Sidhu is still talking. I hear her say, 'Hello? Hello? Who is this?'

I hold the phone to Charlie's ear and unmute it.

'It's Charlie,' he says.

There is a moment's pause while she processes his voice. 'Charlie? Darling, is that you?'

'Reet-Reet,' he says.

I take the phone from his ear and mute it again. Then I lead Charlie by the hand back to the table. 'Look inside that tin,' I say.

On the table is a tin with a pop-off lid. Charlie opens it and gasps. It is full of Haribos. He yells, 'Max, look!' Then he gropes inside and pulls out a handful. Max is mid-jelly, but stops and jumps off his seat to run to his brother.

I activate the voice change once again and unmute the phone. Then I say: 'If you want to see Charlie and Max again, here's what to do. Wait until 10.00pm. Unhook the receiver of your room phone and place it on the bed. Then go outside your hotel room and tell the policeman on duty – his name is Jeff – that his wife, Mary, is on the phone asking for him. He will be confused for a moment. He will not expect her to call your room. Just smile and be patient. Jeff is very close to his wife so he will want to take the call. Wait until he is fully inside the room, then shut the door, run to the end of the corridor, turn right then a sharp left into the fire exit. Descend to street level. You will be in Adeline Place. Run south to Great Russell Street, then east towards Russell Square. From there, take the tube to the IMDB labs. Go straight to your own lab and wait. If you mention our conversation to anyone else – I don't care who it is – neither you nor your friend will see the children again. If you need any proof of my credentials, then think of Barry Townsend and John Scott, then just recently Robert Fleet and Mark Fox. I killed them all.'

I hear her gasp.

Then I click off and return to my guests.

55

Pine, Stone, Varcy and Kendrick were down in the
interrogation suite. Renton had been moved from
1A to 2A, where he was being questioned by SOCA.
They had enough on Renton to charge him. Not
with the Scott and Townsend murder – Varcy was
still working on that one – but with a string of
violent offences. Varcy fully expected them to do so
long before the twenty-four-hour deadline expired.

His plan now was to press Pine as far as he
could. Make him uneasy. Maybe he would tell him
something valuable. Supply the missing piece of
information that was driving him nuts. Something
to tie it all together. The case against Pine was
decent without him slipping up. After all, they had
established a link between him and Renton,
between him and the spy software on Scott's
computer, between him and unscrupulous
business dealings that adversely affected Scott.
He'd had the opportunity to organise the hits on
Scott and the mistaken one on Townsend, and he
had the motive too. John Scott had damning
evidence on his son. *His baby*. Rita Sidhu had
helped supply it. That was motive enough. The
murder of Townsend when the real target was
Sidhu was more of a leap though. To get a jury to

go for that would take a lot of effort and a bit of luck. Varcy didn't like luck. If he couldn't nail it completely, he preferred to wait until something happened that meant he could. So the case against Pine was robust, but not robust enough.

Pine had taken his jacket off and loosened his tie. His face was redder than Varcy had seen it. Stone's face was impassive. His hands were clasped before him in a controlled, waiting position. Varcy had a file on the desk in front of him. It was full of photos, reports and documentation. He had taken what he wanted for this first round of interrogation from the stack of material the team had collected. He wanted to have Hooper in with him for the questions about Pine's business dealings – and in particular those with Scott and the guy found in the Ashford lake – but Cole told him she had gone off to Companies House to check on a handful of firms that Pine had a stake in. He would wait for her before he proceeded with that particular line of questioning. For the first part of the interview he would content himself with what he could sink his teeth into. He pulled a sheet of paper from the file. Katz called it a data sheet. It had a lot of technical jargon on it concerning a software application known as *I-Spy*. *I-Spy* was a bespoke software programme that was adaptable to the demands of the user. In a nutshell it allowed remote viewing of someone else's computer. Keystrokes, passwords, emails and browsing histories all recorded. Varcy tossed it towards Pine and said, 'Do you know what this is?'

Pine glanced at it. So did Stone. Varcy could see Pine's eyes scanning the words.

He lifted them from the sheet and said, 'It's a data sheet. A spy programme. One that allows you to view someone else's computer.'

Varcy nodded his head. 'You ever use it?'

Pine nodded. 'On numerous occasions. Sometimes for business, sometimes personal. It's very useful.'

'Did you set one up to view John Scott's personal computer?'

'No comment,' said Stone immediately.

Varcy looked at Pine, inviting him to say something, but he remained silent.

'Scott had that particular spy software on his computer,' said Varcy. 'Someone was hacking him. The computer doing the hacking is registered to Amonto Oil. We've checked.'

Stone leaned forwards and commented, 'There are hundreds of computers registered with Amonto. A few thousand different users too. How can he know what each one is doing?'

Again Varcy looked at Pine. Pine stared forwards and said nothing.

Varcy let the moment ride on. There was a long silence. Varcy assumed Stone would be used to playing mind games. He wasn't sure Pine would. So he gazed at the two men further, going from one to the other as though he was following a tennis ball back and forth across the net, expecting one of them to smash it down the line.

Neither did.

Eventually, Varcy pulled his gaze away and went back to the file. This time he fished out a photograph of an ambitious, clean-cut young man who shared little resemblance to the wreck he was today. Varcy pushed it towards Pine and said, 'This man drove for your son, I believe. Do you recognise him?'

Pine glanced at the shot and nodded his head. 'Yes, I remember him,' he said.

'I went to see him yesterday,' continued Varcy. 'He's under psychiatric care. He knocked down and killed a child while driving your son to a meeting. He's never recovered from it.'

Pine said nothing.

'He wasn't too complimentary about your son, either,' said Varcy. 'Said he walked away and left him to deal with the dying child.'

Silence.

'Is that the sort of thing your son would have done?' Varcy asked.

'Enough of that,' said Stone. 'We don't need character assessments. Confine yourself to relevant questions.'

Varcy smiled benignly, pulled out two more shots and pushed them towards Stone and Pine. These two were high magnification shots of what looked like long strands of hair. They were coloured, glossy and impeccably focused. One shot had the tag #1 written in ink at the top right hand corner, the other #2. Varcy turned them around so that they faced Stone and Pine. 'Any idea what these are?' he asked.

The two men gazed down at the prints trying to

decipher them. Stone looked up first and said, 'Where are you going with this?'

'It's camel hair,' said Varcy. 'The stuff they make coats out of.'

Then he eased out a shot of Kimberley Westfield. It was a headshot. She was smiling shyly at the camera. 'Do you know who this is?' Varcy asked.

Again the two men studied the print. Stone glanced at Pine, trying to gauge if he might know her, but Pine shook his head.

'Her name is Kimberley Westfield,' said Varcy. 'Or was. Her body was found in woodland about two years ago. She'd been strangled.'

The two men said nothing.

'When she was found,' Varcy continued, 'she was wearing a camel hair coat. These two strands,' he pointed at the high magnification shots, 'come from that same coat. The strand in #1 has been plucked straight from the body of the coat; the strand in #2 was found in a Bentley owned by your son, Mr Pine. The strands have blood on them too. That puts him in the frame for her murder.'

'Hold it,' said Stone, standing up and waving his arms. 'This finishes right here. You're fishing. If you had something concrete you'd have stated it by now. If you want to carry this on, then arrest him. If not, we're leaving.'

This was the response Varcy wanted. 'Are you happy with that?' Varcy asked Pine.

'He's happy,' said Stone.

'He hasn't answered,' said Varcy.

Stone stepped away from the desk and tucked his chair underneath the table. Pine did the same.

'Your son was a thoroughly unpleasant character,' said Varcy. 'Isn't that the truth?'

'Ignore him,' said Stone.

'Don't you want to set the record straight?' asked Varcy.

'He took his own life,' muttered Pine. 'Isn't that enough for you?'

'Not if you've taken revenge for it, it isn't,' said Varcy.

'I've not taken revenge for anything,' said Pine.

'But *your baby* is a killer,' said Varcy. 'I'm out to prove it. Frank Davies said your son was a little shit. I'm not surprised. Are you happy with that kind of legacy?'

'Ignore him,' Stone repeated as they moved to 1A's exit.

'He sounds a thoroughly despicable character,' said Varcy, standing up and following. Pine turned. His face was blood red.

'A complete waste of space,' said Varcy loudly. 'A spoilt rich kid who hides behind Daddy's money. The worst kind of stinking brat.'

Pine's face contorted into a kind of snarl. 'Fuck you,' he said and lunged forwards. Varcy drifted backwards, away from his grasp. Kendrick jumped in and grabbed Pine around the chest. He drove forwards and the pair of them fell back against the wall. Stone moved in and wedged his arm between the two men. He began pulling. Trying to separate them.

'Is that what happens when someone tells it like it is, Mr Pine?' said Varcy. 'Is that how you react?'

Pine was growling. Varcy opened the door and Kendrick manoeuvered Pine towards it. Stone's arm was still stuck between them. 'Wonder what happened when John Scott told you what he had, eh?' added Varcy. 'I bet you did more than just paw at him, didn't you?'

Pine's head was drooped downwards. He pushed hard like a rugby forward in a scrum. Kendrick held him.

'Calm down,' said Stone. 'Everyone calm down.'

The three men shuffled to the left. Stone pulled his arm free.

'Scum will always float to the surface, Mr Pine,' said Varcy. 'You can count on that.'

56

Rita Sidhu's heart was racing in her chest. After the call, she'd collapsed on the bed in her hotel room. Thoughts of the kids, of Meg, of everything she held dear crumbling into dust before her. She'd phoned Meg but it went to voicemail. Since then, she had phoned a dozen times with the same result.

Rita was in no doubt about the type of person she was dealing with. John Scott, Barry, Robert Fleet and now Mark, all slaughtered.

Mark.

She had phoned him in disbelief. Trying to make contact. To reach out. But it too had gone to voicemail. She'd tried again and again.

Images of Mark, Robert and Barry bubbled together in one contorted mess. Then her brain would jump away and she was confronted with the faces of the children. Meg's babies. Her precious godchildren.

Tears streamed forwards. No voice. No sobbing. Just the numbing realisation that the worst nightmare had come. She checked her watch. Its hands were agonisingly slow to move.

The voice had told her not to tell anyone. She would obey that with every fibre of her being. She would not risk anything that might harm Meg or the kids. The stakes were as high as they could get and she would do whatever it took to make it right.

So she waited.

Then at ten o'clock, she carried out the instructions exactly as the voice had given them to her. They worked like a dream. Now she was on a tube train rattling towards Broadgate and the IMDB labs.

57

Varcy checked his watch. It read 9.45pm. Another late one. The building was empty, except for the night duty staff, cleaners, maintenance workers, himself and Kendrick. Kendrick was at the photocopier; Varcy still in his office brooding about Pine. They had agreed to let him go in the end. Varcy was happy with that. He didn't want an arrest. Not yet. It would be a waste. The encounter had had the desired effect anyway. He had made an impact on both Pine and Stone and that was what he wanted. They would be rattled, and liable to make mistakes. If they did, he would be waiting. In the meantime, he would gather as much as he could on Pine and let SOCA do their stuff on Renton. The reopening of the Kimberley Westfield cold case was something he'd have to escalate. Not a priority for now, but something that had to be done.

Varcy picked through Pine's interrogation in his head, checking it for clues, for inconsistencies, for just about anything that might let him in and make the final connection. Join the final dot.

The office phone sprang to life. Varcy picked it up after the first ring. It was Hooper. She was slightly breathless, but her voice was clear and strong.

'Sorry about this afternoon, Gov'nor,' she said. 'I

got bogged down.'

'I hear you were collecting more dirt on Pine,' said Varcy.

'I'm certain he was being blackmailed by Scott.'

'You think?' asked Varcy.

'I've traced money – lots of it – that left Pine and found its way into accounts held by Scott.'

'Okay,' said Varcy. 'Good stuff. Where are you now?' he asked.

'I'm just finishing up,' she said. 'Then heading home for a hot bath.'

'Don't blame you. You can bring me up to speed tomorrow.'

'No problem,' she said. 'Night, Gov'nor.'

'Oh, by the way,' Varcy said quickly. 'Do you like Chinese food?'

'Love it,' she said.

'I know a great place in Soho. Do you fancy coming on Saturday night?'

'Sounds good to me,' she said.

'Can I pick you up around eight?'

'Okay, I'll be ready,' she said.

'Excellent.'

'Night.'

Varcy replaced the receiver as Kendrick drifted in. He was unrolling his shirtsleeves and tying the buttons on the cuffs. 'I'm done,' he said.

Varcy nodded.

'I'm going to The Gun for last orders. You coming?'

Varcy nodded again. Then he said: 'Can I ask you something?'

'Fire away, Gov,' said Kendrick.

'Well, *confide* in you more like.'

Kendrick sat on the seat opposite Varcy's desk. 'Go for it.'

Varcy paused. 'I've started to take an interest in Hooper.'

'What sort of interest?' asked Kendrick.

'A romantic one.'

'Really?'

Varcy nodded.

'You asked her out?' said Kendrick.

Varcy nodded again. 'We've been out once. Going out again at the weekend, but I'm unsure how to play it.'

'How do you mean?' said Kendrick.

'I mean it's not done is it? To go out with a member of the team.'

'You worried *his eminence* will find out?'

Varcy nodded. 'I don't want to complicate matters. Officially it isn't sanctioned. If he found out, he'd have to take action.'

'But he isn't going to find out, is he?'

Varcy shrugged his shoulders. 'I hope not.'

'He isn't,' said Kendrick sitting forwards and resting his elbows on his knees. 'How much do you like her?'

'A lot,' said Varcy.

'Then you should go for it. Go and enjoy yourself, Gov'nor. God knows you deserve it. If it gets serious later then deal with it then. Besides, it's no one's business but yours and Hooper's. That includes *his eminence*.'

Varcy watched Kendrick's face for a moment. Broad and ruddy. Honest and open. Varcy smiled. 'Thanks,' he said.

'No problem,' said Kendrick. 'You coming?'

Outside, the evening air was cool and soft. Alfresco drinkers and diners spilled onto the pavement from the bars and the cafés along Spitalfields. The Gun's clientele was mainly male and suited. Mainly corporate. Drinking spirits and chatting in corners. Varcy found a table in an alcove while Kendrick ordered the drinks.

Removing his jacket, Varcy got comfortable. It had been a long day. He stared through the window towards Crispin Street. The air was full of chatter and laughter and cigarette smoke. One group got his attention. Two men, two women. Varcy assumed they worked together. An easy familiarity existed between them, one that came from sharing an office five days a week. They posed, they drank, the girls flicked their hair and laughed. The men had jackets slung over their shoulders, shirt buttons unfastened, ties loose at the neck. The girls were well groomed in corporate suits. Blue and grey. Not masculine at all. One of the girls had coffee-coloured skin. Indian probably. She reminded Varcy of Rita Sidhu. The other girl was dark too but not her skin. That was pale. It was her hair that was rich and shiny and black. There were four of them. Two men and two women. Four people. *Four*.

Varcy sat upright in his seat just as Kendrick swung into the alcove with the drinks.

'You okay, Gov'nor?' he asked.

Varcy stared ahead, thinking about Frank Davies, Pine's driver. Sedated, overweight, depressed. Re-living the horrors of the past. 'There were four of them,' he said.

'Four of who?' asked Kendrick.

'Four people who visited Frank Davies. He told me I was the fourth one to come asking about James Pine. I took no notice at the time, but it should have been just three. Me, John Scott and Rita Sidhu. Davies said I was the fourth. There was someone else that I don't know about.'

'He's spaced out on drugs,' said Kendrick, placing a Guinness on the table in front of Varcy. 'He probably made a mistake.'

Varcy shook his head. 'No. He didn't make a mistake at all. I did. I missed it.'

Varcy's mobile phone sprang to life. He reached for it.

'Gov'nor?'

It was Jeff. The constable on duty outside Rita Sidhu's hotel room.

'Yes,' said Varcy.

'I've cocked-up.'

'How?'

'Sidhu's left her hotel room and I can't find her.'

'Left or been taken?' asked Varcy.

'Left,' he said. 'She called me into her room on a pretext. I went in, she slammed the door and bolted. She could be anywhere.'

'Okay,' said Varcy. 'She's a grown woman – it's up to her. Stay there in case she comes back.'

He hung up and replaced the phone in his

pocket.

'Problems?' asked Kendrick.

'Sidhu's left the hotel. Jeff can't find her.'

'Stupid bitch,' said Kendrick.

'Maybe,' said Varcy. 'Maybe not.'

Varcy's phone rang again. This time it was Cole. He was outside a lock-up at Gun Wharf in Bethnal Green. He had responded to a call from a patrol car.

'Gov'nor,' he said, 'you'd better get over here right now.'

58

At Moorgate, Rita jumped the barrier and ran the escalator to street level. Outside the streets were quiet and dark, nothing like the area's daytime persona. Street-cleaning vans crawled the curbs sucking up the dust, dirt and rubbish after a full day's worth of bustling action. She turned east onto South Place and walked the five minutes into Broadgate. It too was deserted except for a few late nighters and stragglers drifting away from The Crispen. The circus was deserted too. So were the merchant banks and insurance firms that surrounded it. Retnel Biotechnology's ochre glazed frontage blended with the rest. It might have been a private equity firm or an insurance syndicate.

Rita pushed the large revolving door that led into a carpeted lobby. On the walls were high-magnification prints of proteins and enzymes and immunoglobulins, taken with a scanning microscope – lit beautifully, every nuance captured. Rita usually thought them exquisite. The highest form of art, but today she didn't even see them. She saw only the security guard. He wore the Retnel colours of blue and yellow and a black shiny cap. He glanced at her. She flashed her pass and he nodded an acceptance.

Lab 3467 was on three. Rita avoided the elevator and took the stairs. She gobbled them up two at a time and pushed through the fire exit at the top. The corridor was dimly lit and it seemed to her like an alien environment. So familiar during the day, so much a part of her normal life; part of her soul even, but not now. Tonight had nothing to do with carefree days spent in these labs when her biggest concern was a biochemical assay she was running, or a PCR cycle that needed attending to, or a tissue culture procedure that had gone wrong. Tonight her concerns dwarfed everything else. Would he have the children? What would she have to do to get them back?

Her lab was four doors up on the left. She strained to listen for unusual sounds. Sudden movements. She couldn't hear or see anything out of the ordinary. She could feel plenty though. She felt the dryness in her mouth, sweat on her neck, an ice block in her chest. She moved forwards. 3467 was shut. Underneath the number was a perspex square containing a collage of photographs showing the lab members smiling or serious or awkward. Rita remembered Robert taking hers on her first day. She looked at Robert's photo now. His kind face. The small goatee that everyone teased him about. She glanced at Meg's too. She looked stern in hers, cheekbones high and sharp.

She turned the handle and pushed. The door creaked loudly and swung inwards. A gust of cool air escaped into the corridor and Rita peered in. There was a thin sliver of light coming from the tissue culture hood which threw shadows onto the ceiling. The lab gear was scattered across the workbenches as if thrown in disgust. Dark shapes loomed from the walls. The minus forty-five freezer hummed in the darkness. Rita reached for the panel of switches on the wall. She threw them two at a time. The tubes groaned and stuttered. Then they kicked in and the lab was bathed in light.

It was empty.

59

Gun Wharf was a small industrial site set on the edge of The Cut. It contained two dozen lock-ups. Small businesses trying to scratch out a living. Mechanics or washing machine repairers or small-time manufacturers. There was parking for two medium-sized cars in front of each, and room inside for a couple of large workbenches, a small winch and maybe a lathe or two. Varcy and Kendrick went via the armoury on Wentworth Street where Kendrick had used his blue ticket to book out a Glock 26.

Driving towards the red steel gates that separated the wharf from the road, Varcy could see Cole standing outside the furthest lock-up. The one on the water's edge. Next to him was an ambulance. The back doors were hanging open and light from inside spewed onto the tarmac.

Kendrick swung the car into Gun Wharf and yanked up the handbrake. Both men leapt out and ran towards Cole who was talking to a man in workman's overalls. He turned and jerked his thumb towards the lock-up. 'Two kids, Gov'nor. Drugged. Rita Sidhu's nephews.'

In the centre of the space were two paramedics kneeling over a mattress placed on the floor. Two children were lying on it side by side. They each had a high colour, both were sweating, in a deep sleep. Their breath was even and regular. A good sign.

'What's the drug?' Varcy asked.

One of the paramedics glanced over his shoulder. 'Not sure,' he replied. 'But we're trying to clear it.' Varcy watched him hook a couple of bags of fluid to a frame, pull lines down and attach a cannula to each. He inserted a needle into both children and held it fast with sticking plaster. Then he set it dripping. His colleague moved towards the entrance holding a TETRA radio. Varcy heard him calling for back-up.

Varcy glanced around the lock-up. There was a network of shelves on the south wall, loaded with workshop accessories. Gas torches, small tools, screws and rusty bolts. The east wall was empty except for a chest freezer pushed into a corner. The north wall had two tables pushed end to end. On them were half-eaten sandwiches, cup cakes, chunks of jelly and a jug of orange squash.

'Seen those?' said Kendrick, pointing to an area of wall.

Hung on the wall above the tables were two photographs, side by side, printed onto canvas. About four foot square each. Both showed exactly the same image. It was a sunny day on a beach. The child in the centre of the shot was young – maybe five years old – male, sweet. He smiled shyly into the lens. He was hunched down in the sand, a plastic bucket between his feet, and he was making castles. He was thin, had freckles. There was a lick of fair hair that stood up at the back of his head, and something in Varcy connected.

'I've seen this child,' he said.

'Where?' asked Kendrick.

Varcy shook his head. 'I'm trying to think. I recognise the hair.'

Kendrick moved to the freezer and opened the lid.

Cole appeared at the entrance. 'Gov'nor? You want to talk to this guy? He was the one who raised the alarm.'

Varcy nodded. 'I'll be there in an minute.'

He moved towards the photographs. He watched the child in them; the face, the shy smile. Then he focused on the bucket. The green bucket. Same shape, size, and colour as the buckets at the murder scenes of John Scott and Barry Townsend. Varcy thought back to an episode in his office during which Nash had told him the bucket was symbolic of the killer's camel's back moment.

Something shifted in Varcy's brain.

The bucket is at the feet of the child. The child and the bucket are one. They go together in the photograph and in the mind of the killer.

Varcy glanced over his shoulder at the paramedic who was fussing around the two children on the mattress. Two innocent children. He glanced back up at the photographs.

One innocent child.

One *dead* innocent child.

Varcy's glance fell onto the party table. He noted the half-eaten food, the brightly coloured plates, the tin of Haribos. Then he saw something else. Something small. Something that should not have been there.

It was on the edge. Next to a plate of half-eaten cup cakes. Black and thin and metallic. Varcy picked it up and held it to the light.

A hair clip.

Varcy gasped when the realisation came to him.

He turned and ran to the entrance. Kendrick called after him. Varcy ran over to Cole's car and rapped on the window. Cole had the interior light on and his decision log was on the dash. He opened the door.

'That guy you were talking to. Where is he?'

'In that lock-up,' said Cole, pointing to a building twenty yards away.

Kendrick emerged onto the tarmac and sprinted towards the car. 'What's happened?' he asked.

'I know who it is,' Varcy said.

The door to the mechanic's lock-up was open, and light from within escaped into the darkness. The man was in a small lobby getting out of his overalls. He had one leg free and stood for support on the other. Varcy was breathless as he bundled in.

'Describe the woman to me,' he said.

60

The back of the car was in chaos. Varcy's brain had accelerated into a loop of mixed thoughts and reasons. Kendrick was driving fast. They had the siren on loud. It flashed and pulsed and got traffic out of their way.

The questions, the scenarios, the failures had gripped Varcy's mind the moment he realised the truth. He suddenly understood everything he needed to know about the killer and why the killings had taken place. The puzzle came to him in a moment of blind clarity. Suddenly it all made sense. The killings made sense, the spyware on Pine's computer made sense, the profile Nash gave made sense, the camel's back moment made so much sense. So did Frank Davies and his fourth visitor. Like a powerful magnet that sucks up metal shards, Varcy's mind sucked the disparate parts of the puzzle together and held them tightly.

He was mad at himself for not seeing what was so obvious. Mad because he knew what would happen now. He knew Rita Sidhu would be next. That she would be the last one. That there was just one place to go. One place the killer would lure her. The place where the deception was concealed. The locus.

Only one question remained in his mind. Would he be too late?

61

The Retnel pass I stole from Robert Fleet has been enough to get me past the guard. I doctored the photograph. Made some slight alterations in the syntax. It wasn't hard to do. As I suspected, the guard did not even look at it. I check my watch: 11.05pm. I have left it late. This is a deliberate ploy because I want Rita Sidhu to sweat. To become more fearful and more docile. By my calculations, she will have been in the lab for around forty minutes.

Floor three is empty. It is dim, cool and quiet. Lab 3467 is up on the left. The door is closed. I unloop the backpack from my shoulders and arrange my gear in the corridor. I am careful to be extra quiet. I don't want Sidhu to hear anything just yet. The backpack is a GoLite. It is wide and deep. I remove three items. The bucket with its contents, the half hatchet axe and a rope.

The axe is for chopping, the bucket for containing, the rope is for finishing.

I set myself steady outside the lab door. I close my eyes as I always do when preparing to embark on something profound. I centre myself for a moment then I open my eyes and focus on the door. I could open it easily just by turning the handle, but shock is what I'm after, so I raise the axe and bring it down heavily against the frame. I smash it three separate times. The sound it generates shatters the quiet. I then open the door and step inside.

The lab is quiet, cold and empty. Empty except for Rita Sidhu. I recognise her instantly. She's crouched low by the leg of an aluminum desk, like a small child lost in a game of hide-and-seek. She doesn't move or say anything and I try to gauge the assortment of emotions she is feeling right now. I know fear will be paramount – it always is – but usually other emotions are present too. A feeling of disbelief perhaps, or one of anger. Usually the physiological responses are much more predictable than the emotional ones. A clammy kind of sweat that mottles the skin is almost always present, so is heart stutter. Her mouth will be as dry as desert dust. She is unlikely to scream or shout, or try to use physical violence against me. In my experience these flight or fight mechanisms seldom kick in. Her bladder may well give out.

I know all these things because I have played this game before. In the past it's been non-personal. Just what I did best. Tonight is different. It *is* personal. Achingly so.

On normal days, Sidhu loves this place. I know that too. It's as familiar and as comfortable to her as her childhood bedroom. The order of it calms her and this is why she spends so much of her time here. I also know that she is considered very accomplished at what she does.

This much at least we have in common.

My eyes sweep the cool, sterile environment and

note the stainless steel instruments and bleached white tiles, the digital displays and metal trays with perspex covers. I hear the low hum of a machine somewhere deep in the lab, and finally, directly opposite the door I have entered – about twenty feet away – is the reason I have come. Set into a plain grey wall is a touch pad. Behind it is the safe. I stride towards the pad and enter an eight-digit code that I got from Robert Fleet. I listen to the long, satisfying beep that tells me the combination has been accepted.

But the code isn't enough. There are another two requirements before the safe will yield.

I lay down the axe; move to retrieve the bucket from the corridor. I grope inside and pull out a waxy, soccer-ball-sized sphere. The underside is puckered and lumpy. In parts it is flecked with deep colour. I grip it by a tuft of matting on its top and it spins slowly. I glance at Sidhu to check if she's watching. She is. Her eyes follow the undulating ravines and elevations of its surface. I make sure she sees every inch of the ball because soon she will make full sense of it. The eyes are pink and vacant; a thin jagged mouth is turned downwards and sparse tufts of tangled facial hair puncture the flesh. Suddenly Sidhu gives out a low, guttural moan.

I dangle Robert's head in front of the keypad and the retinal scanner accepts the information. Then I toss the head back into the bucket.

Still the wall does not yield.

Another scan is required to corroborate the first. Sidhu must surely realise by now that I know whose scan is needed. I take up the axe and move towards her. She's too strung out to resist. Instead her body flails spontaneously against the floor tiles, like a freshly caught fish on the dockside. I'm moving swiftly now. I have no desire to prolong her ordeal.

I'm not a monster.

I come alongside her and push my boot into the side of her face, holding it tight to the floor. I hear a crack and I'm certain I have shattered her cheekbone. I raise the axe and notice her body at once becomes still and compliant. I'm grateful for that.

In a moment it will be over.

62

Kendrick sent the BMW into a skid turn at the top of Moorgate. The car bumped along Eldon Street and he mounted the curb, hitting the brakes. He and Varcy sprawled forwards. Varcy unclipped his belt and jumped out onto the pavement. Kendrick shut down the siren and joined him. They ran into the Broadgate complex and into the Retnel building.

'What floor?' said Varcy as they bundled through the revolving door.

'Three,' said Kendrick.

Cole had called the guard ahead of time and he was out of his seat ready. A constable from the Bishopsgate station was standing next to him.

'Anything happen?' asked Varcy.

'Just got here, Gov'nor,' said the constable. 'Take the stairs,' he said, pointing to the doors at the far end.

They galloped up the stairs, Kendrick ahead, Varcy struggling to keep up. They emerged onto floor three, breathless and sweating.

'Where?' said Kendrick.

'No idea,' said Varcy, hunching over to get his breath.

The corridor was dim and quiet. Varcy steadied himself before moving forwards. There was a series of doors ahead. All shut, except one. The farthest. There were three deep divots torn out of its frame. Varcy moved towards it. Pushed the door gently inwards. It squeaked.

He stepped forwards. The lab was dimly lit but he could clearly see Rita Sidhu. She was lying on her back. The killer stood over her. A boot was held fast against Sidhu's face and an axe hovered overhead. It was about to fall.

Varcy screamed: 'Hooper!'

63

The axe quivered a fraction and Hooper's eyes moved from Sidhu to Varcy. Cool and focused, she flicked back to Sidhu then said in a soft voice, 'Hello, Gov'nor.'

'Katy, what are you doing?' asked Varcy.

'Finishing,' she said.

'Don't,' said Varcy. 'Think for a moment.'

'I can't do that,' said Hooper.

'Yes, you can, Katy,' Varcy said. 'You can do anything you want.'

Hooper smiled at that.

'Katy, I know about Philip.'

Hooper's head jerked up on hearing her son's name.

'I know he was knocked down by James Pine's Bentley,' Varcy said.

'*Killed* by his Bentley.'

'And I can imagine how that must make you feel.'

'No, you can't.'

'I lost a child myself,' Varcy said quickly. 'He was just a baby.'

Hooper flicked her eyes back to his momentarily. 'Then you know what I must do.'

'Not if you stop to think.'

'I've done little else these past few years,' Hooper said. 'Piecing it all together.'

'I understand all that.'

'No you don't, Gov'nor,' she said.

'I understand that if John Scott or Rita Sidhu had gone to the police with what they had on James Pine, Pine would not have been around to kill your son.'

'But Pine was around, wasn't he?' said Hooper.

Varcy nodded. 'Yes, he was.'

'Because they all kept a dirty little secret. A secret they stored in that safe.' She flipped her eyes towards the retinal scan plate. 'Philip's dead because of it. My life ruined.'

'You have a choice, Katy,' said Varcy.

'Choice?' she said. 'What choice do I have? What choice did my son have? Me in the army, my son at home with his father. Then Pine. That little prick with all his money and connections. He should've been nowhere near my son. He should've been doing time in some shit-hole prison for murdering the Westfield girl.'

'I agree,' said Varcy, 'and we've opened the investigation again. We have proof that Kimberley Westfield was in his car.'

'We always had proof,' Hooper sneered. 'It's too late anyway. Too late for Philip and for me.'

'Is that what the rope's for?' Varcy said. 'For you?'

She waited a few beats. 'You ever seen a hanging?'

Varcy shook his head. 'No.'

'I have,' she said. 'Many times. I've hanged a

few myself – Pine included. It's quick and clean. I'll take that.'

'What's the bucket for?' asked Varcy.

'For collecting,' she said. 'Decapitation mess. I need her head to open the safe.'

'But what you want from the safe isn't there any more, is it?' said Varcy, pleading. 'We have that evidence already. You've seen it. There's no reason to cut off her head to get it.'

Hooper smiled. 'You'll never understand. I need to see her dead eyes opening that door. There's no turning back.'

She arched her spine. Steadied the axe at the top of its arc. Threw it forwards and down.

Varcy screamed: 'No!'

Two things then happened simultaneously. One of them a fraction ahead of the other. A sound first. Loud and sudden like a fire-cracker. Then an eruption. Red vapour shooting upwards. An urgent spurt to the side. Hooper's head imploding. Her body lurching backwards.

Kendrick was at Varcy's shoulder, his arm was extended, a Glock 26 gripped in his hand. His face was set with concentration, brow dappled with moisture. He held the stance and time slowed. Hooper's body crumpled. Blood gushed from her head and made a thin lake on the linoleum. She twitched a couple of times then lay still.

Rita Sidhu was still on her back. She remained where she was. Completely still. Varcy's eyes flicked around the lab. There was silence. There was calm.

64

The lab was sealed off quickly. Twenty minutes after Kendrick fired the shot into Hooper's head, the hallway was full. Police, SOCOs, DPS officers and Retnel managers. It was like a packed tube train in the rush hour.

Varcy and Kendrick had moved outside. They sat on the palisade that ran around the ice rink. They didn't talk at all. Kendrick stared forwards. Occasionally he brought a lit cigarette to his lips and took a long drag. Varcy had his arms folded and gazed out into the middle distance. His thoughts, his feelings, his emotions all numb. Like a drug had been injected into his body.

Fifty minutes ago, they had watched the first ambulance drive to the edge of the Broadgate complex and a team of medics spill out and run into the Retnel building. They carried Rita Sidhu out on a stretcher. She was clothed with a blanket and her eyes were wide and staring. The medics bundled her into the back of the ambulance and clamped the stretcher to a frame. Then the doors slammed closed and it sped off towards Blomfield Street. A second ambulance had now taken its place. This one was for Hooper. Hooper was dead, of course, but she would need to be transported to the morgue. Not yet though, not before the forensic boys had photographed, measured, brushed and analysed.

It would be a long night.

65

Two weeks later

Early September was as bright as August had been. Warm mornings and hot afternoons. The city crowd gathered in the parks and public spaces in the lunch hour and after work. Jacketless corporate guys with tailored shirts and designer shades, women with short skirts and thin blouses. They lay on the parched grass and ate ice-cream, or they smoked cigarettes and drank cappuccinos outside the coffee shops. They were young and good-looking and cool.

Varcy had called a lunchtime gathering upstairs in the meeting room. He had arranged take-out from S&M. He invited Kendrick, Cole, Katz and Daniel Nash. Ray Johnson – the CI – was invited too. It was informal. No big deal. Not a celebration exactly but a wrap-up before they concentrated on the next case. The puzzle pieces had been located and studied and placed. Varcy had interviewed, reviewed, and assimilated all the data. He had spent time with Rita Sidhu. First in the hospital and then at the hotel. He understood her. He understood Hooper too. He had examined everything he could find on his colleague. There was masses of it. He understood what had made her tick. He had a complete picture of it all. The facts stood out like neon signs in his mind. All connected, intertwined, perfectly understandable.

The men drank Coke or plain water as they waited for their food. Varcy made a small speech about the case and the difficulties they'd encountered on it. He thanked them all for their input and for their effort. Then he sat down and picked up a remote. The projector was pointed at a white screen. They all knew the basics, the general themes. Each team member knew their own area well, but Varcy wanted to pull it all together. Just one time. Then he could throw it off and move on. There were still grey areas, of course. Points of interest no one was certain of, including Varcy himself. Nevertheless, he had them sketched into the play and they fitted well enough.

Varcy said: 'The start of it was not the murder of John Scott as I had assumed. It was the killing of a child. An accidental killing of a boy called Philip Greenwood. He was knocked down and killed by James Pine's Bentley on Cheapside. The boy's mother was Kate Hooper. DS Hooper. The killing changed her life.' Varcy glanced over at Nash and added, 'It was her camel's back moment.'

Nash nodded and sipped his water.

Kendrick pulled a few documents from a file on the desk in front of him and said, 'We thought the killer was ex-military. The MO on Scott and Townsend was interesting. They each had a horrendous arm wound – a radial artery gash – that caused their death. However, they both had a smaller wound too, made by a knife. Townsend had one in his leg, Scott in his shoulder. The Gov'nor made the connection with the so called "control wounds" that were noticed by the military during the Bosnian conflict back in the nineties. Used by the insurgents as a prelude to torture. We believed both Scott and Townsend were tortured. Dr Nash came up with a profile. A profile that included some sort of breakdown that signalled the end of the killer's military career. We searched military records for soldiers who had left the army under such circumstances.'

Nash set his water down and cleared his throat. 'The interesting thing about this case – at least from my point of view – is the sex of the killer. In cases of this kind, almost always the killer is male. My profile reflected that. To find a woman who acts so much like her male counterparts is both fascinating and regrettable. It means, of course, I was wrong, and my profile reflected the error.'

'I was wrong too,' said Varcy. 'I was looking for a killer – a serial killer – who had been hired by someone else to do a job. That's why Charles Pine bounced onto the radar. He knew John Scott was seen with him some time before he died. He was the stalker on Scott's computer and, best of all, Scott had evidence that put Pine's son in the frame for the Kimberley Westfield murder. Pine was connected with Paul Renton too, who visited the Amonto office after receiving a call from him. But that call was faked. Made by Hooper after I told her I was trying to link Pine with Renton. It was a neat fit. Too neat as it turned out.'

'So what happens to Pine now?' asked Cole.

'Nothing,' said Varcy. 'At least nothing for us to worry about. He might be charged for irregular business dealings or even fraud but that's someone else's problem. He had nothing to do with the Scott and Townsend murders, that's for sure.'

'But he must have known what Scott had on his son,' said Cole.

'He did,' said Varcy. 'He was watching Scott like a hawk. Monitoring his every move, stalking his computer and as nervous as a kitten. Pine was paying Scott to keep quiet but he could never be sure he'd stick to it. But it gets more even more complex than that. I always assumed Pine had a mistress – those types usually do. Hooper found evidence to suggest that was true.'

Varcy squeezed the remote and the telephoto shot of Pine on the beach with a bikini-clad woman appeared on the screen. 'That's Rachael Knight,' said Varcy. 'She's a thirty-five year old ex model who now runs a high-end clothing boutique in Mayfair. All paid for by Pine. I wondered how Pine's wife might feel about that. Whether she accepted it, or ignored it, or was ignorant of it. Then I remembered something Scott's housekeeper said. Something about his trips down to Surrey. I knew Pine's house address was in Surrey, although he spent most of his time in London. I knew Pine and Scott moved in the same circles. Something clicked in my head. So last week I went to see Pine's wife. I took a picture of John Scott with me. She was dignified and demure, but tearful. She admitted having an affair with Scott for many years. I asked her if Pine knew about it and she said no. However, I don't believe that at all. I think that guy knows everything. So maybe that's the reason he ripped Scott off on the pharmaceutical company deal.'

'So what about the email you got from him?' asked Kendrick. 'The one asking to see you.'

'I've thought about that,' said Varcy. 'Scott must have assumed Pine was watching him. He knew enough about Pine to assume he would be monitoring his on-line activity. I think the email to me was sent to "concentrate" Pine's mind.' Varcy made speech marks in space. 'To keep the pressure on him so that he kept paying.'

'So where does that leave us?' said Katz.

'Right here,' said Varcy, squeezing the remote once again. Six four by six photographs were projected. Six men. Same size, same colour. Varcy depressed the remote another time. Two more photographs slid in from the right. One showed a woman. The other a child.

'We'll start bottom left,' said Varcy pointing at the screen. 'That's Hooper, of course. Hooper had an interesting career before joining the police force. She left school at sixteen to join the army. Signed up with an artillery division – 6 platoon B Company 2 Rifles – and ended up in Afghanistan. She was stationed at Forward Operating Base Inkerman, five miles north of Sangin, in Helmand. She rose to the rank of second lieutenant. Had an immaculate record. Saw active service and was commended in two separate actions.'

'I thought women soldiers couldn't be on the frontline,' said Cole.

'They can't officially,' said Varcy. 'But if they find themselves out on patrol with the infantry, as they often do in Helmand, what are they supposed to do? The Afghans aren't picky about whom they attack.'

'What was she commended for?' asked Ray Johnson.

'She had a role supporting the medics,' said Varcy. 'Officially she had to help treat any casualties, stabilise them and get them onto the helicopter.' He eased out a sheet of paper from a tan arch-file on the desk and began reading from it. 'During one action, the patrol came under fire from machine guns hidden in a tree line. One of the patrolmen in an advanced position was hit in the chest. Hooper and the medics surged forwards to give assistance, then came under fire themselves. Hooper returned fire, moved deep into enemy territory to continue firing and took out a couple of Taliban soldiers. On another occasion she mixed with the enemy at close quarters and killed a man with SOG powerlock.'

'What's that?' asked Kendrick.

'A knife,' said Varcy.

There was silence.

'I spoke to Hooper's commanding officer,' Varcy continued. 'He said she was as hard as nails.'

More silence.

'Now, I want to talk about the child,' said Varcy, gesturing towards the white screen and the photo next to Hooper's. 'This was Hooper's child. His name was Philip Greenwood. Hooper fell pregnant at nineteen. The father was a soldier in another platoon. They were briefly married and shared custody of him. The army allowed them to rota on and off. When one was on a tour, the other was home. Frank Davies knocked down and killed Philip Greenwood while driving James Pine to a business meeting. This was the start of it all. I've read Hooper's military record. When they told her what had happened to her boy, she collapsed. She never recovered from it. A few months later she left the army.'

'Then she joined the police?' asked Johnson.

'After some time,' said Varcy. 'SVU first, then financial investigations. Finally to us. However, we have found out that she wasn't just working for us – she was taking other jobs too.'

'What kind of jobs?' asked Nash.

'The violent kind,' replied Kendrick.

'All the while tracking down those responsible for the death of her boy,' said Varcy. 'She went to see Frank Davies just as I did. She was the second one of four to visit him. The first was John Scott.' Varcy got up and moved to the white screen. The first photograph in the top row was of Frank Davies. Varcy pointed at it. 'I think she intended to kill Davies, but changed her mind when she met him. She saw how it had torn him up. She could relate to that. Davies told her about John Scott's visit and the questions he was asking about James Pine and why. She realised the implications of that so she went to see Scott herself.' Varcy pointed at the second photograph in the row. 'Scott told her everything. He told her about blackmailing Pine, about the evidence he covered up; he told her how he had got it, who was involved and who analysed it. He told her where the evidence was stored too.'

'All this under torture?' said Katz.

Varcy nodded. 'While blood from his radial artery poured into a bucket. I always felt Scott was resigned to his fate. Like he almost expected it. When Hooper came to see him and he realised who she was and how her son's story fitted with his decision to cover up the Pine evidence – he crumbled. That's when Hooper decided there were three main culprits involved with covering up the Westfield murder and protecting James Pine. Scott – who engineered it, Mark Fox – who arranged for Sidhu to examine and store the samples and Rita Sidhu herself who – innocently as it turned out – provided the evidence.'

There was a light knock on the door of the room. Two women appeared carrying large foil covered oval plates balanced on brown trays. Underneath the foil on each plate was the house special: mashed potato and sausages. The women handed out the plates and distributed sachets of English mustard and HP sauce, setting a plastic jug full of onion gravy at the centre of the table before leaving the room. There was silence as the men dressed the food and tucked in.

Then Cole leaned forwards and jabbed his fork towards the white screen. 'Did James Pine hang himself or did Hooper do it for him?' he asked.

Varcy chewed a mouthful of food and swallowed. 'I checked the dates,' he said. 'Pine was killed two days before Scott. Hooper made him her first target. I could never understand why they found a full cup of coffee in Pine's kitchen. It meant he abandoned it to hang himself. It didn't make sense. Neither did the rope he used. People usually hang themselves with something around the house, like electrical wire or washing line. Something to hand. The rope used on Pine was pristine, three-strand, twisted natural fibre rope, as if it had been bought for the purpose. Which it had, but not by Pine. I think Hooper carried it over to his apartment and just knocked on his door. She knew the type of guy he was. So she smiled sweet and shy. Maybe she dressed up for him too. He let her in without any hesitation.'

Varcy and Kendrick exchanged glances. There was clinking of cutlery on plates. Scooping sounds as the men attacked the food. Katz pointed to the fourth photograph. 'Who's that guy?'

'Mark Fox,' said Varcy. 'He was murdered just before the incident in the lab. Stabbed in the back of the neck.'

'By Hooper,' said Kendrick. 'She was following the trail Scott had given her.'

'But she didn't kill him right away,' said Cole, as he lopped the top off his pile of mash.

'That's right,' said Varcy. 'We now know from talking to Sidhu that Hooper had an affair with him instead,' said Varcy.

Nash dropped his knife and fork and clapped his hands. 'Fascinating,' he said.

'That's why Sidhu broke up with him,' Kendrick went on. 'She discovered them together. Sidhu recognised Hooper when she burst into her lab.'

'Why didn't she kill him right away?' said Johnson.

'Uncertain,' said Varcy. 'Maybe she was using Mark Fox to get a clearer picture of what happened. Who was responsible for what. Who was involved in the cover up.'

'But she got all that from Scott,' said Katz.

Varcy nodded. 'True.'

Nash cleared his throat. 'She was feeling vulnerable at that stage,' he said. 'Something happened that shook her. Made her feel insecure. It had nothing to do with using him for information. She used him for emotional support.'

'She got over it soon enough when it came to knifing him,' said Kendrick.

Nash nodded. 'When her emotional need had passed.'

There was a short silence.

Varcy flicked his fingers. 'Anniversary,' he said. 'She started the affair around the time of the anniversary of her son's death. Rita Sidhu told me she'd discovered the affair between Hooper and Mark Fox late last year …' He groped in his inside pocket for his decision log. He flipped the pages and stuck his finger into its spine to save his place. Then he rummaged through the lever arch file and pulled out a photocopy of a newspaper headline.

'Here it is,' he said. 'He was knocked down and killed on the 7th December two years ago.' He spread open the decision log and peered at his notes. 'Sidhu discovered the affair about then. She thought it had been going on for a few weeks.'

Nash clapped his hands together again. 'Perfect,' he said.

Katz rested his cutlery either side of his plate and chewed thoughtfully. 'Where does Barry Townsend come in?'

'Next,' said Varcy. 'But he was not planned. Doesn't fit the pattern at all. He had no knowledge of what had gone on. Wasn't responsible for any part of it. He just happened to be in the wrong place at the wrong time. Hooper decided to hit Sidhu on the Friday, in the morning. She had watched her for weeks and knew what time she left the flat for work every day.'

'But when she got inside the flat, Sidhu was gone,' said Kendrick. 'She had left early to present a pitch for a Retnel research project.'

'In her place was Barry Townsend,' said Varcy. 'Asleep in her bed.'

'Hooper freaked out when she saw Townsend in bed and no sign of Sidhu,' said Kendrick.

'So she tortured Barry Townsend to find out what happened?' asked Katz.

Varcy nodded. 'To get information out of him. To see if he knew anything. She was on a mission. She had to cover all her bases. But Barry Townsend yielded nothing because he knew nothing.'

'But she had still messed up,' said Kendrick.

'We found the Swiss Army knife she used on Barry Townsend in the bedroom,' said Varcy. 'That would not have been left if things had gone as she expected.'

'And after that?' said Johnson.

'After that, she regrouped,' Varcy went on. 'Readjusted her plan and then went after Rita Sidhu's boss.'

'Robert Fleet,' said Kendrick. 'He was killed because Hooper needed his retinal scan to corroborate Sidhu's. That was the only way the safe would open. She simply took him off somewhere – probably the lock-up – killed him and removed his head. Probably with the same axe she tried to use on Sidhu.'

Nash shifted in his seat. 'The fact she still wanted access to the safe is interesting. By the time she came to murder Sidhu, it was unnecessary. The evidence had already been revealed. She could have shot Sidhu, or stabbed her, but she still wanted to remove her head and open the safe with it. It had become a ritual. The bucket was part of it. A symbol. The symbol of her child. The safe was also a symbol – that was where the evidence had been hidden all along – that was the centre of it all.'

Food silence descended once again.

'Which leaves Rita Sidhu herself,' said Varcy. 'A brilliant student. Highly intelligent. Great career ahead of her.'

'Poor choice in men,' said Kendrick.

'Remarkably poor,' agreed Varcy.

'What's the future for her?' asked Katz.

Varcy shrugged. 'Who knows? I doubt she'll recover from this any time soon.'

'Why did she change her name?' said Cole.

'For the reasons she gave,' shrugged Varcy. 'I thought she was lying, but it stacks up. Her father was absent. On the booze. He had little to do with her upbringing so she changed it.'

Katz dabbed his mouth with a napkin. 'She should have stayed out of it,' he said. 'It would have saved so much grief.'

'It would,' said Varcy. 'But she didn't, and the consequences were horrendous.'

Epilogue

Building a relationship with my readers is the very best thing about writing.

I've written an epilogue to this novel and if you'd like to read it please go to:

www.stevedavison.net/deadinnocentepilogue

and download it onto your Kindle. It's free of charge and will automatically join you to my VIP readers club where you will receive information on new books and deals plus a lot of free content.

About the Author

Steve Davison graduated in Immunology from King's College, London. He then completed his MPhil in Molecular Genetics at Cambridge before training as a Chiropractor and setting up his own successful practice in south-east England. He lives near London with his wife and children.

FOR MORE INFORMATION ON STEVE DAVISON PLEASE VISIT:
www.stevedavison.net

In the Varcy and Kendrick Series

Kill&Cure

His fate hangs on a drug trial gone wrong. Can he keep his family safe when he becomes a target?

London chiropractor David "Stitch" Stichell is desperate to hold onto his adopted daughter. Already struggling with deteriorating health, his heart breaks when her birth father returns to take her away. But his life spirals into chaos when the other man is suddenly murdered.

As his experimental cancer treatment mysteriously self-destructs, the people around Stitch start dying – leaving him as the prime suspect. Vowing to find out who's behind the assassins on his tail, he must dodge acid-laden syringes and hails of bullets.

Will this frantic dad stop his enemies before he's

filled full of holes?

Kill&Cure is the gripping first book in the Varcy and Kendrick crime thriller series. If you like flawed characters, British settings, and fast-paced action, then you'll love Steve Davison's intense page-turner.

Buy *Kill&Cure* to diagnose a pattern of death today!

The Hunted Kind

A horrifying secret. A bloody coverup. Can one detective end a gory obsession with vengeance?

London, UK. Vincent Crow clawed his way to the top of his multimillion-pound empire. But even with his pockets lined with cash, he can no longer ignore the pain of his abused past. And putting his dark demons to rest means satisfying his revenge-driven bloodlust until not one of those pedophiles is left standing…

Nailing low-life crooks is all DCI Terence Varcy has after losing his wife and child. So when a shooting at the precinct leaves a desperate woman on the run from a twisted cabal, he and his partner leave no stone unturned to flush out the culprit. But their hunt for clues becomes a race to find a killer when the trail uncovers a string of gruesomely arranged bodies.

Oblivious to the cops hot on his heels, Crow continues to mete out his grisly justice with meticulous brutality. And to save innocent lives, Varcy will have no choice but to slice open the city's sickening underbelly.

Can the world-weary detective put a corrupt ring of sadists behind bars before a vigilante executes his own deadly sentence?

The Hunted Kind is the gritty third book in the Varcy and Kendrick Crime Thriller series. If you like hard-nosed detectives, sinister secrets, and shockingly graphic scenes, then you'll love Steve Davison's riveting novel.

In The Merge Series

Merge: The World Is The Game (Book 1)

His perfect game became a deadly gateway. Can
one genius save reality from fright-fueled
domination?

2070. Reclusive prodigy Memphis Garrick turned
tragedy into a tech empire. Heading up the
ultimate immersive experience not only brings him
worldwide success, it allows him to visit the family
he lost during childhood. But when a tyrant from a
parallel universe hacks his virtual paradise and
merges it with reality, Memphis is loaded into a
battle to stop the coded spread of terror.

Plunged into an archaic Tudor world, Memphis
partners with an enigmatic beauty to reverse the
cruel program turning their fear into fuel. But in a
realm where resistance means death, the pair's last

hope to restore billions of fallen souls rests on a daring high-stakes hard-code reset.

Can the gifted visionary rescue humanity from dread-driven destruction?

MERGE – The World is The Game is the cutting-edge first novel in the MERGE dystopian science fiction series. If you like cyberpunk action, unimaginable realities, and brilliant protagonists, then you'll love Steve Davison's nightmare tale.

Merge: The Illusion Virus (Book 2)

Will be released Summer 2020

Printed in Great Britain
by Amazon

43123821R00217